3/26/19

THE BELOVED WILD

THE
BELOVED
WILD

MELISSA OSTROM

SQUARE
FISH

FEIWEL AND FRIENDS

NEW YORK

SQUARE
FISH

An imprint of Macmillan Publishing Group, LLC
175 Fifth Avenue, New York, NY 10010
fiercereads.com

Our books may be purchased in bulk for promotional, educational, or business use. Please
contact your local bookseller or the Macmillan Corporate and Premium Sales Department
at (800) 221-7945 ext. 5442 or by email at MacmillanSpecialMarkets@macmillan.com.

Library of Congress Cataloging-in-Publication Data

Names: Ostrom, Melissa, author.
Title: The beloved wild / Melissa Ostrom.
Description: New York : Feiwel and Friends, 2018. | Summary: In 1807,
   Harriet Winter leaves her family's New Hampshire farm with her brother to settle in
   the Genesee Valley to avoid being pushed into marriage with her neighbor, Daniel Long.
Identifiers: LCCN 2017017604 (print) | LCCN 2017035743 (ebook) |
   ISBN 978-1-250-29465-4 (paperback) | ISBN 978-1-250-13280-2 (ebook)
Subjects: | CYAC: Frontier and pioneer life—New York (State)—Fiction. | Brothers and
   sisters—Fiction. | Sex role—Fiction. | Genesee River Valley (Pa. and N.Y.)—History—
   19th century—Fiction. | New York (State)—History—1775–1865—Fiction.
Classification: LCC PZ7.1.O85 (ebook) | LCC PZ7.1.O85 Bel 2018 (print) | DDC [Fic]—dc23
LC record available at https://lccn.loc.gov/2017017604

Originally published in the United States by Feiwel and Friends
First Square Fish edition, 2019
Book designed by Liz Dresner
Square Fish logo designed by Filomena Tuosto

10 9 8 7 6 5 4 3 2 1

AR: 5.9 / LEXILE: 840L

For Michael, Lily, and Quinn,
and the happiness we make together

PART ONE

CHAPTER ONE

A March wind roared and dipped down the chimney to tease the flames. I welcomed its frigid breath. The fire, combined with the activities of nine people, made an oven of the house. I regretted wearing the winter longies under my skirt. This was no night for woolen flannel.

In preparation for the sugaring, my father and brothers, along with our neighbor Mr. Long, had turned the industry of spile making into a contest, and a continuous shower of sumac shavings fell around the hearth. We would need at least five hundred of these spouts to tap into the maples. I divided my time between helping Mama clean up after supper and returning to the fireside bustle to sweep the floor, deliver mead, collect spiles out of the dust, and turn the metal rods on the coals so they stayed hot, ready to burn out the spouts' centers.

Betsy and Grace, instead of making life easier by lending a

hand, added to my labors. Greatly overestimating my interest in their latest skirmish, my two sisters followed me.

Before I could sidle away again, Betsy grabbed my arm. Her glare, however, was all for Grace. "Last week it was the headache. The week before that she whined about her blood feeling tired. Whoever heard of an eleven-year-old with tired blood? Ha." Betsy, who was two years older than Grace, stared accusingly at the youngest. "Too weak to do her chores but not so ill to refuse the last cake. She's not remotely sick."

Grace, languishing against my shoulder, contradicted her with a series of honking coughs.

"A slight chill is all," Betsy insisted, speaking louder to drown the hacking. "I caught the liar pinching her cheeks right before Papa returned, hoping to give herself a consumptive air."

"A talebearer and an actress: Who's worse?" I swatted Betsy's leg with the broom. She'd stepped right in my dust pile.

Stumbling out of the way, she said in a vicious rush, "*I* know what she's about. She wants Papa to pity her so he'll let her have her pick of Mitten's pups."

"That's not his way." I returned the broom to the closet, confronted the maple-sugar buckets strewn by the back door, and began stacking them. "He wouldn't single her out for a spaniel."

"But he might let her name them, and she'll choose stupid names again." Betsy shot Grace a scornful look. "Mitten. Next we'll have a Boot and a Pretty Coat and a Sock and—and—a whole trousseau of foolish titles."

Grace coughed. "You're so cruel to me. You'll be sorry about that when I'm dead."

A call for more mead interrupted Betsy's retort. I detached my sleeve from her fingers and turned to the Invalid. "Don't be a goose. You are getting devilish tedious." Wrinkling my nose, I filled the mead pitcher. "Plus you reek."

Grace gave her arm a tentative sniff. "Mama rubbed me down with sulfur and molasses."

"That explains it." I picked up the pitcher. "Now move." The girls shuffled out of my way.

Mama had joined the gathering, her round face rosy and hands placidly folded in her lap. Her small feet kicked back the rocker, and as I turned from Luke's replenished cup to fill our neighbor's tankard, she gave me an approving smile. "Harriet's a great help to me, Mr. Long. She made the bread we ate at supper— always does now, in fact. How she manages such a fine crumb and glossy crust, I don't know. And she makes that mead at strawberry time. Good, isn't it?"

Our neighbor took an obliging sip. "Very good."

"Almost as good as her ginger beer," Mama added with a meaningful wink and a hand brandished in my direction, like a peddler advertising a shiny pot.

I narrowed my eyes at her.

Mr. Long picked up the spile he'd started. "I think I remember that beer being uncommonly delicious."

"If inebriation's your aim," I said, "you're in the right company." Indeed, except for Gideon, my favorite brother and also the only sensible one, the boys looked well on their way to gross drunkenness. "Mead, beer, currant wine"—I topped off Matthew's drink—"I could run a tavern."

"Harriet," Mama scolded.

Mr. Long merely smiled and finished his spout.

Passing her on my way to the kitchen, I answered her reproving expression with a grimace.

Mama had abandoned every effort of subtlety. We'd always seen a lot of Mr. Long. He was our nearest neighbor, not yet the age of my oldest brother but already the sole proprietor of a farm larger than our own. His parents had died of influenza almost three years ago. An only child, he'd escaped the contagion's deadly clutches and, afterward, somehow managed his grief and the family farm at the same time. More than managed. The property had thrived under his care. He was still my brothers' close friend, but his greater responsibilities set him apart, made him seem older.

Before he'd turned seventeen last year, my mother had stopped calling him Danny and started addressing him as Mr. Long. "You don't call an accomplished gentleman *Danny*," she'd explained when I had questioned the change. Her deference irked me because she expected me to share it—and because, in recent months, she'd decided to make him her son-in-law with or without my endorsement. She was the one who had invited him to dinner, surely hoping an evening involving whittling spouts would give him the chance to shine, for everyone in Middleton, New Hampshire, knew that Daniel Uriah Long had a special genius for carving wood. It would be impossible not to know this. Each thing he built, from the topmost rafter of his house to the armrest he fashioned for the end of his meetinghouse pew, bore his initials and a date: D.U.L. 1808, D.U.L. 1806, D.U.L. 1809.

There was nothing specifically wrong with Daniel Uriah Long. I'd be the first to admit that he *was* an excellent farmer. And yes, he boasted a strong frame capable of handling the most arduous task, a handsome if reticent face, and expressive gray eyes that showed an appreciation for the absurd even when his unsmiling mouth didn't. As for his initialing, I really couldn't accuse him of vanity, since, in all fairness, most men of my acquaintance signed their handiwork. In fact, south of us, one whole side of Ebenezer Felde's barn sported, in large letters, his entire last name. Daniel Long was simply a great one for puttering with wood. This, of course, resulted in a surplus of initials.

And those initials, shy of one letter, said it all. His every aspect lacked impetuosity, mystery, devilment. It was difficult to work up a romantic passion for Mr. D.U.L. Yet, inexplicably, he'd managed to stir within his plodding heart an interest in me. It was no secret in Middleton that the man hoped, in the near future, to fix me with his tedious initials.

Just the thought of this expectation raised my hackles. After I finally folded the towel in the kitchen and joined the fireside circle, now raucous with my brothers' ditties, I was feeling particularly mulish and shook my head when Papa requested a song.

The scent of singed sumac hung in the air. Plenty of spiles filled the few maple-sugar buckets between Matthew and Gideon, but Mr. Long continued to whittle away at one, from time to time answering a question or sharing a brief observation, usually without looking up. In the reddish light, I could see that along the spout he'd carved a tiny but intricate leafy vine. "Rather fancy for a spout, isn't it, Danny?"

My father frowned at my waspish tone, but Mr. Long nodded. "Habit."

His mildness goaded me to add, "You forgot to etch in your initials."

Quick as a snap, his eyes met mine. "So I did." He rectified the omission and held out the spout. "For you."

Surprised by the gesture, I didn't immediately take it. Then, just as I leaned forward to accept the gift, he retrieved it, leaving my hand dangling stupidly.

His mouth quivered. He suppressed the smile and murmured, "Perhaps I ought to carve your initials in it as well, since it will be yours." He raised his eyebrows expectantly.

I folded my arms. "I doubt there's room for anything else on the little thing."

"I'll squeeze them in. It's *H* then . . . ?"

"*S*," I offered grudgingly.

"*H.S.W.*, Harriet S. Winter," he said evenly as he carved. "What is the *S* for? Sarah? Sally?"

I tightened my mouth and shook my head. I despised my middle name. If only the *S* did stand for Sarah or Sally.

Betsy the Tattler, sitting at Papa's feet, offered, "Submit. That's what it stands for."

For the first time that night, Mr. Long laughed. "*Submit*. Oh, that's rich." As he presented the spout, he asked, still grinning, "And do you?"

I took it with a slow, ungracious show of disinterest but answered curtly and quickly enough: "No. Never."

CHAPTER TWO

I woke early the next morning. Dawn began to drift into the loft, reversing the darkness, like a tea un-steeping itself. Sliding out from under the quilts, I took care not to disturb my sisters' slumber, then made use of the chamber pot and broke the ice in the pitcher to wash my hands and face. The brisk water swiped away the vestiges of sleep. With a shiver, I hurried out of my nightdress, slipped speedily into my clothes, and climbed down the ladder plank to the keeping room.

My father, kneeling by the hearth, was kindling the fire. He smiled at me over his shoulder. "Morning, kitten."

I greeted him with a kiss on his bristled cheek.

Mama glanced up from the potatoes she was chopping. "At least two of our six rise to work in this house, David."

Papa stood and dusted his knees. "The boys likely wore themselves out looking to the fences yesterday."

I sniffed. *Looking to the fences.* Was that cant for drinking oneself into a stupor? I plucked my apron from its hook and pulled it over my head.

A wet snore erupted from the borning room, where Matthew and Luke slept.

Mama and I grinned at each other.

"They're pretty well knocked up," she murmured, scooping handfuls of potatoes and transferring them to the soup pot. "But Gideon's out and making ready to haul the dead hickory that fell by the pond. Want to eat and take him his breakfast?"

"Certainly." We could have the chance to talk. My brother seemed distracted lately. I wondered why. "I'll take mine and have it with him."

"Don't linger." Mama gave the pot a stir. "You didn't finish your Latin yesterday."

I made a face. We lived too far from town to attend school, so our mother educated us, which I didn't mind when the subject was geometry, history, logic, or literature. Latin was another matter. I hated it. Sighing, I tied the apron strings at my waist and, without bothering to repair my braid, hurriedly wrapped a half-dozen warm biscuits in a towel and donned my cape.

A cold westerly wind whipped me the second I stepped outside. After tucking the bundled biscuits against my stomach, I tightened the cape around me with my free hand and made my way toward the pond. The straggly remains of Mama's kitchen garden occupied the yard closest to the door, but along the rotting ropes of squash vines, snowdrops bloomed: harbingers of spring. I stooped to admire the little white bells before continuing, first circling the well sweep, then passing the shed. Only small patches of snow dotted the property, but frost furred the ground. Under my boots, the matted grass crunched and, all the way to the stand of uncut timber, gleamed like silver in the early sunlight.

I passed the barn and climbed over the stone fence. Gideon stood far beyond the pond, near the burial place. He was a familiar figure even from this distance, with his peculiar forward slouch, like a man always heading into an impossible wind. Overhead, pink edged the clouds, and, encircling us, mountains towered like blue giants curled in sleep, great guardians of whatever fantastical lands and seas rippled out on their other sides. I inhaled deeply, glad to escape the house, liking the brisk air that stung my lungs. It was a glorious morning.

I tossed him a biscuit half by way of hello.

He caught it with his left hand. "Thank you"—he wrinkled his nose at the honey on his palm—"for making me sticky."

Smiling, I perched on the toppled hickory he'd already trimmed for hauling. "So what's the problem? You've been moping all week."

He shrugged and ate the biscuit half in two bites. "Not moping. Just thinking." He wiped his palm on his trousers; then, with the ease of practice, he sank his ax into a stump before sitting next to me, shoving his dusky fringe from his forehead, and inhaling appreciatively.

"Here."

The biscuits were still warm, their split centers luscious with melted butter and golden honey. Gideon groaned as he bit into another one.

"Thinking about what?"

"The Genesee Valley."

I stilled. I'd heard about the Genesee Valley. Its wilderness. Its availability for purchase.

After hazarding a peek my way, he gazed around at the beautiful morning. "If this were all mine, Harry, I'd never go. But it isn't. Plenty of New Englanders are already emigrating, pushing the bounds of civilization and improving the territories in western New York. And why not? Farms have crowded this area. The soil is thin, the forests gone, wild game rare. Out that way, land—fertile, forested land—is selling cheap. Prodigiously cheap. I can save enough money in less than a year to purchase a hundred acres from the Holland Land Company."

His vehemence astonished me. When I recovered, I demanded, "What good are a hundred acres of friendless, strange wilderness?"

"Sounds like heaven," he answered bluntly. "A land thick with virgin forest, all species of wood, and mine, mine, mine: completely mine, not a single brother to work for or share my parcel with."

" 'All species of wood,' " I muttered. "You sound like our whittling neighbor."

Gideon grinned. "Daniel Long undoubtedly would appreciate the rich variety of so many trees. I wonder if he'd sell his farm and commence a pioneer life with me."

"You'd make a lovely couple." I shoved the biscuit bundle into his arms and stood.

My mind whirled. I replayed his words, sensibly argued but nevertheless impossible for me to process. His enthusiastic reasoning so thoroughly twisted my expectations, what I understood to be my past, present, and future, that I wouldn't have been surprised if the cardinal on the hemlock overhead suddenly took flight upside down. Gid was my best friend. Home meant Gid. Where would I be without him?

I wandered to the burial plot and leaned against a post.

Without turning, I said, "I guess you've made up your mind." *With no thought to my feelings.*

He must have heard the hurt in my voice because he said in a cajoling way, "What can a youngest son hope for here? The rockiest, scantest portion of a mountain? A stretch of bog and clay? Should I try my hand at preaching to earn a living?" He appeared at my side and frowned over the fence. "I don't belong in a place if there's no room for me there."

"You belong with your family, and family always makes room."

He grunted and folded his arms.

Opposite the fence, two dozen grave markers faced us like grim pages in an unfinished book. The inscribed names reflected my ancestors, not Gideon's. By blood we weren't siblings or even half siblings. I was the single product of my father's first marriage, and Gideon the youngest of his mother's. Only Grace and Betsy could call our current parents their own.

By long habit, my eyes immediately found my birth mother's marker: MRS. SUBMIT FAITHFUL WINTER, WIFE TO MR. DAVID WINTER, DEC'D OCT'R 10 1792 IN YE 18 OF HER AGE.

I had been taught little more about my mother than what these shallowly inscribed details provided. My father, while far from coldhearted, was not sentimental. He never led me to believe he still mourned his loss and certainly didn't wallow in romantic recollections. Plus, his second wife, hardworking, cheerful, handy in the kitchen, and quick with the needle, well pleased him, as she did all of us. She was the only mother I'd ever known, and I loved her as if she were the one who'd borne me.

But I frequently wondered about this Submit Faithful Winter.

The handful of letters and numbers, encircled with a scroll border and topped with a winged skull and crossed bones, told a sad story. The most telling detail, of course, was her death date. It coincided precisely with my birthday.

The other headstones looked similar to hers, all jutting out of the winter-ravaged ground, as if this ragged oval plot were the mouth of the earth, baring its teeth. The predominant surname was Knowles, my birth mother's maiden name. She had been the last Knowles in these parts, and my father, having married and outlived her, had inherited her home: the land, the house, and this, all that was left of her family's remains.

More females than males occupied the lot, since many a Knowles man had lived to enjoy two, even three, wives in succession. The women's names, especially Patience, Thankful, Mercy, and Temperance, either amused or piqued me, depending on my mood. Today I found them thoroughly irritating. Every man got to be himself, a plain Richard or a regular Edward. These women, however, had to grow up lugging around the weighty expectations tied to whatever names their parents had chosen for them.

" 'Mrs. Hope, wife to Mr. James Knowles, deceased June 17, 1775, aged nineteen years.' That was my mother's mother. Hope." I sniffed. "All these women could play a part in an allegory."

"An ironic one, considering when your grandmother passed away. Hope died fast."

"They all do." I scanned the markers. Hardly a woman buried here lived to see her twenty-first year. "A stranger might gather each married a bluebeard."

With his best Scottish burr, Gideon sang softly, " 'Loup off the steed,' says false Sir John. 'Your bridal bed you see. For I have drowned seven young ladies. The eighth one you shall be.' "

"Very nice. Of course, in the tale, the last bride's brother gallops to the castle to rescue her and dispatches the monster in the process. I suppose, since my favorite brother plans to pioneer in the wilds of the Genesee Valley, I'll end up like all the others in here: young and dead." I shot him a sour look. "Perhaps you'll return for a visit after your first great harvest. You can rest a pumpkin on my little plot as a token of remembrance."

He nodded and took a step back, resting a heel on his sleigh. "You are excessively fond of pumpkin pie. Ouch." He rubbed his arm where I pinched him. "Don't be dramatic, Harry. Chances are you won't marry a wife killer." He waved an airy hand to indicate the crowded little lot. "Disease probably scotched most of the unfortunates here."

"Note their ages, stupid. The women obviously died giving birth to their babes."

"Well, you can't blame the poor husbands for that."

"Who else would I blame?"

He looked stumped for a moment. "A drunk midwife?"

"No." I slowly shook my head. "Childbirth's a common way for a woman to die." I eyed the excess of female appellations on the markers and added dryly, "Particularly in my family. According to Old Nancy in the village, my birth mother was very slight, not made for easy birthing."

He gave my back a brisk pat and, as one determined to look on the bright side, said, "But she was also a noted beauty."

I grunted. If there was one thing I had learned about Submit Faithful Winter, it was that. Among family and acquaintances, I'd frequently heard about the Knowles women's famous beauty. Apparently, it was inheritable. Until I came along. I was a typical Winter: spare, pale, and lanky.

"Cheer up, Harry. I can't see you suffering the same fate. You're almost as tall as me—certainly no slip of a girl."

I tapped the top of his head. "*Almost?* I'm just as tall."

"But with more bones than skin, as Papa says." He smirked.

"He makes me sound like a walking skeleton."

"Yes. Rather. But you've got a lot of yellow hair and an interesting face," he said before ruining the already-tepid compliment with "though your mouth is too wide and your eyes too big. And you could better mind that sharp tongue of yours if you tried." He grinned. "Otherwise, though, I think you're perfect."

I snorted.

"So does Daniel Long."

I glared toward Mount Chester. Mr. Long's estate was nestled at its foot. "Too bad Mama can't take a second husband. She holds His Dullness in such high esteem."

Gideon smiled at me quizzically. "I can't understand why you don't. He's an honest friend, kind, industrious, fair, generous, intelligent—"

"Handsome?"

He refused to rise to the bait. "Sure. Handsome as well. Frankly, I like him vastly better than our brothers. I don't know why you don't."

I shrugged. How did I explain a reaction I couldn't entirely reason for myself? Perhaps it had something to do with getting written into someone else's story, without a chance to tell my own. "I'm handy; that's all. A practical way to bridge the two farms."

"You underestimate Daniel Long."

"Is it wrong to want something more than practicality in a marriage?"

"If you think that's all he sees in you, you're foolish." Then, with a sidelong twinkle: "Not to mention rhetorical." He started making his way back to the downed hickory.

"I suppose you, with your frontier ambitions, are the only one of us who gets to choose excitement."

"Mr. Long has the best farm in these parts. If I were a woman and he proposed, I'd marry him faster than Luke can tipple a bottle of rum."

I smiled. "Faster than Matthew can hazard his new boots at the card table?"

"Faster than Betsy can spill a sacred secret."

"Even faster than Grace can sniffle her way into a hot mustard footbath?"

Grinning, he retrieved his ax from the trunk. "Even faster than that. Anyway, I'd like to see you good and settled before I leave next March."

Before I leave next March. The words stole the smile from my face.

Gideon was more than the brother who matched me in age, nature, and size. He was my best friend. We'd grown up shadowing each other, collecting tadpoles in the stream, playing one-a-cat, racing our sleds in the winter. We hadn't been grown long enough for me to forget our childhood games. Contemplating losing him pained me. I turned away to hide the sting of tears, and for a moment the mountains blurred into the clouds above them. I blinked and took a steadying breath.

But when I could see clearly again, the range persisted in looking strange. Though yet like lolling giants, the rocky formations no longer seemed to guard the faraway lands. Rather, they struck me as a meaner front: the stern keepers of here.

I shivered. Wishing I'd remembered my mittens to stave off the nip of the March morning, I fisted my hands under the cape and slid them into my apron's front pocket.

There I encountered something hard. Taking hold of it, I realized it was the spile Mr. Long had carved for me. I must have stashed it in the pocket and forgotten it.

I brought the spile out into the daylight, ran a finger over the intricate vine, and turned the spout to find his initials. Just as I was about to stuff it back into my pocket and return to the house, the other set of initials seized my attention. *"What?* The devil!"

Gideon, roping the hickory onto the sleigh, looked up.

I stomped to his side and, borrowing from our older brothers' vocabulary, muttered a string of what I reckoned must be terrible expletives.

He took the spile I'd thrust in his face and straightened. Instead of sharing my indignation, he threw back his head and laughed.

"I don't find presumptuousness amusing." I snatched the spout out of his hand.

As far as I was concerned, there wasn't an ounce of humor in Mr. Long's making my last initial an *L* instead of a *W.*

CHAPTER THREE

Besides warning me to keep his secret to myself, Gideon didn't discuss his pioneer plans in the following weeks. Silent as he remained on the matter, however, his discontentment with his present situation became increasingly noticeable. He wasn't sullen, but more and more he found ways to detach himself from the other men's labors. For instance, he left the splitting of rails to Papa and our brothers and chose to work in the woodlot by himself, felling a fine oak and preparing it for spring seasoning with nobody's help but that provided by Trouble the ox.

He chose the oak with floor timbers in mind. For a long time now, Mama had spoken wistfully of a good wooden floor to replace our hard-packed dirt one. Gideon confessed to me he planned to make the oak-plank flooring a parting gift for her. I didn't want to hear this—nor whatever he had in mind for *my* farewell present. Nothing could reconcile me to his leaving.

Winter clung to March. Just as the green spears of daffodils nosed through the ground behind the toolshed and we began to smile hopefully at the cloudless skies and believe the worst of the weather had ended, we woke to a snow thick as a curtain. The spell persisted for the last three days of the month. Mama grew impatient with the men crowding the house, getting in the way of our spinning, and making a mess by the hearth with their tool sharpening.

Finally a northerly kicked at the trees, and though the temperature didn't rise above forty degrees by day, neither did it sink below twenty at night. On a morning in early April, after breakfast, Papa stood in the open doorway, peered at the sky, and held out a hand for a moment as if weighing the wind. He shut the door and returned to his chair. "Sap will be flowing properly now."

Sharp freezes at night, free thaws by midmorning: sugaring time. Its arrival, more than all the green shoots and tweeting birds, foretold spring.

Matthew greeted the announcement with a holler. My sisters cheered. Quite literally, there was no sweeter time: the sap collecting and boiling, then the sampling and celebrating. Sugaring was work, but of a social kind, for some of our neighbors would aid us in the enterprise.

I didn't doubt all of us felt the thrill of anticipation. But Gideon stood so quickly his chair tipped over. He pounded across the room and wrenched open the door, apparently to see for himself the day's conditions.

When he turned, his face was alive with excitement. "Shall I ride to the Welds place and let them know?"

"Certainly." Papa pulled on his boots. "Tell Robert he can take home a tub of sweetening for pay if he joins us."

Betsy studied Gideon with a sly smile. "I'm sure the pretty cousin staying with them also might like to earn a sugar bucket. We can always use some help tending to the stirring and boiling."

Mama nodded complacently. Already my older brothers were rushing to catch up with Papa, shrugging on their coats and mumbling about checking on the firewood supply in the sugarhouse. I rose hurriedly, too.

Gideon's reaction to Betsy's comment, however, stopped me in my tracks. She'd meant to tease him with the reference to Robert's cousin, and I could tell she'd succeeded. He looked irked and flushed, like she'd guessed something he wanted to keep private.

I stared at him dumbly. *Another* secret? I tried to dredge up a recollection of this new neighbor. She hadn't been in Middleton long enough for me to meet her more than once, and that had been at meeting. Since the Welds family sat in a pew behind ours, I'd failed to get a good look at her. I only vaguely recalled a dab of a girl, red-cheeked and curly-haired. Yet I suspected from Gideon's expression that he'd attended to her much more closely.

How closely? Had he seen her since then? If so, was she a passing interest or more than that? And just how did she figure into his frontiersman scheme?

It took a whole week to get some answers. Half of it we spent at our farm, the other at Mr. Long's. But whether at our sugarhouse or his, the days matched: the men, bundled in coats and fur caps, disappeared into the woods, driving their ox-pulled sleds, and every few hours returned, their barrels brimming with sap. They'd stop at our bonfire to drain the contents into the cauldron, then head back to the woods.

Mostly, the womenfolk stayed near the kettle—me, Mama, my sisters, and the Weldses' cousin, Rachel. Stirring the sap and adding wood to keep the fire going for a steady boil didn't require much focus; I was given the freedom to imitate nosy Betsy and, during the few times when Gideon's and Rachel's paths crossed, examine the subjects' faces to see what kind of romance was brewing between the Winter and Welds households.

But whenever Gideon made a visit to contribute his full barrel, he neither stole more than a searing glance at this girl nor uttered a single word. It was impossible to determine their degree of familiarity.

Still, during the week, I had plenty of time to examine our new neighbor. I decided I couldn't like her.

She was missish.

Her responses to Betsy's inquisitions invited this conclusion. Running the long-handled ladle over the bubbling surface to skim the sap, my sister would ask questions: "So, from what parts did your parents come, Rachel?" "Have you any siblings?" "Do you like Middleton?" "Isn't your cousin Ed the most half-witted fellow you ever met?" "Did you leave behind a beau?" "Would you settle in this country for good, do you think?"

We didn't call Betsy the Intelligencer for nothing.

Rachel's answers disclosed that she was an orphan, with no nearer relatives than the Weldses. During the year after her parents' passing, she'd stayed in Massachusetts, working as a spinning girl for the prosperous family that owned the mill before saving enough to pay for her stage fare and traveling to the Weldses. The new living arrangement, she confided, was a happier circumstance, since the Weldses, though poor, were a cheerful bunch. "And I do love caring for the babes, cuddling their precious persons, telling them fairy tales, and teaching them games. They're the dearest things, round and romping. Full of juice! I adore children."

Her glowing recital happened to coincide with one of Mr. Long's appearances, so he was present when I grunted and remarked, "You're in the right place, then. The Welds house veritably teems with brats." Ten in all: the four youngest of whom made for a daily hell of snotty noses, soiled diapers, sticky hands, cries, accidents, and constant demands. I shuddered.

Catching my expression, Mr. Long's mouth quivered. But he mostly attended to the cauldron, ladling sap and watching it closely as he poured it back in a slow trickle. He handed Betsy the wooden utensil. "Too thin yet." Then, to Rachel: "I'm sure Mrs. Welds appreciates your help."

Rachel, blushing prettily, gave a modest little shrug.

Mama, who'd been bestowing an approving smile on the paragon of would-be motherhood, turned to Mr. Long. "A large family's a blessing. Just wait until all of those Weldses grow up. So many helping hands would make short work of this business." She tilted her head to indicate our sugaring. After casting a sidelong peek my way, she inquired innocently, "Do you think you'll be wanting a big family yourself, Mr. Long?"

For heaven's sake. I flared my eyes at her.

He answered blandly, "Oh, without a doubt. I should guess ten or eleven children."

"Eleven," I gasped. So I was to be a broodmare? Not if I could help it. I glared at him. "Why not make it a round dozen?"

His mouth curved for an instant before straightening. "Good thinking."

Grace began moaning by the stacked wood, complaining about a bellyache.

Mama glanced distractedly her way. "What now, child?"

She whimpered and rubbed her stomach. "I don't feel at all myself. What if I'm getting a touch of the influenza?"

With a frown, Mama hurried to her youngest and relieved her of her armful of wood, while Betsy exclaimed into the cauldron's steam, "Fiddle! Miss Lazy needs a touch of the switch; that's what she ought to be getting." She passed me the ladle and strode, arms folded, to Mama's side, sneering, "I'd like to know how many times she's spilled syrup onto the snow for sampling. Bet she made herself sick on candy."

Rachel smiled indulgently at my obnoxious sisters.

Mr. Long, used to their squabbles, was looking at the sky, his expression content. "As long as we keep getting these light snowfalls, the sap will run. We might be sugaring off into next week." He tugged on his mittens and winked at me. "Keep stirring, Harriet Submit Winter." He pronounced my name succinctly, as though he was savoring every single syllable.

I gripped the ladle. How gratifying it'd feel to thwack him over the head with it.

"Oh." Rachel fixed me with her round blue eyes. Those eyes annoyed me. They were so perpetually surprised. "Is that your full name? Very pretty."

I muttered a thank-you and said to Mr. Long's parting back, "Yes, Harriet Winter, not Harriet *Linter*. Too bad your spelling isn't as good as your whittling, Mr. Long."

He turned to flash me a grin. "Perhaps you can stitch me an alphabet sampler, and I can work on my letters."

"I *hate* stitchery."

"I imagine you'd rather be hard at work distilling strong spirits." He delivered a sigh in the new girl's direction and explained,

"Miss Winter plans to open a tavern when she grows up. Someday. Hopefully." His expression clarified that the last two words modified the growing, not the tavern opening.

I shook the ladle threateningly in the air.

Rachel, ever wide-eyed, made a perfect O with her mouth, then said doubtfully, "I wonder your parents would let you."

He clucked. "Yes, well, she's their cross to bear. If only she'd give needlework a try. Most girls happily *submit* to that labor." He shook his head and ambled toward the sled.

I growled, but before I could lash him with a retort, he'd started talking to his young cousin, Jeb.

And Rachel was chattering again.

"So you dislike stitchery? Do you mean that truly? I find plying a needle a very productive activity. Quite soothing, too, and almost as pleasant as singing." She bent to nudge another piece of firewood into the flames. When she straightened, her hand fluttered up to smooth a curl from her forehead. "I've never known a Linter, but back in Juneville, I knew a Linton—many Lintons, in fact. Rather friendly, the Lintons—or Mrs. Linton, at least. I would have rather hired myself out as her dairymaid than as Mrs. Walkley's spinning girl, except the Lintons got the notion to make the great trek westward. The morning they departed, Mrs. Linton gave me a gift of some fine lace and made me promise, when I was finally in the position of exploring the legendary Genesee Valley myself, that I'd indulge her with a visit, and she said I'd be welcome to stay as long as I liked. I nearly joined her then and there, for to see a whole caravan readying for departure—the wagons weighted with furniture and farm equipment, the livestock tethered and nervous, the dogs yapping—oh, it filled me with such great excitement, and I—"

"Did you say the Genesee Valley?"

"Yes. Wondrously rich land, I hear." She glanced around, as if to ensure no one was eavesdropping, then added in a near whisper, "Cousin Robert and Cousin Ed are keen on the notion of journeying there as well." A small frown creased her forehead. "Nothing official yet, of course. They haven't even told their folks—avoiding their mother's tears and opposition as long as possible, I imagine. I learned of it by chance, actually. But they've extended the invitation to me, and I couldn't be more grateful."

I stared at her for a moment. "Ah."

And to myself: *Aha!*

CHAPTER FOUR

One need not grow up with or live for any great length of time in close proximity to five other children to learn this: There is never anything so desirable as that which is desired by another. Mention a hankering for the last potato in the pot, and before you know it, every other young person just *has* to have that potato or risk death from the craving.

Betsy and Grace fought over a rag doll for the better part of a year until they tore it in half. Matthew and Luke, to this day, vied for the same coffee cup. Gideon's situation always proved particularly treacherous. This youngest and smallest son could not compete with the meaty-armed, thick-fisted oafs who comprised our brothers. He learned early on to make silent his joys and discoveries. An unusual rock worth keeping was quietly palmed and furtively pocketed.

Chances were that *this*, more than anything, explained his reticence around Rachel. A show of proprietary fascination would have incited our brothers' competitive urges. If one weren't I (the person who knew Gideon best) or Betsy (our family's version of a Bow Street runner), one probably wouldn't discern any particular interest on Gideon's part in this person who, as far as I was concerned, sported more hair than wit.

Of course, this unfortunate aspect of human nature also explained his reluctance to disclose his pioneer plans to the family. Sure, he didn't want to upset Mama too soon. But he also didn't want to plant a seed of interest in Luke's skull. He might decide to join him, and Gid wanted this adventure all for himself.

On the evening of the last day of sugaring, when Daniel Long's great room filled with spit-shined boots and Sunday-best skirts, when maple cakes (baked by Widow Barnes, Mr. Long's housekeeper) fragranced the air, and when sleigh bells heralded each new arrival outside while laughter and the fiddler's string tuning stirred the interior, only Betsy and I probably detected anything peculiar about Gideon. If his cheeks looked ruddier than usual, well, many of us were a bit blistered from a week of working in the cold wind and tending to a big fire.

So, with Rachel, he did not behave like a dog guarding a ham bone. Not overtly. He escorted her to the dance floor just once: for a cotillion. His bow was polite, his conversation (at least that which I managed to overhear) punctilious. Afterward, he walked her to a chair and procured a glass of currant wine for her. He observed every nicety with this new neighbor. He even promptly released her to her next partner. Then, making his way around the couples who were arranging themselves in the new set, he quite rightly asked a languishing Mildred, the doctor's homeliest daughter, if she'd favor him with a dance.

Yet I saw past the pose. He breathed a mite too quickly and watched the rosy, laughing Rachel rather too closely. He was like a cloud hiding a bolt of lightning.

And I could tell that Gideon, in some strange and secretive and un-Gideon way, was utterly shattered.

I didn't demur when various Middleton boys asked me to dance, not even when Mr. Long was the one asking. Frankly, I was too distracted to devise a tart rejoinder and perform my customary show of churlishness. I stood up for most of the dances but didn't do so very gracefully, too busy spying on my brother to attend to the steps.

Before the last reel ended, Mr. Long, my partner, blew a long-suffering sigh and shuffled me off the dance floor.

I blinked at him in surprise. "Are you winded, Mr. Long?"

He drew me to a chair near the punch bowl. "No. Injured. You keep stomping on my feet." He passed me a cup of punch and stood by my chair, watching me in amusement as I quaffed it. Then he glanced at Gideon, who was leaning against the wall and doing his best not to glare at Robert, who danced with the gaily giggling Rachel.

Mr. Long's expression turned thoughtful. "Ah." He gave me a sympathetic smile. "You're worrying about losing your best friend." Absently, he reached down and brushed a strand of my hair behind my ear.

I gaped at him. The impulsive gesture obviously surprised him as much as it did me. For a moment he didn't seem to know what to say or where to look, and finally he simply tucked his hand in his armpit, as if not trusting it to stay put.

He cleared his throat, and after a minute the awkwardness passed. I resumed frowning at Gideon and wishing the boy hadn't turned into such a ridiculous fool.

Mr. Long handed me a second cup of punch. "Poor Harriet," he mused quietly. "It's hard getting older."

Bluebirds arrived, Easter Sunday came and went, rain turned parts of the farm into watering holes, the brook rose and flooded, a spell of sunshine dried the worst of the muck, spring plowing began, many ripped seams were mended, many stockings were darned, many wristbands were stitched, and all of April passed before Gideon spoke of the Genesee Valley again, saying a little about the Welds brothers, verifying their similar pioneer plans, and mentioning how much money they'd already put aside, enough to allow them to leave for the wilderness months before he would.

All of this sounded like a preface. Sure enough, he asked abruptly, "What do you think about their cousin Rachel?"

I worried the flattened end of a nail with my thumb. We were in the forge barn, where he was making nails to improve his savings. Though we all had chores that contributed to the family's earnings and helped maintain the farm, if we chose to do more than we were assigned, we could make spending cash, what Mama called "pin money." Gid hid his personal savings under the plank where I stood. The pile of coins was growing into quite the cache. After a moment of silence, while I deliberated telling him my true opinion, I tossed the nail in the pile and shrugged. "She's pretty."

"Yes, very pretty," he sighed, and hammered a nail rod to a point with unnecessary force. "Every Middleton boy thinks so."

Hope leaped like a blaze in a wind. So Rachel was much

admired? Good. Perhaps she was a flirt, and Gideon would grow disgusted with her. Or maybe some richer Middleton boy would pursue and win her, and my brother would decide the Genesee Valley didn't sound so wonderful after all. I didn't say anything else, about Rachel or Gid's pioneering, and to my relief, the conversation waned.

I was not the kind of person to handle a problem. I ignored it and prayed it'd disappear.

But this problem didn't, as I learned the first Sabbath in May, after meeting.

The Sunday started so well. Spring was new enough that I hadn't forgotten what the meetinghouse was like in winter. How wonderful not to haul foot stoves into the unheated church, not to watch Pastor's stormed message make clouds in the bitter air around his red face, not to shiver in our muffs and under our furs for the wearying hours of worship, not to bite into half-frozen communion bread, and not to fear that the icy baptismal waters were going to smite the unfortunate wintertime newborns with a deadly chill.

The day was blissfully mild. I felt unencumbered. Free.

It was even warm enough for some of the Middleton folks to walk barefoot to the meetinghouse and thus save the shine on their shoes. They waited until they reached the doorway to slip them on and button them.

Those of us who lived too far away to walk traveled on horseback or in carriages and wagons. We arrived just as the Weldses did, and though my older brothers jumped out of the wagon and rushed to the fence where the horses were hitched so they could examine a neighbor's new bay, Gideon quickly strode to greet the Weldses. Looking extraordinarily pleased, he lent Rachel his hand to help her step down to the rutted road, before any other young man could beat him to it.

Overhead, a hawk wrote curvy letters across the blue sky in soaring sweeps, looking more like a creature playing than hunting. With the help of the wind, the trees and bushes dotting the yards twitched their young leaves like frisky colts. Early miniature irises, ice blue, formed a pretty trim around the white church. The blacksmith shop was quiet, the tavern windows dark. No vendors cried their wares, and no spinning wheels whirred. Besides murmured conversations and the occasional caw of a crow, the only sounds to disturb the Sunday peace came from approaching parishioners, their wagon wheels crunching the gravel on the roads and, upon reaching the bridge, thundering the loose planks.

It was too fine a day to rush into the church. Folks dallied outside, shaking hands, inquiring after one another's farms and relatives. Some loitered by the fence; others strolled across the scruffy grass into the graveyard. Children played on the ground and promptly reversed the positive effects of their Saturday night washings by digging into the flower borders and yanking loose fat worms.

When at last we shuffled in, most of us had worked out the worst of our fidgets, and the congregation settled down to listen to Pastor Cartwright's morning-long sermon with good grace.

Though he kept us on our knees for one too many interminable prayers, we enjoyed some distractions. Mama brought a store of nuts and dried fruits for munching. Mr. Underwood entertained us with his amazing spitting skill, shooting his tobacco juice down the middle aisle, sometimes as far as the altar. Once, the dogs in the neighborhood set up a racket; then, as if led by a singing master, in one accord they started to howl. And halfway through the service, Widow Harrison, who lived behind the church, popped out of her pew to try to capture one of her chickens, which had wandered through the open doorway. Whenever she got close enough to seize it, the hen eluded her with a *brawk!* and a nervous flapping of wings. The fun came to an end when the bird clumsily flew up and landed on the pulpit. The reverend trapped its legs in a speedily shut Bible.

Finally we sang the closing hymn, received the benediction, and went outside. We lived too far away to commit our afternoon to the second round of worship. Stretching our stiff muscles and blinking at the noon-high sun, we prepared to leave. I was looking forward to a few hours of rest. But then three things happened to ruin what promised to be a perfectly lovely day.

First, after climbing into the wagon and sitting back to wait for the rest of my family, I spotted Matthew and immediately noticed something strange in my oldest brother's demeanor. He detached himself from the crowd by the church doors, looked carefully behind him, and sidled to the end of the fence. Then followed this worrisome sight: Matthew and Isaac Rush deep in conversation. Rush was the worst gamester in Middleton and the man most responsible for arranging the various local gambling parties and blood sports. Mothers, in particular, despised the man. He all too efficiently encouraged their boys to empty their pockets in wasteful plays for money stakes.

The Winters didn't have the luxury of a fortune to gamble away, but there was no mistaking the secretive passing of a fat purse that took place between my brother and Mr. Rush. How in heaven's name had Matthew scraped together such a bundle? Even if he'd set aside a year's worth of pin money, he never would have saved that much, not unless he'd gotten lucky at the card tables and managed to grow his cash. If that was the case, it was a short-lived luck. The money was gone now.

After sliding the purse into his coat, Mr. Rush wandered across the street. Then my oldest brother trudged back to the meeting-house. No one, not even our sister Grace, could have worn a sicklier visage. His skin was pasty white, and his eyes, as soon as they met mine, bulged in alarm. He immediately looked away and veered toward the crowd outside the doors.

Where this money had come from, how much it amounted to, and why it had left Matthew's possession were worrisome questions. They made me extremely uneasy. No one but I, however, seemed to have witnessed what had happened. Indeed, Matthew and Mr. Rush had enjoyed almost complete privacy in their exchange. That was because of the second shocker.

After the service, nearly the entire congregation had flitted toward a carriage to welcome the late-arriving Goodrich family. I had heard about the Goodriches. I knew Mr. Goodrich had inherited the mill and was already stirring Middleton's curiosity with his plans for improvements. What I hadn't known was that Mr. Goodrich, besides sporting a single son, had fathered a pack of beautiful daughters. From my wagon perch, I could examine all of them: five elegantly dressed, prettily mannered, fashionably dark-haired, dark-eyed beauties.

Mr. Long already seemed on very good terms with the oldest. Similarly tall and handsome, they stood facing each other right outside the meetinghouse doorway like a newly married couple. Though I couldn't discern the particulars of their conversation, they obviously spoke naturally, like good friends. And, every so often, Miss Goodrich's laughter trilled like a merry bell.

I sniffed and folded my arms. It was a wonder she found anything to amuse her in Mr. D.U.L.'s conversation. She was probably as foolish as Rachel Welds.

And that was the third circumstance: Rachel. She had also squeezed her presence into the welcoming crowd, but as she turned away from two of the Goodrich girls, she ran smack into my brother.

Luke, not Gideon.

A teasing encounter ensued. Luke joked. Rachel tittered and blushed. Luke joked again. Rachel tittered some more. And directly behind Luke, Gideon stood and seethed.

Poor Gid. He was a mite short for Rachel to spot behind the beefy Luke and too worshipful by far to engage her in the kind of breezy flirtation Luke was so good at.

Worst of all was Luke's expression of intrigue. Rachel had captured his notice. Gideon, standing stiffly behind the bold Luke, was probably recollecting every instance his older brother had wrangled something dear from him: the favorite pup, the favorite piglet, the favorite toy, the favorite treat.

Stiffly, Gideon turned and stomped to the wagon. Perhaps the sympathy I felt for him was written across my face, because he quickly looked away from me and busied himself by hitching the oxen.

After climbing into the wagon, he sat heavily, hunched and somber, his eyes downcast, his hands loosely folded. We observed the silence until the crowd began dispersing. I noted with a sensation as sharp as vinegar how charmingly Mr. Long took Miss Goodrich's hand as they said their good-byes. I supposed he saved his great store of sarcasm just for me.

Gideon's sigh interrupted my peevish thoughts. He began

talking, softly but earnestly. "I'm tired of wanting things I can't have, Harry. I need my own place and can almost afford it. I hope you understand why I have to leave." The entire time he spoke, he stared straight ahead, eyes burning, face rigid.

I said what I knew he needed to hear. "Yes, Gid, I understand."

But I didn't say what I'd started thinking. *Maybe I need the same. Maybe there's nothing—and no one—here for me, either.*

Maybe I'll go with you.

CHAPTER FIVE

Though the idea of joining Gideon had initially sprung like an inspired and viable course of action, it almost as quickly lost its appeal. In fact, I felt ill simply thinking about leaving Middleton. Home became a cherished picture constantly adorning my thoughts. The fact that in this vision, among my family and the rolling, springtime landscape, Mr. Long had also begun to appear . . .

Well. That was a development I preferred not to ponder.

Chores prevented me from dwelling too deeply on this disturbing shift in my sentiments. It was May, and May didn't wait for humans to exercise their feelings. May could care less about a person's hopes and fears. May was the season of the plow.

The month began with a warm spell, and the men spent the first week after that fateful Sunday turning the soil, letting what hid all winter long greet the sun and saturate the air with the scent of earth. The following Monday, they began planting the Indian corn.

That day, in an hour of rare harmony, Betsy and Grace talked gaily while taking turns at the butter churn. I listened from where I stood over the stew pot. Their conversation made my mouth water, for what they anticipated was true: Mama would contrive some *very* good things with the results of this planting, from johnnycakes to Indian pudding. Luke, having returned to the house to collect the ax handle he'd left seasoning on the spit hooks, leaned over the girls to add his own personal vision of paradise: "And don't forget the corn whiskey."

By midweek, the weather took a turn for the worse. Nevertheless, Mama, who wore out the almanac in her efforts to time our planting according to the constellations, put me to work in the kitchen garden. The moon had begun to decrease, and she insisted it was time to commence the radishes.

"What difference does it make?" The afternoon was wet, yet here I was, planting radishes and looking as mud-caked as a freshly dug root vegetable.

"Radishes taper downward, dear," she murmured. She was just as damp as I was and on her knees two rows over, worrying about the progress of her peas and searching their curly tendrils for blight. "You need to plant them downward at the decrease of the moon."

A strand of wet hair had plastered itself across my face. I peeled it away and muttered, "Stuff and nonsense." But I kept digging.

By the end of the week, the garden was planted. I resumed my inside chores, the ones that kept me busy regardless of the season.

The men, in contrast, had few consistent labors. Their duties changed according to nature's whims and schedule, and in May, nature demanded a lot. This was a good thing, particularly for Matthew. As the month progressed, between the cooking, mending, and scrubbing, in the early mornings and the late evenings, I kept an eye on my oldest brother. I hadn't forgotten what I'd witnessed at the beginning of May. It was a relief the plowing and planting yoked him to the land. He had no time to ride to town, neither to work extra jobs nor to squander his earnings at the card tables with the likes of Isaac Rush.

That changed toward the end of the month. Most of the planting was done, a worrisome circumstance when it came to Matthew, who started slipping to town again, but a good thing for Gideon, who could now steal away from the farm to improve his savings. I helped. It was pole-wood season, for the trees were vibrant with sap, and their busily spreading bark was easily removed. Gid and I cut long poles from the hickory and white oak saplings in the woodlot's lowland, then kept most of them soft for splitting and pounding by fixing them under rocks in the rushing stream. Armfuls of splint wood and hoop poles promised a fair bit of money from the town cooper, but we wasted a few of our poles on swordfights. Gid usually managed more hits than I did, but I almost always got my revenge by pushing him into the creek. I would have liked to have devoted more of our time to fun, but he wasn't as easy to tease into foolery as he'd been in the past. He was on a mission.

His single-mindedness influenced me, and I also ensured some personal savings by turning splinters into baskets. Mama approved of these endeavors. Perhaps she thought my newfound interest in moneymaking reflected a womanly impulse to supply myself with a dowry.

Marriage, however, had never seemed less likely.

The fact was, Mr. Long didn't appear as interested in me as he once had. This turn of events occupied my thoughts as I spent the final week of May weaving baskets.

He still passed a great deal of time with us, or at least with the men. Like most farming neighbors, we lent our aid to him to quicken an industry, and he reciprocated. Though Papa and my brothers had handled without assistance the cultivation of the corn—hoeing, weeding, and hilling it—Mr. Long and his cousin Jeb had helped my family with the more arduous task of stump pulling in the field my father wanted widened. In return, my brothers had sharpened their froes and split enough wood shingles for Mr. Long to use to replace his bark roof.

But our neighbor's recent weeks were not all work and no pleasure. If Betsy could be counted as a reliable source of information, he was also spending a fair share of his time in Middleton with the Goodriches.

I refused to feel betrayed when it came to Mr. Long. If he wanted to bestow his precious person on a pack of silly town girls, that was fine with me. Let them grow bored watching him whittle every handy piece of wood. No doubt, when he got to know them well enough, he'd make them the new objects of his caustic comments and observations. I couldn't care half a farthing.

My mother, unfortunately, could.

June arrived and brought with it bright, cheerful weather. Mama, in contrast, was pure gloom and doom. Betsy, who enjoyed accompanying Papa whenever he had business in town, started bringing back interesting news regarding Mr. Long. The gossip vexed Mama. Her worries made the strawberry season, normally quite a lovely time, a painful period of ominous predictions and gentle scolds.

We began picking the fruit in the middle of the month, and on the first day of this endeavor, Mama sighed, "Those Goodrich girls are very ladylike." She cast a disapproving frown at my dirty apron.

I shrugged. Given our enterprise, I wasn't sure how she expected me to preserve an immaculate appearance. We were in the meadow, foraging diligently for the wild berries—or at least Mama and I were. Grace was just eating them.

Betsy, intent on witnessing the mild lecture Mama was dealing me, mostly stalked us.

I gave her a mean look. "Go away, Miss Nosy."

"I hear the oldest plays the pianoforte," Mama continued, dropping a handful of sweet red fruits in her bucket. She shook her head slowly and tragically, as though the Goodrich chit's accomplishment bespoke automatic victory in the matrimonial contest. All hope was lost.

She interspersed the subsequent strawberry-related activities with additional details, all sighed mournfully. "Those girls' dresses are store-bought," she moaned through the mashing for jam. "The oldest girl paints—in *oils*, no less," she groaned through the strawberry bread mixing.

Halfway through preparing berries for drying and tea making, she stopped and demanded, "Do you know what the Goodriches have in their parlor?"

"A pianoforte?" I was nipping the caps off the berries with vicious pleasure, like a vengeful peasant beheading greedy aristocrats. Indeed, my hands were stained a bloody red.

"Well, yes," Mama said impatiently, as she arranged another

capless strawberry on the clothed table. "But also a sofa. A real sofa!"

As opposed to a fake one, I supposed.

I tried not to let her death-tolling headshakes perturb me.

Her funereal fixation on the supremacy of the Goodrich girls' upbringing and talents persisted and reached a climax on the day of the strawberry festival. It was held every year during the strawberry moon, but this time, the prosperous Goodrich family had offered to throw open their grand doors and host the evening's ball.

I dreaded it.

After trimming my best gown in new lace, yanking the brush through my snarls, dressing my hair, and smoothing and patting and circling me, Mama took a step back and scrutinized my appearance with the fierceness of a military leader strategizing an ambush. Then she leaned forward and pinched my cheeks.

I jerked back.

She followed me and took hold of my cheeks again. "Just trying to give you a little color, dear."

"Ow!"

Whether my bruised cheeks maintained their artificial blush all the way to town, I couldn't say. But the circumstances at the Goodrich house cheered Mama immensely.

At least initially.

Within minutes of our arrival, while I was still gaping in speechless wonder at the six-piece orchestra, the chandelier that sported more blazing candles than the Winter household lit in an entire year, and an actual French dance master liltingly calling out the figures, Mr. Long secured my first dance. He teased me in his usual fashion whenever the cotillion brought us face-to-face. I fired back sharp retorts. We resumed our raillery as though several weeks hadn't slipped past us with nary a conversation.

But afterward he danced with many others, including the three oldest Goodrich girls. He acted just as politely charming with them as he had with me—and (if their laughter was any indication) equally teasing. In fact, he struck me as shockingly popular with the ladies. Practically a *flirt*. The official beau of the ball! So busily occupied did the Middleton maidens keep him, he couldn't bother chatting with members of his own sex. The only man with whom he talked was Mr. Goodrich. I overheard some of this conversation and discovered that Mr. Long was doing work for the older gentleman, specifically helping him harness the mill wheel's power and improve the business's efficiency by building additional machines.

My location on the famous Goodrich sofa put me in a position to learn this information. Rachel Welds briefly stopped by and tried to engage me in a nonsensical chat about ribbons before admiring my sprig muslin gown and delivering the dubious compliment that I reminded her of the beautiful, young sunburst locust tree that stood "grandly tall and golden and perfectly straight" outside the front door of her former Massachusetts home. Then she flitted away.

I heaved a sigh of relief. I wasn't good at girlish gab. Girlish anything, really. Feeling awkward, out of place, grotesquely long, and as wooden as a sunburst locust, I glanced down at myself, wondering how it was that my birth mother had been a famed beauty while her sole child had turned out like a clumsy filly, all skinny legs.

I was sitting hunched over my cup, sipping (gulping) some thankfully potent punch, watching the dancers, and, in the short lulls between the songs, listening to Mr. Long and Mr. Goodrich chat about cogs, hammers, and bellows a few yards away, when Gideon appeared and settled beside me.

He looked happier than usual. I assumed this was because he'd danced twice with Rachel, two times more than Luke, who'd failed so far to outmaneuver the other swains intent on winning her hand. Plus, Rachel had arranged in the topknot of her hair a lush, red flower that looked suspiciously like one of Mama's peonies. I wondered if Gideon had ridden all the way to the Welds house earlier in the day to give her a bouquet of the June blossoms.

My brother's eyes followed his love interest's progress across the floor in the contra dance. I studied the floor for a different reason. Mr. Long had just joined the dance, this time leading the oldest Goodrich daughter. Hadn't he danced with her once already? Miss Goodrich laughed her little silver-bell-tinkling laugh. I made a face at the couple. Heavens, they were awfully familiar. Perhaps seriously familiar. Maybe they planned to announce their engagement tonight at the end of the festivities. Well, I'd be the first to stand and cheer.

"Strange to think this could be the last civilized event I attend before I leave," Gid said.

I tore my eyes off Mr. Long and shook my head. "There'll be a few more dance assemblies before March. And even on the frontier, folks surely scrape up some reels. As long as there are people, there'll be music and dancing." I cast a critical eye around the Goodriches' immense parlor, swollen with the millings of laughing ladies and gentlemen in their Sunday best and wastefully aglow in countless candles. "Though probably not in such a fancy setting."

"I'll miss these occasions. Our neighbors, our friends. You, especially, Harry."

"Well, you don't need to miss me." *Because I'm not sticking around here, either.* Mama had hardworking (if tediously inquisitive) Betsy to help her. Papa didn't require me to darn his socks; even sickly Grace could do that. And Mr. Long . . . he obviously wouldn't miss me. Why stay and witness his and Miss Goodrich's courtship?

Yet I hesitated to declare my intention to leave. Home, home, home: It still held me in its familiar embrace. Plus, as busy as I'd been sentimentalizing Middleton, I hadn't thought of a good way to disclose to Gid my idea of leaving it, to frame this agenda in such a manner to make it sound reasonable.

But perhaps, while the music and dancing afforded us a measure of privacy, now would be the time to speak. Staring straight ahead, squashing my reservations, I blurted, "You don't need to miss me because I'm going with you."

He turned to face me. A while passed before he stammered, "But—but—there's Mama and the girls and—and what about him?" He waved a wild hand toward Mr. Long, deep in conversation with Miss Goodrich.

My mouth tightened. "What about him?" I glared at our neighbor. He aggravated me to no end, first assiduously attending to me for months—nay, years!—and so faithfully it seemed all of Middleton shared an understanding of our pending nuptials, then thoroughly ignoring me, to the extent that, for the past six weeks, I had been forced to endure an onslaught of pitying glances every Sabbath at meeting.

And then here, tonight: starting off with his old friendly jabs and jokes then promptly ditching me for the rest of the evening.

I felt toyed with. That I'd taken him for granted in the past and thus earned this treatment, I didn't want to admit. I longed to show him—and everyone—that I was my own woman, quite capable of orchestrating my future without anyone's help. I wasn't going to hang around to see if our neighbor thought I was good enough for him. I wasn't going to linger just to get tossed aside. Either way, the waiting made me a loser. Staying in Middleton would be like the quadrille now under way: a perfectly sedate dance, politely dictated by custom, all figured out step by step, up one long line and down another. Fine but predictable. Someone else had made up the dance. I shouldn't have to follow the steps.

I wanted an adventure, too.

Gideon was looking doubtful. "I don't think our parents will let you."

"Well, for that matter, you don't know if they'll let *you*. And if they do, they might be grateful to me for agreeing to go with you. After all, who'll set up your housekeeping while you're working on your parcel, chopping down trees, and taming the wilderness?"

His gaze drifted toward Rachel.

I snorted. "I won't interfere with your romance, Gid. Go ahead and court her. If she agrees to marry you, after the happy occasion I'll leave you two to your love nest." I knew I sounded sour, but I couldn't help it. I had never imagined Gideon would prove so susceptible to a ninny. Most likely, after the featherbrain lost her youthful shine, he'd find her to be a terribly dull companion. I folded my arms. "Regardless, I can't see marriage happening before you've cleared enough land to build a house and grow something."

He nodded slowly. I could tell he was mulling over my points and finding them sound. "That's decent of you, Harry. I'd sure love your company. Truthfully, leaving you behind was the one consideration spoiling my anticipation." His smile turned tentative. "But if things work out with Miss Welds and me . . ." He cleared his throat, stared at his boots, and finished awkwardly, "Where would you go?"

"Back to Middleton, I guess."

Even as I said this, I couldn't really believe it. What would home be like without my best chum? The farm I knew featured Gideon racing me, coming to my aid when one of our brothers tormented me, making me laugh during the most boring activity. His absence would more than sadden me; it would permanently alter my world, turn it barren and cheerless and unfamiliar, as if a person hadn't gone missing but a whole chunk of the landscape had disappeared—a big mountain, an entire stream.

My gaze found Mr. Long. He was leading Miss Goodrich from the dance floor and looking pleased. With her, probably. I experienced a sinking sensation. Once Gid left, I'd never find anyone to fill the void. Better that I go with him.

CHAPTER SIX

Being made aware of (and now a pending participant in) Gideon's ambitious plan turned me into a quasi member of a secret club I hadn't known existed. This club, before me, had been an organization of three: Gideon, Robert Welds, and Robert's younger brother Ed.

On the first occasion of my attendance, I glanced around the graveyard where we were holding the meeting and asked, "Where's Rachel?"

"Dunno," Ed said, shrugging. "Minding the children, I expect."

Given the number of sticky, stinky siblings these two brothers shared, his explanation was all too plausible. Poor Rachel. I didn't particularly like her, but I wouldn't wish that much snotty-nosed torture on anyone.

Robert eyed me with displeasure. "Like she's supposed to be doing."

I smiled blandly. As long as Gid said it was fine for me to hang around, Robert would just have to put up with me.

The three men's feverish conversations, covertly shared behind the meetinghouse on Sundays and during rare visits arranged away from the farm, fed my excitement and, at least intermittently, lessened my dread of leaving home. They got their hands on a map and plotted their journeys, arguing where they ought to ford the Genesee River. And, with the help of the three letters Rachel had received months ago from Mrs. Linton, her old Massachusetts friend, the boys pieced together tidbits to improve their travel decisions and parcel choices. For instance, they learned that the main highway, called the Ridge Road, while the best means to penetrate the wilderness, was little more than an Indian trail. And certain available lots, particularly those below the lower falls, along the banks of Allan's Creek in the new town of Carlton, were swampier than others and produced many plants ideal for foraging, like morels and elderberries, but were also home to any number of rattlesnakes.

And of course there were bears, wildcats, coyotes, and wolves. Thankfully, less terrifying creatures occupied the thick forests, too, including beavers, hedgehogs, raccoons, and quail, all suitable for eating, according to Mrs. Linton. While the boys discussed the best techniques for crossing brooks with their teams when no bridges spanned them, I pondered the prospect of eating a hedgehog and wondered how one set about preparing the animal for cooking without getting speared by a bunch of quills.

Throughout the planning, I listened but didn't propose any suggestions. The fact was, while the Welds brothers knew that Gideon had made me privy to their plot, they didn't know he'd agreed to let me make the journey with him.

"Why can't we tell them?" I demanded, one early summer

evening behind the barn. I carried a pail of cherries, my favorite fruit, and selected a plump, firm one from the top of the mound.

I'd chewed and spat out the pit before Gideon finally answered. Rubbing the back of his neck, toeing the dirt, and looking altogether sheepish, he admitted, "They don't want a female messing with their adventure."

"But Rachel's going."

"Not to stay with them." He frowned and, with annoying primness, lectured, "It wouldn't be at all seemly for a proper young lady, neither sister nor wife, to keep house for them. They're to escort her to the Lintons', where she'll take up residency."

"For how long?"

He gave a stiff shrug. "Until she marries, I suppose."

I could tell it bothered him that he was unable to add a *me* after the *marries*. But Gideon was an honest fellow, and he couldn't yet claim to have won any major portion of Rachel's heart. She handled him in a friendly fashion: warmly, cheerfully, and exactly as she treated every other panting suitor.

I grinned. "So that's where you'll be doing your courting."

He gave me a nasty look.

July sprang over the countryside in a purple carpet of clover, and I put up an entire cellar shelf's worth of dandelion wine. Beyond the whir of Mama's spinning wheel, the twitters of birds, the hum of dragonflies, the buzz of bumblebees, and in the evening the roar of crickets and tree frogs, came the hiss of the sweeping scythes. Haymaking had begun. Yet the Winter family still didn't know that two of theirs were preparing their thoughts for departure, hearts filled with equal parts anticipation and anxiety, faces frequently turned westward, gazes intent with the determination to leave.

The temperature turned insufferably hot. We sweated our way to town for the Independence Day celebration and, surrounded by the din of clanging church, school, and farm bells, ate the marchpane cakes that had already started melting in Mama's basket. The sun scorched the air and baked the fields until the wheat didn't smell just like green growing things but a bit like the bread it was destined to become.

The only place hotter than the roasting fields was the summer kitchen. Betsy and Grace bickered incessantly, and every day I could feel my own mood reaching a boil quicker than the stew. More and more, I looked for ways to escape, and since the men took most of their meals in the fields, bringing them their nooning became my respite from the sweltering house.

On one such occasion, they didn't even notice my approach, so focused were they on their haying. Before I could distinguish brother from brother, I could hear their music. The scythes sang notes as the blades cut the thick air.

I reached the line of windbreakers, stood still in the shade of the first tree, and admired the practiced, graceful ease with which they cradled the field of grass. Papa had hired Robert and Ed Welds to help, and they, along with Gideon, brought up the end of the scythe team.

I searched for Mr. Long's broad back, and when I realized he wasn't part of the line, I immediately felt piqued, rashly concluded he'd squandered a haymaking day by visiting the Goodriches, then became irritated with myself for caring. To shut up my disordered thoughts, I called across the field, "Dinnertime!"

Papa was the first to turn. His face shimmered with sweat, and when he got to my poplar's flickering shade, he blew a sigh, pulled off his hat, and swiped his face and head with his sleeve before giving my braid a little tug by way of hello. He accepted the switchel jug and guzzled gratefully. "Ah!" he gasped. "Thanks, kitten."

The others joined us. I should have returned to the house and left the men to their nooning, but it was too pleasant idling beside them as they picnicked in the nearby shock of hay. They ate enormous amounts of bread, cheese, and meat and, between bites, joked and tore into one another with grinned insults. Even Gideon seemed at ease.

I mostly attended to the Welds brothers, who would become my constant companions once we reached the Genesee Valley. At this stage, I couldn't call them much more than acquaintances, despite their closeness to Gid. The nature of my chores kept me penned up most of the time, and I didn't enjoy many informal occasions like this one to rub shoulders with the boys. The handful of furtive would-be pioneer meetings hadn't deepened our friendship. The brothers had resigned themselves to my presence but clearly didn't like it.

Now, however, exhausted to the point of garrulousness, they gave me a glimpse of their true selves. And from what I could tell, in many ways they were just as silly as Rachel.

Robert had a way of responding to my older brothers' jests with rancor, as though he couldn't discern mere teasing from genuine offense, and Gideon stepped in to smooth his friend's ruffled feathers in such an automatic way that I figured he was accustomed to doing so. Ed, meanwhile, gazed blankly around him and was a good five beats behind in his guffaw whenever a joke stirred the team. Sometimes he entered the conversation with a completely aberrant comment or question: "I shouldn't like switchel if it weren't for the ginger, unless nutmeg instead of ginger flavored the drink, in which case I'd love it even more, because nutmeg beats all." "Have you ever heard of mango fruit? How do you suppose a mango tastes?" "Do my boots look purple to you?"

I experienced a fissure of alarm at the prospect of taming the wilderness with these two, Mr. Hot Temper and Mr. Stupid Gudgeon.

Then I checked myself. What was I thinking? I wouldn't be doing the taming. I'd be in the house doing what I always did: cooking, spinning, stitching, washing, cleaning.

Though the younger men kept up their raillery, Papa grew silent, his eyes on the sky. He abruptly stood. "I'm not liking the looks of those clouds. Best get the hay rolled before the rain can rot it."

The others obliged him by hopping to their feet, shouting their thanks to me over their shoulders, and resuming their labor. I took my time packing up what little remained of the food and shoved the field keg deeper into the shade of the tree so the drink would stay cool.

They'd begun a song. I watched them scythe to the rhythm of their tune. Gideon had told me they sometimes raced, too. They'd work hard and steady, until nightfall or even later if the worrisome clouds held off and the moon could shine.

I would have liked to learn how to mow, to whet my blade on the grindstone before rushing to best Gideon's pace, to hear my alto waver alongside Luke's handsome baritone. My brothers would set me to raking fast enough if Papa would let them.

But he wouldn't. He never would.

I trudged back to the house.

CHAPTER SEVEN

Lammas Day arrived, and we celebrated this first of August as we always did, by cramming ourselves into the wagon at dawn and making the journey to meeting. Mama, dignified in her best dress, held wrapped on her lap a beautiful round bread, the first from the new grain. The pastor would consecrate it, and the blessed loaf would become the center of our dinner table later.

My father looked pleased as he drove us to town, remarking on the sights along the way: the orange tiger lilies fringing the woods, an indigo bunting alighting on a branch in an iridescent flash, and the attractive stone fence Mr. Long and Jeb, his cousin, had built last month to replace the split-rail barrier that had been too short to hold their new horse.

Papa's good spirits infected all of us in the rumbling, lurching wagon. The first sheaf of wheat he and the boys had harvested had been a good one. There was reason to be grateful.

Five hours later, when we finally returned to the farm, Mama spurred the girls and me into a whirl of work. The harvest table would reflect poorly on us if it didn't offer the plentitude nature had made possible this year. By the time we began delivering steaming bowls and laden platters to the holding boards outside, the Winter men, along with Mr. Long and Jeb, occupied the benches on either side of the main table. When the Weldses arrived, the second table's benches quickly filled. Mrs. Welds and her girls contributed the sweeter dishes to the feast, and the male company pronounced Rachel's offering especially remarkable—no contest, the clear favorite.

What the boys really meant was that *Rachel* was the clear favorite. It was hard not to roll my eyes at their cajolery and her blushing demur. Her jam cake was good but not remarkable.

Mama, on her private mission, refused to let the pretty Rachel cast me in the shade. She lost no time in promoting me to our neighbor. "Have you sampled Harriet's blackberry wine yet, Mr. Long?"

I snorted. She knew perfectly well he had. She'd poured him his first cup.

"I'd better try some more." He smiled at me. "Still experimenting with the spirits, I see."

I narrowed my eyes but merely said, "This is from last year's berry crop."

"Tasty. Does the beverage improve with age?"

"It certainly gets more potent. Drink up, Mr. Long, and we'll see how well you navigate the maze."

Betsy, putting her devious mind to good use, had designed this year's turf maze and directed our brothers, in accordance to the configuration of her planned paths and openings, to turn up the sod. She called it Betsy's Bower.

Not only had Mama not fretted about the foolishness mazes were wont to encourage, but she banked on this foolishness. Ever vigilant, ever hopeful, ever plotting, she offered, "I can send Harriet in with you, so you don't get lost."

"Why, that's a very good idea." His smile widened at my expression. "Would you mind guiding me and my befuddled senses, Miss Winter?"

Why ask me? Is it because Miss Goodrich isn't here to escort you? "I don't know that I should." I took a swig of the blackberry wine. "I'm foxed, you see."

Mama shot me a fierce frown. "You are not."

He laughed. "Then we'll just teeter and topple our way through together."

This image appealed to my sense of the ridiculous, and a laugh escaped me.

He must have taken my humored response as acquiescence, because, a few minutes later, while most of the others, stuffed silly, languished at the tables in desultory conversation or, in the children's cases, lolled on the ground, he stood and eyed me expectantly. "Ready?"

I rose slowly, nervous and self-conscious. Silently we passed the benches and the children playing in the grass.

"Watch this, Mr. Long," Grace called. She knelt by the makeshift table we'd used as a buffet. Almost nothing remained in the serving dishes now, but on one end, the toy farm boy that Mr. Long had made for her tapped his hoe onto a surface board, up and down, again and again, until the weight hanging like a pendulum behind the balancing figure stilled. Grace raised her wondering gaze to her benefactor and announced reverently, "I *love* it."

"I'm glad." To me, he said, "I've been wondering what other versions of this toy I might make. Maybe a washwoman slapping a shirt against a rock?"

"Or a boy with a fishing pole," Grace suggested.

Mr. Long nodded. "Or a man bobbing on a horse."

"How about a person digging a grave?" I asked.

Grace wrinkled her nose, but Mr. Long grinned. "Morbid. I like it."

We wandered toward the old hayfield Papa had agreed to let us spoil for the sake of the maze. Across the land, harvest stacks gleamed like little circular thatch-roofed houses. Cicadas buzzed in the trees behind us. The family's and friends' voices softened into another kind of buzz. By the time we reached the maze, we were quite alone.

Feeling stupidly flustered, I stole a peek at my companion. Something about his profile jarred me. A moment passed before I realized precisely what it was. Though tall and broad-shouldered, he also looked very *young*. Daniel Long so capably handled his farm that I often forgot he was only two years older than me.

I was mulling over this fact when he cleared his throat and said, "I've been meaning to speak with you, Miss Winter, and I'm glad we have a moment alone, so I can do so."

My mouth dropped open.

Did this mean what I thought it meant? Heaven help me, what was I to do? Say? Think? Heat stole into my face. I threw a desperate look around us and burst out with, "Yes, well, here we are, Betsy's Bower, and if we're going to find our way through it, we'd best get started, because my sister has enough wit to make this thing a challenge. You can see we take our mazes seriously here. No mere sheaves of wheat scattered across the grass for us. Oh no, we dig up an entire field. Betsy says the puzzle covers at least a mile of twists and turns, and after that meal I just inhaled, I'm feeling ready for some activity, so let's not tarry. Shall we? Ah! Here's the labyrinth's opening. Watch your feet. If you trip over a clump of sod, rescue won't be easy, and I'll be hard-pressed to carry you on my back. Ha-ha-ha-ha . . ."

Mr. Long listened to my maniacal chatter with a bemused expression. When my false laugh petered out (much in the same way the mechanical toy's hoe had stuttered to a standstill), he began leading the way through the maze and said over his shoulder, "I was wondering if—"

No, no! I wasn't ready! I hadn't decided! Absolutely certain the moment of truth had arrived, the critical moment that Mama, with her tricks and ploys, dash it all, had done her upmost to hasten, I interrupted wildly, "Did you know the Puritans banned all maze games by law? How sad to have to acknowledge our ancestors. What dead bores they must have been, praying morning, noon, and night, only breaking the monotony with hard work and the occasional witch hanging. Oh, those prosy Puritans! Makes me sick, just thinking about them, preaching left and right, never giving anyone any peace but thrusting their judgments down everyone's throat."

"Harriet?"

"Yes?"

"Will you please shut up? You're rattling on so, I can't think which way to turn."

We'd worked ourselves into a corner with no exit. In my

prattling panic, I'd not only failed to exercise the least bit of strategy in solving the maze's route, I'd also afforded Mr. Long the very privacy I should have been preventing. "Sorry." I gulped, closed my eyes, and took a few steadying breaths through my mouth. "Go ahead." I steeled myself for the marriage proposal, my mind spinning in a state of electrified indecision.

He didn't say anything.

I opened my eyes.

He wasn't even looking at me. His head was cocked, and he wore a frown of concentration. He put his finger to his mouth.

And then I heard it: a rustle. Not the slither of a snake, not the frisking of a squirrel, not the flutter of a bird, but the sounds of a bothersome Betsy shuffling behind a haystack, her ears undoubtedly pricked.

The little sneak.

Loud and clear, I said, "I'm glad you let me bring you here, Mr. Long, because what I have to say isn't the sort of thing Mama and Papa will want to hear. The truth is, I'm concerned about Betsy." I winked.

He grinned. "Ah, yes, Betsy. She's something else."

"It's not just her inquisitiveness that worries me. Sure, everyone knows her for being the most obnoxious, horrid, tedious Nosy Nelly in all of Middleton." I heard a gasp a few yards away and had to swallow my chuckle. "That's nothing new. What really troubles me is the peculiar fanaticism I perceive in her prying tendencies, the crazy glitter that lights her eyes. Let me be frank, Mr. Long. Her curiosity has become a sickness. In short, I'm convinced Betsy is utterly deranged. Mad, through and through. And I can think of no easy way to disclose her madness to our parents without breaking their poor hearts."

A growl had replaced the gasp, and as Betsy made her outraged exit from her secret lair, I called after her stomping figure, "Let this be a lesson to you, Busybody Betsy!" To Mr. Long, I laughed. "Wait until she gets to my mother, starts tattling, and ends up admitting to the eavesdropping. Getting caught in her own snare. Good. She'll give proof to my insults, and I hope Mama boxes her ears for the offense."

" 'Thou find'st to be too busy is some danger.' "

"*Hamlet*." I stared at him, impressed. "Do you read a great deal?"

"And whittle." He smiled. "They're pleasant ways to pass the quieter months." His expression turned serious. "I'm afraid you might accuse me of being as tedious as Betsy or the Bard's spying Polonius with what I want to ask you."

I gazed at him mutely. This didn't sound like the beginning of a proposal. Wasn't he supposed to fall on his knee and spout avowals of love and other such flummery? "What do you mean?"

He tapped a boot against a clod and folded his arms. "It just seems as though the Winters, my longtime friends and neighbors, are lately all torn up with secrets. There's Gideon, and now *you* and Gideon, whispering with the Welds brothers whenever you get the chance to tiptoe off together. Then there's Matthew . . ."

I shoved aside the first half of his observations, more concerned with the second. "What about Matthew?" He hesitated, so I offered, "Some weeks ago, I caught him handing over a fat purse to a ne'er-do-well."

"Isaac Rush."

I nodded. "Matthew's not in more trouble, is he?" My oldest

brother seemed normal enough lately. I'd been hoping he had gone back to his former self—not that I particularly liked that self, as frequently intoxicated and rude as it was, but it beat a Matthew who gambled for high stakes.

He gave his head a shake, as if banishing a dark thought. "What about you? Gideon and the Welds boys are concocting a scheme, that's obvious, and whatever it is, it's got the three of them distracted. Now you've joined the fuss." A small frown creased his brow. "Do you want to tell me about it? May I help in any way?"

I bit my lip. Whether he thought to offer for me or not (perhaps saving his tender words for the fancier Miss Goodrich), Mr. Long had been a good and constant neighbor—to be honest, at times more than that. He deserved a warning of my impending departure, but how could I disclose it when Gid and I hadn't told our parents, when I hadn't even come to terms with leaving? "I can't speak of it," I finally said. "It's not my secret to tell." At least not mine alone.

He nodded slowly. "Just so you know, you can come to me if you need anything. I count you one of my closest friends." Surprise must have shown in my face, for he smiled, turned, and began to lead us through the maze again. "It's all well and good to be Mr. Steady and Respectable around here, directing my cousin Jeb in the ways of running a farm, but the role gets tedious. Frankly, it wearies me. Sometimes I feel like I never got my fair share of childhood. I went from playing hoop wars in straightaway races with Luke to figuring out how to fix the well sweep. There are days I loathe my dull duties." Over his shoulder, he gave me a lopsided smile. "Despite my initials implying otherwise."

I had the grace to blush.

"Anyway, when everyone else treats me like a stern stick-in-the-mud, you never stand on ceremony with me. You make me laugh and don't hold back on the teasing." After a pause, he coughed and said gruffly, "I want you to know I appreciate your friendship."

This admission, not at all the proposal I'd expected but somehow more endearing and wrenching, left me speechless. I finally stammered, "I—I thank you, Mr. Long. You're, well, a friend to me, too." As soon as I said the words, I realized their truth and, more comfortable, confided, "To speak plainly, I always do look forward to devising new ways to tease you."

He laughed. "You're very good at that."

We managed the rest of the maze in a comfortable silence. Nothing was obviously different. I wasn't Miss Harriet Winter, soon-to-be Mrs. Daniel Long. Nor was I Miss Harriet Winter, the confirmed spinster who'd squandered her chance to be mistress of her own home. I hadn't told him about my pioneering ambitions, and he hadn't disclosed the specifics on what he knew about Matthew's plight.

But when we found the exit to Betsy's Bower and walked back to the party, with the evening sun looking as heavy as a ripe peach in the sky and the fields awash in warm light and our two lengthened shadows side by side, I felt a change in us, a change *between* us: a sweetening.

It was a change that required consideration.

CHAPTER EIGHT

The next weeks passed in a blur of harvesting and pickling, storing and drying. I saw very little of my brothers, even less of Mr. Long. And if I'd packed fat onto my skinny bones from the Lammas feast, I completely lost it again by shooting up and down the cellar ladder hundreds of times. Hauling and preparing food, then shelving it in the dim coolness of the underground pantry, was the pattern that filled my days.

Across the mountains, the first smudges of red appeared like small wounds on the heads of soft maples. Days shortened. Papa and my brothers cut and shucked the corn, and the crop was so plentiful, they ran out of room for it in the loft and had to build a cratch to stow it in. By the time all the grain was thrashed and the hay stacked, Mama, my sisters, and I had reduced the garden to pickled beans, pickled beets, pickled tomatoes, pickled cucumbers, pickled whatever-doesn't-poison-you. And I reeked of vinegar.

Apple season arrived to save me from the kitchen. I was happy to relinquish the last of the preserving to Mama and my sisters and spend my time climbing the ladders braced against the fruit trees, plucking maiden's blushes and Cooper's russets from the limbs, while all around me, in the tall, browning grass, insects made a chorus with their racket.

Soon the second-best apples would enter the kitchen for drying or go to the mill for cider. The third-best, those poorer apples that had fallen to the ground or hidden themselves in the upper branches of the trees, would become butter, sauce, and yes: more vinegar.

But the fruits I selected first from each variety were the prime eating apples. These I picked cautiously, my cotton gloves protecting them from rough handling. Mama tucked the choice ones, stem up, in straw-packed boxes. They'd wait in the cellar for us, a welcome, raw sweetness to munch on when so much of everything else bore the taste of preserving.

I wondered how many of these apples would yet linger in winter storage when Gideon and I left home.

The first picking was a slow process, requiring meticulous care. I should have been happy to have Rachel Welds as a harvesting companion, for she was a stout worker, worthy of every bushel Papa would give her to share with the Weldses as payment for her assistance, and very gentle, never rendering an apple unfit for packing with rough pulling or heedless squeezes. But the girl created more noise than the insects did.

At first I thought I'd go mad listening to her prattle on and on about her baby cousin's rash and the pelisse she was sewing and the best way to prepare a potato. Eventually, however, I learned to respond to her talk instinctively without absorbing a single word, murmuring in a vaguely consoling way when her voice turned fretful, obliging her with a surprised grunt when she subjected me to something apparently startling, and laughing absently when her tone tittered into happiness.

But when she described the trip she'd recently taken to Middleton, in the company of her aunt, uncle, and two of her cousins, and the stop they'd made at the Goodrich house after Mr. Welds had finished his business with a merchant, I found myself listening and prompted, "You stopped to see the Goodrich family?"

Rachel might have been silly, but she was also kindhearted, too much so to snub my abrupt interest. After hours of insulting her with ill-masked boredom, I deserved a rebuff, and she had every right to thwart me. However, she enthusiastically nodded, sending her pretty, dark ringlets in a merry dance around her face. "So Auntie Welds could deliver the cloth she'd woven and dyed. Mrs. Goodrich ordered it some time ago. The lady inspected the material; then, gracious as can be, she invited us into the parlor for tea and biscuits. I could hardly believe the sight that met my eyes."

She paused dramatically, affording me an uncomfortable and (since this was Rachel, after all) unusual moment of silence for conjecture. I pictured the parlor door shooting open to reveal Mr. Long and the eldest Goodrich girl in a passionate embrace, or Mr. Long on his knee proposing to a simpering Miss Goodrich, or, at the very least, Mr. Long standing by the pianoforte and dutifully turning the pages of sheet music for the accomplished Miss Goodrich to play.

Lord knew, ever since Mr. Long and I had shared that warm exchange in Betsy's Bower on Lammas Day, the man hadn't spared three whole minutes for me. Maybe Miss Goodrich was keeping him too busy. I focused on the apple in my hand. "So what did you see?"

"A harpsichord!"

"Really?" Relief made me smile. "Yet another fine instrument. Don't tell my mother. She's always comparing me to the oh-so-great Goodrich girls with their superior talents."

Rachel shrugged. She was sitting on a low branch of the apple tree opposite the one in which I'd similarly perched. She crossed her legs at the ankles and confided, "No doubt the Goodrich girls have added harpsichord lessons to their schooling, for there was never a family more passionate about the science of music. But I couldn't like the new songs they took turns strumming for us. Tame stuff. Perhaps I'm too simple to appreciate such sophisticated entertainment, but I'd take one of the old ballads any day." And with this announcement she sang, in just about the loveliest voice I'd ever heard, " 'On Friday morning he did go, into the meadow and did mow. A round or two, then he did feel a poisonous serpent at his heel.' "

" 'Springfield Mountain.' Very nice. I like that one. Start it again, and I'll sing harmony."

From beginning to end, we belted out the tale of the mower fatally bitten by a rattlesnake. Our voices blended beautifully, and we grinned through every tragic verse, each visibly pleased with the other's skill.

"How do you sing harmony like that?" she exclaimed.

"I'm not sure, really. I just can hear it." I happily swung my leg and took a bite out of the apple I still palmed. Around the mouthful I said, "Your voice is extraordinary. I've never heard the like. Do you happen to know 'The Children in the Wood'?"

She answered by humming the opening refrain.

And before I knew it, we completely forgot our apple picking in the process of testing each other's recollection of all the ditties we'd ever heard. With relish we hashed out grim songs of painful death, jealousy, violence, lost love, betrayed affections, and even a particular favorite of mine about the murder of illegitimate children. Then we decided to skip the hymns in favor of the seafaring songs we knew: tunes about floods, shipwrecks, and piracy.

When we exhausted our common ground, she taught me two ballads I'd never heard, one about domestic trickery, the other about a streak of impossibly good luck.

I returned the favor by teaching her a song I wasn't supposed to know. "Luke sings it all the time," I said. "It's called 'Corydon and Phyllis.'"

"Let's hear it."

"'Ten thousand times he kissed her while sporting on the green, and as he fondly pressed her, her pretty leg was seen. And something else, and something else, what I do know but dare not tell.'"

She laughed. "How deliciously vulgar. Sing it again, so I can try it."

Her enthusiasm prompted me to reveal my familiarity with a few more bawdy tunes, including "Old Maid's Last Prayer" and "The Female Haymakers."

We were still in our apple trees, sticky from chomping on fruit between songs and making up a naughty verse to add to the already obscene "The Farmer's Lass," when the sun sank in a pool of violet. Twilight stole into the orchard, and Gideon called for us from the direction of the house.

We reluctantly climbed down from our trees and found our

baskets, suspiciously light given the number of hours we'd supposedly spent harvesting.

But I didn't regret the day's poor pickings. As we returned to the house, hauling our fruit, we shared a last duet, choosing "The Deceitful Young Man" as our encore.

It was a great song. Not the least bit missish.

According to Mama's almanac, "The moon of September shortens the night. The moon of October is hunter's delight." We were in the thick of October, and it *was* a hunting period, literally and in more subtle ways.

Though the sorghum squeezing and cider milling filled a good portion of our time, the harvest rush had ended. Mama resumed our school lessons, and Papa and my brothers enjoyed a vacation from work with fishing and hunting. A spell of Indian summer cooperated with the men's ambitions. They left early in the morning and stayed out until the late afternoon, when a strange blue haze filtered the sunshine and made a dream of the flaming foliage and flickering shadows. October drifted along as lazily as the leaves floated past us, and at the end of each day of sporting, the warm sham-summer wind carried cheerful whistles across the land and heralded Papa and the boys' return. They arrived at the house looking relaxed and pleased, proudly bearing their day's catches like scaly and furry trophies.

Perhaps his hunting successes emboldened Gideon. Or perhaps the three Weldses' looming January departure gave him a sense of urgency. Regardless, my best brother set out to court Rachel, less bashfully than before and with more regularity.

There were many opportunities for him to do so. Rachel spent a great deal of time at our farm, largely by my request. We were getting along quite well, and I guiltily wondered how much of her previous chatter had been inspired by nerves, a jittery attempt to lighten the heavy mood my unfriendliness had perpetuated. She generously never mentioned my former coolness—not that we suddenly took to conversing like chums. Rather, ever since the two of us had discovered our mutual, if rather questionable, passion for tavern tunes, we simply sang.

These duets happened whenever work brought us together. We sliced apples for the splint drier and paddled the big pan of boiling sorghum syrup to the tempo of our songs.

At first, Gideon and the rest of the Winters listened in bemusement. In October, on the evening of my seventeenth birthday, when Rachel joined us for a special celebration, she and I entertained the gathering with exuberant singing. The next day, Mama, smiling through a wince, suggested we might try sounding a *wee* less cheerful while crooning about the gruesome murder of the innkeeper's daughter at the hands of her jealous highwayman lover. But since Rachel and I assiduously avoided the tawdrier tunes when others were about, the family got reconciled to our little concerts and even began requesting ballads.

Sometimes Gideon would take advantage of a lull in our singing to sidle in, sharing with Rachel a towel full of the late raspberries he'd discovered in some woodland thicket or bringing her a pretty songbird feather.

He was less successful, however, when he brought the whole dead bird, and not even the assurance that he hadn't actually killed the hummingbird convinced her to handle the ruby-throated creature.

One afternoon, after the men returned with their catch of fish for our supper, I listened in silent amusement as Gideon tried to enthrall Rachel with his clever rabbit trap, showing her the reed that held up the trick door, pointing out where the bait would hang, explaining how to trail the lure, then vividly describing the lightning speed with which the bent reed would trigger the shutting of the front. His voice practically vibrated with coaxing enthusiasm.

She was conspicuously unimpressed. After listening with a frown and gnawing on her plump lower lip, she murmured, "I can't like the deceitfulness. It seems kinder, somehow, to just shoot the unfortunate thing."

"A man needs more skill in snaring than he does shooting."

"But then you leave the poor animal alive in its little coffin— for who knows how long—until you get around to finishing it off. That's cruel."

"It's got plenty to eat while it's stuck in there."

"What if the sad animal left its young in a hole? They'd starve without her. You could be killing a mother rabbit and, as a result, her babies, too."

I finished scraping the scales off a fish and shook my head. "Murderer."

He scowled at me and shuffled off with the bunny killer cradled in his arms.

Rachel shrugged and went back to teasing out the tiny bones along a fillet. "You know, Harry, October's passing quickly and it will soon be wintertime. Maybe we ought to consider what we can do with some Christmas carols. . . ."

It was peculiar watching how coolly Rachel received amorous advances from not just Gideon but also Luke, Matthew, and her handful of bachelor suitors at meeting. I suspected she didn't plan on committing herself to anyone when she'd already promised Mrs. Linton she'd join her in the Genesee Valley.

One time, however, she confided, "I haven't heard from her recently." A little frown creased her brow. "Months, actually. And yet I'm sure she still needs me. Her children are a trial, and Mr. Linton"—Rachel sighed—"well, he's a bit high-strung, too. You know, the missus was a great support to me when my parents took sick, and I swore, if the opportunity arose, I'd help her in kind. When she first left, she begged me to join her, and now that I have the opportunity, I feel obligated to do so. I can't disappoint her at this late stage in our plans."

"I'm sure your Mrs. Linton would understand if marriage prevented your going."

"Perhaps," she murmured, then changed the subject.

Middleton wasn't going to keep Rachel, either because of her promise to Mrs. Linton or because she had no excellent reason to stay. One thing was clear: She hadn't pledged her heart to Gideon or anyone else in these parts, at least not sufficiently to alter her inclination. Of course, she didn't yet know that Gideon (who was still keeping his pioneer plans to himself, lest Luke decide to share them) would be following her in that direction. And that I would be, as well.

That was the plan, though I persisted in questioning it. My uncertainty kept me mute on the topic.

Strangely, the singing compounded my uncertainty and reluctance. Most of the old tunes Rachel and I sang I'd learned from my brothers. They were family songs.

And then there was Mr. Long. Our banter after meeting and during his occasional visits had resumed.

The last Friday of October marked a particularly playful

exchange. Rachel and I were making apple butter. This required eight hours of stirring and sweating over the cast-iron kettle. We were singing, as usual, when my neighbor showed up with some neatly penned verses—"to add to your favorite ditty," he clarified with a wink. "Mistress of the Tavern," under Daniel Long's influence, not only trounced every rowdy patron, but demonstrated a singular talent for concocting her own delicious liquor. In addition, this indomitable woman never, under any circumstances, "submitted" to anyone: not her father, not her husband, not even President Madison when he made the mistake of trying to convince her to become his secretary of strong spirits. Mr. Long loitered for a while to hear us try the new lyrics and wasn't at all vexed when I failed to make it through a single verse without succumbing to laughter.

He and I were back to our old selves . . . though now somehow *different* selves. The pleasure I took from our encounters got so great that he frequently sprang as my first thought upon waking and lingered as my last thought before slumber. Indeed, throughout the day, whenever a horse cantered into the yard, I rushed to the door to see if it was him.

At times, however, my desire to stay in this place came from nothing more than the place itself. October passed, and the trees, robbed of their foliage, poked out of the mountainsides like brush bristles. The fields looked dead, lacking their thriving crops and, as of yet, unimproved with a whitewash of snow. And every day, for all of the first half of November, I awoke to a harsh wind slapping the house. But such bleakness only served to make the fire curling under the stew pot that much more welcoming and Mama's steaming sassafras tea that much tastier and, in the loft, Betsy's and

Grace's sleeping frames that much more delightfully warming. I was missing home already, and I hadn't even left.

I carried my premature nostalgia to the woodlot. For the first time in a long while, I lacked my singing friend; Mrs. Welds had a weaving order she needed Rachel's help filling. Cider milling and pressing kept Mama and my sisters occupied, so I spent five days in the middle of November on my own, doing my best to beat the squirrels in nutting. The recent high winds had shaken the treats straight out of the trees. I gathered from the ground big baskets of chestnuts and walnuts and returned home at dusk each day with my fingers stained dark brown from the juices and stiff from the cold.

Clouds shrouded the last day of my nutting. The trees encircled me like endlessly layered shadows, and the first snow began to fall as I trudged toward the house. The flakes swirled, large and light as down feathers. When the woods finally thinned, I stood at their scrubby edge and marveled at the sudden winter scene. Heavy gray swallowed the mountaintops, and snow fringed every available branch. It laced the fields, lined my trail, and veiled the air.

I hunched over my basket and set forth into the wind. Dusk settled around me. Yet the snow resisted the approaching nightfall and gleamed. By the time I reached the house, it had completely frosted the roof. Smoke wafted out of the chimney, and the window by the door beckoned with a golden light.

I shivered, more from a wave of bittersweet longing than from the cold. It was a beautiful sight, familiar and strange and magical at once.

Home.

CHAPTER NINE

When I entered the house, I paused for a moment on the threshold, the blowing snow and languishing light of the day behind me, the no-less-beautiful firelight before me, the nut basket heavy in my arms, and my heart heavy with love—love for hearth and home, for kin and neighbor. One neighbor in particular. In fact, I was so bursting with exquisite feeling that had anyone inside greeted me at the door, I would have kissed him on the spot.

As it was, although the family sat talking among themselves at the dinner table, only Matt acknowledged my entrance, and that was merely to look up from his plate and order, "Close the door. You're letting in snow."

So much for the ties that bind. I set down the basket. "And hello to you, dear sibling."

He grunted.

While I turned to shut the door and latch it, Papa sighed, "Please don't leave the nuts in the middle of the room."

"I wasn't going to," I said through my teeth, collecting the basket.

Betsy glanced over her shoulder. "Why don't you add a log to the fire?"

"Why don't *you*?"

"You're closer."

I put the basket down. Again.

Betsy reached for a roll.

Grace rested her head on Papa's shoulder. "Remember that day after meeting when Harry didn't put away the foot stove, and I tripped over it and knocked out the hot coals? I almost broke my leg *and* burned myself."

After using the poker to shift the log into place, I pushed myself up from the hearth, dusted my hands, and gave my little sister an exasperated look. While the others went back to their conversations, I transferred the basket to the chest behind the borning room door and sniffed appreciatively. Mama must have seen me coming. She had my dish ready.

Before I could sit, Luke interrupted what Gideon was telling him to hand me his plate and mutter, "Get me a little more cornbread and gravy, would you?" Without waiting for an answer, he grinned at Gideon and said, "I'd pay to see that. Ed Welds, the drover. Ha. A person ought to be at least as smart as the cattle he's driving to try that for a living."

"Shame on you." Spooning jam onto her bread, Mama clucked. "Poor Ed. He's such a nice boy. You shouldn't pick on him."

Luke shrugged. "What is he *thinking*? Nothing, probably. That's the problem."

I returned and rested the filled plate before Luke.

Instead of thanking me, he held up his tankard. "More cider, too, if you don't mind. A drover!" He snickered.

I sighed and stomped over to the cider jug on the counter. While I refilled the tankard, the din behind me grew louder, with Gideon defending his pal, Grace wishing aloud for a happier ending to *Romeo and Juliet*, the play she'd taken to reading repeatedly, Mama indulging her with smiles, and Betsy badgering Papa to let her have a barn cat in the house for a pet since he'd declined to give her one of Mitten's pups.

During the last few days, my home-loving reflections had all but snuffed my interest in the Genesee Valley. Now the thought of that destination tempted me, tempted me again—the elixir of escape.

It was sad how much more I loved my family when I wasn't actually near them.

As I headed to the noisy table with the brimming tankard, Gid scowled and slapped down his spoon. "I can barely stand to eat with you going on and on about Romeo. 'Romeo, Romeo! Wherefore art thou Romeo?' *Stupid*."

Papa speared a chunk of potato with his fork. "That tongue of yours *does* run like a fiddlestick, Grace."

Betsy grimaced. "Find something less ridiculous to jabber about." Then, under her breath: "Idiot girl."

"Mama! Did you hear what Betsy called me?"

Coming up behind my older brothers, I was just about to deliver the cider when Matthew, perhaps taking advantage of the others' distraction, ducked his head and said quietly, "Be a sport, Luke. Mr. Thompson's going to pay me to help raise the bridge come April. I only need a little to—"

Luke jerked sideways. "I said *no*."

Both brothers jumped when I put the tankard on the table.

Matthew scowled. "What do you want?"

"With a fool?" *A gambler? A scoundrel?* "Nothing."

His mouth tightened. "Here." He thrust his tankard my way. "Fill mine while you're up."

I opened my mouth to tell him he could get his own cider and choke on it for all I cared, when Mama said, "You'll have to help yourself." She rose and started stacking plates.

Giving Matthew my back, I smiled at my mother. Dear Mama. Some of my previous tender feelings returned. Now *she* was a person worth missing.

I dropped onto the bench and drew my plate closer.

Mama squawked. "What are you doing? You don't have time for that."

I stared at her dumbly.

"Your collar's all rumpled, and, *heavens*"—she made a face— "look at your hands."

"I just washed them."

"Wash them better. And do something with your hair. Mr. Long's joining us for dessert. He'll be here any second."

I gripped my fork. "But I'm hungry."

"You can eat later." She shooed me.

Growling explosively, I heaved myself up from the table.

Grace giggled, "Make yourself pretty for your beau."

Betsy's mouth quirked. "I wouldn't be so quick to call him that, when he's on such friendly terms with the Goodrich daughters, not to mention half a dozen other Middleton girls. He's the new favorite, don't you know?"

I ironed my face as I passed them on my way to the ladder

plank, hoping to convey indifference. Inwardly, I seethed. Oh, to escape the drudgery, to enjoy some blessed adventure, to get away from it all—*them* all. My sisters. My brothers. My parents. And Daniel Long, too, if the man couldn't make staying worth my while. It was time for him to own his feelings and declare his intentions. One day he was courting me; the next day he wasn't. I was tired of not knowing where I stood. If he loved me, I deserved to hear it. I couldn't decide my future without that certainty.

When Daniel arrived mere seconds after I climbed down from the loft, I struggled to keep the impatience and irritation out of my expression. If his anxious glances my way were any indication, I didn't succeed. Mama's overt matchmaking, Betsy's sly innuendos regarding *who knew* how many Middleton girls, and my older brothers' high-handedness ("Get me another slice of that tart, Harry"; "We could use some more ale here"; "Move—you're standing in my light"): These did *nothing* to improve my mood.

I was finally eating my (cold) supper when my mother smiled dotingly at Daniel. "Would you like more cream tart?"

"Thank you, but I'm full. It's delicious, though."

"I'll take another slice, please." Gid held up his plate to Mama.

"Harriet made it this morning." She slid the last portion onto my brother's dish. "Her crusts always turn out so tender."

I rolled my eyes. Would have been nice if the family had saved a slice for the baker.

Papa pushed away his dessert plate. "Did you finish the pinion wheel for the saw machinery?"

"I showed it to Mr. Goodrich last night, in fact," Daniel said.

"And did you dine with the family?" Betsy smirked in my direction.

He nodded distractedly and said to Papa, "Wheel should work fine, I think."

I hunched lower over my plate. *The man's like a bloody bee, flitting from one girl to another, a sip here, a sip there.*

". . . and Harriet can help you," Mama said.

I glanced up. Everyone was gazing at me. Their expressions covered the whole spectrum: sly, pleased, hopeful, indifferent, amused, annoyed, curious.

My mother, looming over me, was all encouragement. "Won't you?"

"Won't I what?"

She wiped her damp hands on the end of her apron. "Help Mr. Long carry in the squashes he brought us."

I slapped down my napkin. "Can't a girl eat in this house?"

My mother's mouth thinned. "A girl can eat later."

"Later, later. It's always later around here." Grumbling, I rose and shifted my glare from her to Mr. Bumblebee.

Daniel's smile died.

I stomped across the room. "Come on, then."

Night had fallen. While I waited by the wagon, Daniel pulled the door shut behind him. The lamp in the window illuminated some of the darkness, caught snowflakes in its golden halo, and revealed Daniel's expression, too: trepidation mixed with humor.

But love? What about love, Daniel? Love!

I fought an impulse to shove him onto the snowy ground and took some steadying gulps of air. The cold felt good. It eased a little of my ire and made me glad to be out of the house. I breathed deeply. *Free, free!*

Daniel gazed at me questioningly.

I stared straight back. "Well?"

He coughed, sidled around me, and pulled two crates from the wagon.

I glared at the starry sky.

He shuffled by the crates. "I reckoned your mother could use these. Jeb and I ended up with more butternuts than we'll ever eat."

"That's nice." I crossed my arms and held myself tightly. "Anything else?"

"Um"—he glanced around—"no. Sorry. Just squashes."

I flared my eyes. "Anything else you want to *say* to me?"

He took a step back. After furtively searching my face, he smiled weakly and offered, "The cream tart was tasty."

My breath left me in a hiss. *Seriously?* I stooped to grab one of the crates. "Glad to hear it. I personally couldn't judge. No one thought to leave me any."

"Thank you." I accepted the tea from Lydia Goodrich, and there was a moment when the eldest Goodrich daughter's skin met mine, just touching. Poised in the Goodrich family's parlor, hovering in the lavender-fragranced air, our hands were a study in contrasts. Hers soft and white, mine calloused, the fingers still stained with walnut juice, nails pared as short as a boy's.

Then that second passed, and the four of us—Mrs. Goodrich, Miss Goodrich, Mama, and I—began to sip our tea intently like mismatched people relieved to have something to do that didn't entail talking.

I shouldn't have agreed to accompany my mother here. The decision had ruined a perfectly good Sled Day, particularly this year when sufficient snow had coincided with the first of December, making sledding actually possible.

In truth, though, I might not have finagled a sleigh ride anywhere else but here. My parents had business in town. Mama had packed the bayberry candles Mrs. Goodrich had ordered and then invited me to join her and Papa on the trip. After a long summer of the wheeled wagon bumping in and out of road ruts and muddy holes, I couldn't resist the temptation of the first winter travel.

And I *had* enjoyed that part: the sleekly packed snow, the squeaking of the steel-shod runners, and the constant tinkling of the sleigh bells fastened to the horse's harness. The jingling increased the closer we got to the heart of Middleton, where others' shining sleigh bells chimed in.

Now I anxiously listened for the bells that would signal Papa's return. When would he rescue us?

Abruptly, Miss Goodrich set down her tea and picked up a lady's journal. "Have you seen the latest Parisian fashions for the season?"

I shook my head and leaned closer to her on the sofa. As she turned the pages, I stared at the illustrations. These were gowns I'd never wear. I had absolutely nothing to say about them.

Eventually she abandoned her musings on lace and trim.

During the endless lull, I furtively scanned her. Her dress shimmered over her elegant form in the way only silk could. I glanced down. My best dress was a sturdy article of my own making, comprised of home-produced linen and wool. Not a shimmer in sight.

While my mother gave the parlor her unmasked adoration, the Goodrich matron stoically did her best to keep a conversation going. But Mama and I lived too far away to join in on town news.

When Mrs. Goodrich began to discuss upcoming balls that "winter has *finally* made permissible, now that there's a little time for frivolity in our busy household," my mood swung from uncomfortable to annoyed.

Busy? What did the Goodrich women do that made them so busy? Neither loom nor wheel nor dairy nor hearth tied them down. They didn't sew their own dresses; their stitchery was saved for lace making and samplers. Meals, clothes, cleaning, soap, candles: They had servants to handle all that. In fact, Mrs. Goodrich had ordered Mama's candles not because she didn't have someone to make plenty already, but because my mother's were recognized throughout Middleton for being especially fine.

As if the Goodrich woman had read my mind, she returned her cup to its saucer, cleared her throat, and murmured, "So, tell me, Mrs. Winter: How do you make these beautiful candles?"

Culled from her inspection of a claw-footed table, Mama started. "Well, I send the girls out to pick the bayberries; then we throw them in a pot of boiling water. Their fat rises to the top and makes for a superior candle wax. You won't have to worry about bayberry candles burning out fast or smoking and bending under the heat. The *best* candles, bayberry. Quite sweet-smelling. I've saved a few for Christmas presents. They're very special. Growing up, we always sang, 'A bayberry candle burned to the socket brings luck to the house and gold to the pocket.'"

While Mrs. Goodrich nodded politely, Mama resumed her appreciative study of the parlor. She ran her rough fingers over the polished, half-cushioned arms of the chair. I could clearly see where the fire and bubbling grease and lye from our recent soap making had left burns across the backs of her hands.

The sight brought a lump to my throat. It didn't seem right, in this new nation won for the sake of liberty and equality, that already we'd fallen into such separate classes. Way up there: the Goodriches. Way down here: the Winters. With a pang, I realized that my singing chum, Rachel, probably ranked even lower than us. She was the distant family member who had to pay for her keep by getting hired out to any household that required an extra set of hands, including mine. She never complained, but I couldn't help but wonder if the ever-present need to prove useful depressed her.

Lydia Goodrich broke into these worrisome thoughts. "It was kind of you to bring us a jug of your cider. I have a strong penchant for good apple cider."

Mama and I just nodded. How was one to answer such an inane comment? Everyone loved cider.

She gave a delicate cough and started pleating the skirt of her dress. "Is cider difficult to make? Do you simply, um, squeeze the apple?"

Like a soft peach? I frowned and opened my mouth to explain the process, dumbfounded that there was a person who existed in this world who didn't know the rudiments involved in the making of the most ubiquitous drink ever.

The approaching tinkle of bells distracted me. I peered out the window that framed the bustling street. I recognized the pitch of that jingle. I'd heard it every winter for much of my life. Yet the bells weren't Papa's.

They were Mr. Long's.

A moment later, a servant opened the parlor door and announced him.

We rose, and he entered the parlor, smiling, red-cheeked from the cold, and preceded by a pack of giggling, breathless, snow-dusted girls. I'd wondered where the other Goodrich daughters had gone. Mr. Long must have taken them for a ride.

His smile widened when he spotted me. While Mrs. Goodrich ordered her younger daughters upstairs to change, Mr. Long greeted Mama warmly.

Mrs. Goodrich folded her arms and gave him a cloying smile. "How *kind* of you to give my girls such a treat. And what a *shame* Lydia wasn't here to join you when you set off. She so *loves* a sleigh ride."

I almost gagged. Mrs. Goodrich was too transparent. Where had the eldest daughter been? Probably hushed and hustled into her room to await a later sledding opportunity: a more romantic excursion, one just for two. I mentally rolled my eyes at the woman's blatant trickery. I knew a matchmaking mama when I saw one.

However, the remark, as patent as it was disingenuous, worked. Mr. Long's eyebrows flew up, and he good-naturedly smiled at the marriageable eldest. "I can take you for a turn around town now if you'd like."

She demurred with a bashful stammering yet immediately moved forward as if to pounce on the chance. Mrs. Goodrich's face beamed victoriously, while Mama, at last dragged from her admiring appraisal of her surroundings, perceived the other woman's agenda and frowned in perturbation. It was probably Mama's expression that awakened Mr. Long to the possibility of an ulterior motive. His smile wilted, his eyes flickered my way, and he added hastily, "Why don't you join us, Miss Winter?"

Miss Goodrich froze. "Why—why, yes, that would be lovely."

I raised an eyebrow. Ah, yes, lovely. Quite the enchanting prospect: Mr. Long and his two vying suitors clinging to his arms while they shot evil glances at each other and his sleigh slipped around Middleton for all to see. A veritable spectacle. "No," I bit out. "No, thank you."

An uncomfortable silence settled in the parlor. Miss Goodrich leaped in to fill it by chattering, "I was just asking Miss Winter how her family makes cider. I know the apples need to be pressed, of course, but . . ."

Mr. Long nodded at this shameless demonstration of ignorance and, smiling my way, said lightly, "Miss Winter's the one to ask. She's an expert on the making of drinks."

I didn't smile.

I settled my gaze on the other girl. How could this oh-so-gentrified Miss Goodrich ever think she'd manage a farm? Didn't she know she wasn't remotely suited for all the chores that position required? Or was this what Mr. Long wanted in a wife: an ignorant piece of expensive flummery?

With a savage kind of dryness, I said, "The apples must be milled first." *You do know what a mill is, don't you, daughter of Middleton's wealthy mill owner?* "That crushes them into a thick pomace. The juice would taste thin without this step. Slow bruising, sun, air—they all tinge the drink, make it sweet. Not a pretty thing, milled apples. No doubt you'd find the broken fruit disgusting. But then how much that's just pretty is worth anything? I have no time for pointless prettiness." My disdainful gaze swept the parlor and its inhabitants, including in its peevish path a visibly stunned Mr. Long, an obviously embarrassed Lydia Goodrich, a shocked Mrs. Goodrich, and a humiliated Mama.

Certainly, I was behaving boorishly. Yes, my tone dripped condescension. I couldn't help it. This situation of unwitting rivalry was intolerable.

The Goodrich girl tried to smile. "Interesting," she said weakly.

"Life always saves room for an appreciation of the 'just pretty,'" Mr. Long said quietly. "I wouldn't take to whittling otherwise. And the Goodrich family wouldn't appreciate parlor music. Not everything need be purpose-riddled. Beauty and art justify themselves through the pleasure they provide."

Mama was slowly shaking her head at me, grave disappointment in her face.

I dropped my gaze and studied my hands.

Heat stormed my already (I was sure) pink face when she said in a mortifyingly scolding tone, "Yes, beauty and art and *good manners*: all worth admiring, all worth cultivating, my dear. I believe I hear your father at the door. Propitious timing. Thank you, Mrs. Goodrich, for so kindly entertaining us. We must take our leave."

Head bowed, I slunk out of the Goodrich house. Mama's expression fueled my shame all the way home. And as the week passed, whenever I recollected my rudeness and how readily Mr. Long and my mother had corrected it, the shame flared.

It was sufficiently excruciating to compel me to avoid everyone. I skulked outside as often as possible. The banking-up season had begun, and the minute I realized Papa was shouldering the sides of the house with proper insulation, I seized the opportunity to help, wrangled armfuls of cornstalks across the yard, and arranged them around the house's foundation, mounding the cover particularly high on the north side to keep out the worst of the wind and cold. And since the steady sting of shame quickened my labor, I finished in no time and offered to insulate the barn as well.

Shoveling cow dung along its sides was probably a fitting punishment for someone like me. Of course, what I really needed to do was apologize, particularly to my mother. That I also owed Mrs. Goodrich and her eldest daughter apologies was too painful and impossible to consider.

That week, remorse stuck in my throat and stayed there, every time Mama and I found ourselves alone. It also stopped up my windpipe and choked me when Mr. Long visited the farm and when I saw him at meeting.

Gone was the banter. Extinguished were the titillating glances and laden remarks. He didn't look judgmental—just uncomfortable.

As for me, I still smarted. Even after I recovered from my mortification, I persisted in feeling *teased*. Exactly what (and *whom*) did Mr. Long desire? It infuriated me that I was in this loathsome position of wait-and-see. How lucky to be the man—to dictate action, to shape the future. If I'd held the power, I would have frankly confronted Mr. Long: *Do you love me, Daniel? Yes or no?*

CHAPTER TEN

Christmas passed, but my heavy thoughts prevented me from joining in on the holiday cheer. Where did I stand with Daniel? With Gid and his pioneer plans? I didn't know. Nothing was clear.

As I nursed my woes, problems developed elsewhere, ones I had noticed but failed to address. Then, one winter afternoon, the troubles burst like horrid blisters. It was the first Tuesday in January. Rachel and I hogged the house with our spinning. Papa had bought Mama a superior wool wheel for Christmas, and my friend and I were making use of the new wheel and the old one, side by side. We matched our spinning, moving in unison back and forth by the machines, manipulating the thread in rhythm with the turning, singing at the pace of our measured footwork, while the great wheels hummed, fast and low.

Grace, her nose red with another cold and her small frame hidden under a mountain of blankets, sat in Mama's rocker by the fire and watched our performance with pleasure. Whenever Rachel and I finished a ballad, she clapped, sniffled into her handkerchief, and ordered, "Encore!"

The day marked my happiest in a long time, though it wasn't without poignancy. Rachel and her two cousins were leaving in less than a week to embark on their frontier journey. I'd miss her. Our singing didn't just help me forget the catastrophe at the Goodrich house, now more than a month past; as always, it made labor—even the most tedious chore—fun. I was very conscious of the gracefulness of our joint spinning, how our gliding steps, advancing and retreating, might have been the orchestrations of an ancient dance. We partnered our instruments with an ease born of practice, our left hands controlling the yarn while our right hands mastered the wheels.

At the end of a sorrowful duet mourning the death of Sweetie Abigail, Grace sneezed and said hoarsely, "Do 'American Taxation' next."

I looped the yarn and eyed her skeptically. With the wheel's soft wail, spinning lent itself to more plaintive songs. "Are you sure? It's not a very touching tune."

She blew her nose. "I like it."

Rachel laughed and started: "'While I rehearse my story, Americans give ear; of Britain's fading glory, you presently shall hear. I'll give a true relation—attend to what I say—concerning the taxation of North America. Oh—'"

I was just joining in on the chorus when the door opened and cut short our music.

In a wind-whipped cloud of snow and with the thuds of stomping boots, Mama, the Welds brothers, Matthew, Papa, and Gideon entered the house. Despite the flurry of their entrance, none of them spoke. My mother, red-eyed and drawn, greeted Rachel, Grace, and me with a nod instead of her habitual smile. Her mouth made a thin line across her face.

The door closed. A few seconds later it opened again, and Betsy sidled in, her eyes wide, her mouth puckered in round amazement, the very picture of intrigue.

A sullen din followed: quiet exchanges, the whisper of coats shed and then hung, the clank of the teakettle, the scraping of chairs across the floor. Only the Welds brothers failed to contribute to the activity. They stood silently by the entrance, their expressions decidedly uncomfortable. Robert ran a hand under the scarf at his neck and asked gruffly, "Ready, Rachel?"

"Just about."

While she and I slid the wheels against the wall and safeguarded the yarn in the wool basket on the shelf, Mama urged Grace out of the rocker and nudged her in the direction of the loft. My little sister's blankets trailed behind her like a princess's train. She sniffled and coughed her way up the ladder.

Betsy collected the damp boots and mittens by the door. Under the guise of arranging them on the hearth to dry by the fire, she shot me an urgent look and whispered, "Matthew's in hot water. The Welds boys know a bit about it. They wandered into the barn when Papa was dealing Matt an awful scold, then—"

"Betsy."

She bit her lip at the sound of Papa's voice.

He eyed her in exasperation. "I need you to go to the toolshed and look for the snowshoes I left there. Not the ash plank ones but the hickory splint pair I made last year."

"Now?"

"Immediately."

She struggled to keep the scowl off her face, trudged to the door, shrugged on her coat, and cast a final glance of hungry curiosity over the stiff inhabitants, her eyes lingering on Matthew. She huffed on her way out of the house.

Papa shut the door tightly behind her but picked up where she'd left off in gazing at Matthew, who sat slumped at the table, his head in his hands. It was a hard stare with enough disgust in it to startle me. A mild-mannered person by nature, my father had never, at least to my knowledge, looked so fiercely ill-tempered.

While Rachel laced her boots, Mama pasted a polite smile on her face and walked toward the Welds brothers. "Are you sure you won't take some tea with us?"

"No, no. Thank you. We ought to get back before it gets too late." Robert glanced at the window, still vibrant with afternoon light. Probably realizing the inanity of this excuse, he blushed and dropped his gaze to the floor.

Mama didn't attempt to persuade them. She nodded slowly. "We'll join the party seeing you off Saturday morning." To Rachel, who was tying on her hat, she smiled tremulously. Real affection flitted across her face. "I understand your cousins are escorting you to the Genesee Valley. I pray you make a happy home with the Lintons. We'll miss you here."

Rachel and Mama exchanged a few words of parting. Matthew remained, still as a statue, slumped in his chair. My father continued to observe him with displeasure. Gideon stood by the fire, warming his hands and similarly frowning, for once apparently too distracted to try to wheedle a conversation out of Rachel and get in her good graces, despite the little time he had to do so before she left Middleton.

When I caught my favorite brother's gaze, I raised my eyebrows. What was going on?

He shook his head.

Not until our three friends parted did Papa speak again.

He strode to the fire and delivered his words to the flames. "Your silence bothers me more than anything, Matthew. Given your propensity for gambling, I suspected you in the theft. But Daniel shouldn't have been the one to verify it."

Matthew's hands fell from his head to the table with the force of two angry slaps.

Mama jumped. Then she turned and, with her back to us, went about cutting salt pork and situating the slices in the skillet.

I didn't belong in this conversation yet was reluctant to leave unless ordered to do so. Dreadful awareness, not idle curiosity, arrested me. For months now I'd kept secret the incident of the purse exchange outside the meetinghouse, though I'd often wondered if it was information my father deserved to know.

And now there was this. *Theft.* My misguided discretion dismayed me. Obviously, I should have told.

I waited with trepidation to learn what new sordid situation Matthew had devised. Apparently, it involved Daniel Long. My parents didn't seem to notice me, so I took down the yarns and began nervously organizing them.

"You're right," Matthew finally answered. "He shouldn't have. This is none of Daniel Long's business."

"You made it his business when you borrowed from him."

"Just so he could sport me enough blunt to recover—"

Papa barked a harsh laugh. "At the card tables? No one recovers there." His mouth twisted. "And don't use your cant with me. I'm not Isaac Rush." He spat the gamester's name.

Matthew's hands made fists on the table. "Plenty of men find their amusements in town."

"Cruel, pernicious amusements . . . expensive games and cock-fighting," Mama said. She shook her head. "Wasteful."

Matthew began an angry retort that Papa cut off with a sharp "Watch your tone with your mother."

"I'm twenty years old, yet she treats me like a lad."

"You act like one. If I'd known how often you took advantage of your free time on the farm to skip to the tavern and throw dice in hazard, I would have kept you occupied doing chores alongside Betsy and Grace."

The insult drew Matthew to a rigid posture in his chair. "I don't go for hazard. I play faro with perfectly respectable gentlemen, like Mr. Goodrich, Dr. Davis, and Mr. Underwood."

"I don't care if the prince regent of England sat at the card table with you. The fact is you're not in their positions. Perhaps they have spare money to lose. Perhaps they can afford to plunge heavily, write vowels to pay up later, and talk all that nonsense about bad luck turning. Besides pin money, you have no coins to wager, not that belong just to you." Papa sighed and more gently continued, "Farmers don't make much money. You know that, Matthew. We raise our livestock and grow our food and take care of our own needs. If there are a few things we can't manage, we trade with friends or bring our molasses, butter, and eggs to the store for exchange."

Yes, the molasses and butter that Mama, my sisters, and I made and the eggs we collected—not to mention the feathers we gathered and the candles we dipped. I glowered at Matthew, increasingly irritated with his nonchalant high-handedness. How *little* he valued our labor.

Papa crouched by the fire and, with the poker, shifted a burning log, stirring into the air a spray of red sparks. "Money's hard to come by. It took us three years to save that amount. Three years squandered."

Matthew's head had returned to his hands. He mumbled sulkily, "I planned to restore it—even add to it. It's not like I wanted to lose. And I didn't take it all."

"No. I had just enough to buy your mother the new wheel." He rubbed his brow. "Do you know how I felt when I pulled out the chest from under my bed two days before Christmas and found most of the savings gone? *Sick.* Physically ill." He groaned. "I didn't want to think about one of my own children stealing. Decided to put off confronting you until after the holidays, hoping you'd come forward on your own accord, confess, and apologize. It never crossed my mind the situation could get worse"—his laugh was brief and bitter—"until Daniel visited this morning and admitted you've been going to him off and on, begging for help in paying off your gaming debts. . . ." Disappointment crossed his face. "Oh, Matthew. How *could* you?"

A sob escaped Mama. Shakily strewing the chopped apples into a bowl, she shook her head again.

The sound seemed to penetrate Matthew in a way Papa's words hadn't. His own face briefly crumpled, and his voice was unsteady when he said, "I know. I'm sorry. I'll pay it all back."

"When? How? I wanted to purchase a new ox this spring at auction."

Perhaps it was unfortunate that Matthew happened to glance at Gideon in that moment and become aware of his younger brother's presence, or that Gideon didn't bother to hide his condemnation, for Matthew's expression soured again and he said,

"Ask Gideon to cover the costs. He's squirreling all sorts of cash away. Who knows for what?"

Gideon folded his arms. "I suppose I should be grateful you didn't discover where I hide it."

Matthew snarled. "All I'm saying is I'm not the only person in this house with secrets."

Papa straightened, swiped his hands on his legs, and shot both sons a weary look. "After a year of furious whispering with Robert and Ed? Not much of a secret. I imagine he's saving to follow his pals in their pioneering."

Flabbergasted, I stared at Papa. When I recovered sufficiently, I turned to my brothers and found them still agape.

Under different circumstances, I would have laughed at this: the eldest and youngest brothers—so opposite in physique and nature—abruptly sharing dumbfounded faces as alike as twins'.

But Matthew's deception, not to mention his defensiveness, sickened me and killed any impetus for humor. Who did he think he was, risking the farm, the whole family, for his entertainment? What a selfish fool.

Father's perceptiveness, however, did surprise me. And I grew even more surprised when Mama bestowed on Gid a small smile, somehow understanding, sad, and approving all at once.

"You're a hard worker," she said to him. "It makes sense you'd want to try your hand at keeping your own farm."

Matthew's mouth closed with a snap. His astonishment gave way to a jealous glare. "More like try his hand at catching Rachel."

Gideon scowled. With a sniff, he turned and said to Papa, "I'll put off my plans, if you need the money for the cattle. It wouldn't take me many months to recover."

Papa patted his shoulder but shook his head, while Matthew

made a mocking face and loudly scraped his chair across the floor in his impatience to stand. "No, *I'll* raise the blunt." When Papa's expression turned suspicious, Matthew added with an angry blush, "Not that way. I work hard, too, you know. And if I can't make enough by auction time, I'll—well, I'll work something out."

"I won't have you going to Daniel again," Papa said. "You're already beholden to him."

He grunted. "Fine. He wouldn't mind, though. The man's practically my brother." With a toss of his head, he indicated me. "Everyone knows he and Harry will make a go of it one of these days. And once they're married, his farm's as good as mine." He flashed me a humorless smile, then said to Papa, "Dare say he'd give you an ox or two in exchange for our little wasp nest here."

Papa grimaced. "Don't be so vulgar."

My anger came to a boil. I surged to my feet and clenched my hands. This angst, it had been simmering in me for quite a while, long before the occasion of these revelations, even before my humiliation on Sled Day. It needed only Matthew's arrogance—his privileged maleness—to make my ire explode into words. "If you think I'll marry anyone for *your* sake, you're mistaken."

"Why not?" He gave me a dismissive look. "You ought to feel grateful Daniel wants you. And you're going to have to marry someone anyway. That's what girls do. Even headstrong hoydens like you."

In a furious hiss, I clarified, "It's *not my job* to make your life easier. Haven't you had it easy enough, playing your high-stakes games with the family's meager resources, acting like a dandy instead of what you are, a poor farmer? What bacon-brained plan will you take into your cockloft next? Perhaps a new look to complete your posturing—some shiny boots, a quizzing glass, a starched cravat?" I barked a mirthless laugh. "Wouldn't those make you a pretty picture at the card table? Well, Sir Matthew, you won't be betting me."

The others stared, astonished.

My face felt hot, and a sound akin to a rain-glutted waterfall filled my ears. I stomped toward the door. "You'll likely gamble away the farm one day. It's a shame you're the oldest and so terribly stupid. I wish *I'd* been born a boy." Furiously, and with words I hadn't known I'd buried, with a sentiment kept secret even from my conscious self, I snatched my cape off the hook, glared at the confounded faces of my family, and finished, "This *isn't* Matthew's land. This isn't even the Winters' land. This is *Knowles land*." I stamped my foot. "And it should have been mine!"

CHAPTER ELEVEN

I whipped around to escape and stormed straight into Daniel Long. For a second, in my disorienting rage, I mistook his hard stomach for the door and patted it nonsensically, as if to find the latch.

He took my trembling hand in his and murmured, "Harriet?"

I tore myself free. "Leave me alone." Burning and shaking, I stumbled past Luke, who stood just outside, slack-mouthed and bug-eyed. "What are you looking at?" I muttered, and marched across the dead kitchen garden.

Behind me I heard Mr. Long say, "No, stay here, Gideon. I'll talk to her."

A scarce snow threaded the air. Without acknowledging the man who strode steadily, unhurriedly, in my wake—the man who was my neighbor and sometimes friend and supposed suitor—I forged past the barn, where the cows mooed and Mitten barked like an audience mourning my temper, then over a stubbly field, and around the pond, frozen and snow-dusted.

As I clumsily scaled the stone fence, my skirt caught in my boot heel so that I had to teeter at the top while awkwardly unraveling myself, rending the flounce's hem in the process. Out of the corner of my eye, I watched Mr. Long get closer. My pulse quickened. I hurried over the rocky barrier, hem trailing, and continued my attempt at a dignified walk. *Do not bolt like a naughty urchin; do not give Mr. Long or anyone else the satisfaction of seeing you turn fugitive and run away; do not admit to being wrong.* In this situation, I wanted very much—indeed, desperately—to feel that my outburst was justifiable, if not particularly laudable.

Mr. Long was probably circling the pond by now. The pond, white and round, like Mama's cheeks. She'd stood so pale and still while I'd ripped apart Matthew, spat my vicious resentment toward her family (no, no, *my* family, my family, too), then hurled the Winters against my rancor for good measure. Dear Lord, where had the bitterness been hiding itself all these years?

A sob escaped me. I kept walking but glanced over my shoulder. Mr. Long had paused to gaze across the frozen water.

Years ago, I'd recklessly tested the pond's ice. My parents had forbidden me to walk on it that February. We'd experienced a mercurial stretch of weather, cold snaps and thaws taking turns for weeks on end. The ice had looked thick. I'd thought it would hold my weight. When the bottom fell out from under me, I plunged like a rock. Then, dazedly ignoring Gideon's yells and the dead tree limb he extended in my direction, I made my situation worse by trying to heft my drenched self out, again and again breaking and widening the hole in gasping, sputtering foolishness. Not until Gideon swatted me in the head with the branch did I find the sense to seize it.

I felt like that now. My anger, a dangerous pool, had held me for weeks. I'd practically dived into its deadly waters. And I was still drowning in it, making matters worse and worse. Mama's tragic face, my scorn, my meanness to anyone who dared to take what I wanted, who dared, even unwittingly, to show me my inferiorities: These thoughts teemed and crashed in my head. The tears welled in a rush, tears of remorse but, still, as always, of anger, too: this time mostly directed at myself.

Matthew wasn't the biggest fool in the family.

Dignity forgotten, I raced across the snow, floundering and slipping, all the way to the burial ground, and once at the fence, I clung to a post and sobbed into the rough grain. I hated myself. I wanted to throw my body onto the other side and bury myself alive.

I knew Mr. Long was coming, but when he touched my shoulder, I gasped and jumped anyway.

"Oh, Harriet," he said quietly.

It seemed like the most natural thing in the world to twist under his hand and shove my wet face against his chest, a hard surface but kinder than the wooden post and vibrantly beating against my ear. "Why, *why* didn't you leave me alone?" I sobbed, even as I clutched his coat on either side of my face.

He grunted. "Can't tell you how often I ask myself that." His hands rubbed my back. "I never know if you hate me or want me." After a moment he added, "It's uncomfortable, never knowing."

I shook my head and kept crying. I didn't know, either.

"Would you like to talk about what happened?"

"No."

His chest rumbled a short laugh. "As you wish."

We stood that way for a while: me weeping, then just crying, then eventually sniffling and noisily breathing, a moist, shuddery inhaling and exhaling against Mr. Long's shirt, and him easing his hands up and down my back, in a consoling but matter-of-fact manner. I'd always noticed Mr. Long's strong hands, wondered how such a big man could fashion the smallest details into a piece of wood and whittle so finely. He had sensitive hands, and I felt a rare rush of warm gratefulness that he was letting me recover in his careful, caring hold.

Minutes passed before I finally detached myself from his shirt.

His gray eyes were softer than I'd ever seen them, more like a spring fog than a thundercloud.

"I didn't mean to get so angry."

"I know." He shrugged. "You just have a hot temper."

His casual evaluation of my nature raised my hackles, which was unfortunate, since it proved his assertion true. Straightening, I made a face, then turned and rubbed my eyes. When I cleared my vision, I took in the burial ground, as always searching out my birth mother's marker first: MRS. SUBMIT FAITHFUL WINTER, WIFE TO MR. DAVID WINTER, DEC'D OCT'R 10 1792 IN YE 18 OF HER AGE.

"'Mrs. Submit Faithful Winter,'" I read aloud. "Dead at eighteen." I shot him a sideways glare. "That's where submission lands you."

He snorted. "Then I expect you'll live a long, healthy life, Harriet, because you're the least submissive girl I know."

I folded my arms. "We can't all be biddable Lydia Goodriches. Think how tedious the world would be."

He folded his arms likewise. "Yet how calm and peaceful, too."

"Ha." I narrowed my eyes and, raising my chin in a dismissive way, returned my attention to my mother's—my first mother's—gravestone, with its winged skull and crossed bones. The thought of the mother waiting back home swamped me with guilt. I shook my head. "Did you hear"—I swallowed—"everything?"

"Enough, anyway."

I winced. "I'm sorry I hurt Mama's feelings. I—I don't know why I said what I did." Because it was true? Because I could have wielded so much more power and enjoyed so much more freedom if I'd been born a son? I sighed, my breath still quivering from the long cry. "But I'm not sorry I blasted Matthew. He's a cocksure idiot."

"He's just immature. I think all this trouble cured him of his gambling propensity."

"I should *hope* so. The fool: capering to town, his pockets stuffed with hard-earned money, and losing it all—for what? To impress the oh-so-mighty-and-important Mr. Goodrich?" I made a sound of disgust.

"What do you have against the Goodrich family?"

There was a dare in the question. I retorted curtly, "Nothing."

"Jealous?"

"I am not jealous."

"I think you are. In fact, I think your disposition is inherently jealous."

"Ah. In addition to hot-tempered."

"Exactly."

I growled. For a suitor, the man could improve his love-making skills. "That's a terrible thing to say about me."

"You were jealous of Rachel."

"Rachel's my friend."

"She wasn't at first."

"Well, if you want to go back to the beginning, I guess you're right. I thought she was silly."

"You were jealous of her, jealous of how much Gideon liked her. I don't think you started enjoying her company until you realized she didn't return your brother's feelings."

"Not true!"

"Then there are the Goodrich girls. Remember, I heard how disdainfully you dismissed the trappings of their wealth." He shook his head, as if sadly recollecting. "That speech positively smacked of jealousy." Before I could sputter a rejoinder, he continued: "And of course, there's what you said about Matthew, how unfair it is he gets the bulk of the land on account of being the eldest." He shrugged and said simply, succinctly, "More jealousy."

I bristled. "Not just on account of his being the eldest—on account of his being the eldest *son*. *You*, Mr. Long, can't appreciate what it's like having this await you." I waved an agitated hand to indicate the little graveyard.

"We all have this waiting for us," he answered dryly.

"Not death. *Submission*. Following whatever rules your father, then your husband sets out for you, toiling without ever owning, obeying without ever deciding, having as much freedom and say as a broodmare," I said wrathfully.

"That's only true if you set yourself up with someone who doesn't care for your feelings and wants to knock you down."

"It's true for every girl."

"Who marries poorly."

"Even the ones who marry well. It's always a possibility, if the husband loses his tenderness, interest, or patience. The woman's at his mercy." I fisted my hands. "But who knows? Maybe she won't live long enough to suffer his abuse. Chances are childbirth will kill her while she's still in her prime. Then she can die with everyone vaguely and fondly remembering her as a biddable girl." I breathed a wild cackle and shot my arm over the fence to point at my birth mother's marker. "As a great beauty! What hopes and joys God promises the fairer sex."

Mr. Long took a step back. "What are you trying to say, Harriet?"

"That a woman's fate, whichever direction it takes, fails her spirit and potential, that a woman's options, no matter how I look at them, are offensive."

He stared at me silently for a moment, then said quietly, "Including the option of a loving marriage?"

"*Especially* that option." I was breathing fast, almost gasping. My hands sought out the fence post. The memory of the pond returned, the sluggish, cold water clawing at my cape and filling my gown, the way the icy edge of the opening I'd made with my body came apart in my struggling grasp. "So if you think, Mr. Long, that I'm just another object for sale, a little trinket for purchase, you're wrong. I—" I panted and looked around me, feeling dizzy and sick. The sun had cut apart the clouds again and now streamed over the mountains and fields, spangling the scattering snow, turning the flakes into silky stitches tying up the afternoon.

Like a person who just can't help herself, a person intent on drowning, I finished in a strangled voice I couldn't even recognize as my own: "I won't marry you."

His head snapped back. For a fraction of a second, something horrible and wounded seized Daniel Long's expression.

Then severity smoothed it away. Face hard, he nodded once, buttoned his coat, and with the sort of surgical precision with which he whittled dumb wood into things of loveliness, said softly yet clearly, "Dear Miss Winter, I don't recall ever asking you to."

That night, I raised my head from the kitchen table and gazed blurrily at Mama. A squint was all my swollen eyes could manage. "I have to go."

She slowly wagged her head, her forehead wrinkled, her cheeks damp from crying. "But the Genesee Valley, Harriet? That's so far away. Why . . . I'll never see you."

Her hurt added to my anguish. I couldn't speak, couldn't bear to witness her pain, so I stared over her shoulder. Firelight played against the rough-hewn wall. Gideon's shadow interrupted the wavering display. Then Papa's. The two men joined us at the table, my father beside my mother, his arm bracing her shoulders, my brother next to me. He gave my clasped hands on the table a pat.

The house was silent. I didn't know where my parents had shooed the rest of the family. Perhaps they'd left on their own accord. Probably hiding. Overwhelmed by Matt's duplicity. Terrified of the crazy eldest sister.

Gideon cleared his throat. "I was thinking, now that Betsy's old enough to cover a good share of the inside chores, you wouldn't mind Harry joining me. From what I hear, the land there is thick with endless woods. I'll have to spend days clearing it just to hack out enough space to raise a shelter. It promises to be a tremendous amount of work for one person to endeavor. I aim to purchase two oxen and a wagon at auction next month, and between those expenses and the down payment on my parcel, I won't have any money left to hire hands. Harry would be a great help to me."

My father's hand came off the table, palm up, a bewildered, questioning hovering. "But you can't really want to go, can you, kitten? You love it here. I know you do. Why do you want to leave?"

I mutely stared at him. He was right. I didn't just love it here; I *adored* it—the beauty of this area's seasons, the comfort of its rituals, the way the land fed and fostered us, provided the conduit through which each of us communicated with the other, without having to say a word. Had I ever truly, in my heart, thought I'd leave?

But now I would. Because I had to. Because I'd flayed someone who mattered to me with hurtful words. Because I'd mucked up my relationships here, burned my chances to the ground. Because I hurt. Because I was humiliated.

Because I was sick of being what everyone expected me to be.

I gratefully squeezed my brother's hand and answered weakly, "Gid's my best friend, Papa. He needs me."

Mama's fingers had traveled to her cheeks. "What about Daniel?"

I couldn't talk about him. I just shook my head, squeezed my eyes shut, and admitted my despair with a wet whimper.

We sat silently for a moment. Then Papa sighed. "I appreciate your wanting to be a help to your brother. But he's got Robert and Ed to support him. Gid hasn't been happy here for a long time. But you . . ." He dropped his gaze to the table and worried a gouge there with his thumb. "Perhaps you and Daniel had a tiff, and now you're smarting." He looked at me, and his eyes were stern. "Don't throw away your future out of pride, Harriet. Don't make a decision you'll regret."

I bit my lip. I couldn't explain what had happened. I could hardly explain it to myself. I only knew that, in the span of a half hour, I'd gone from falling into Daniel Long's arms to shooting him down and getting a well-deserved cut in return.

Whatever we'd had, whatever we might have had, was done: irrevocably severed.

"I can't marry Mr. Long." I pulled away from Gideon's clasp and dropped my head in my hands.

PART TWO

CHAPTER TWELVE

On the first of March, the day of our departure, Gid and I, with the help of the family, packed the supplies so early that the sky hadn't yet acknowledged morning. Behind the trees, stars pinned up a darkness that was one shade lighter than the black branches. Wood smoke wafted through the brittle air, while sporadic exchanges—in voices kept low, as if someone were sleeping, as if someone were dying—encircled the ox sled.

Lanterns traveled across the yard like roving moons. By their glow, I was allowed windows of gilded clarity: Papa's somber face as he tightened the canvas covering, a wet gleam on my mother's cheek, Betsy comforting Mama with a pat on the hand, Gideon and Luke's muttered exchange in front of the yoke of oxen, Matthew's approach as he led the cow by its rope, and Grace, uncertain and peering around in wonder.

I understood the littlest one's feelings. Outside was different.

The hour of activity, usually an hour of rest that passed unnoticed, made this most familiar place, our very own yard, strikingly foreign.

The spaniel Papa gave Gid and me as a parting present raised her head, gazed across the inky yard, and barked once before resettling on my boots, warming my feet more thoroughly than a down-filled pillow.

Leaning into the sled, Betsy inspected the contents of the basket Mama had packed, then demanded over her shoulder, "Did you have to give them *all* the cakes?"

"Don't be so greedy." My mother nudged her aside and reached across my lap to tuck in the loose corner of the blanket. "You wearing your flannel longies, dear?"

The question tugged up a corner of my mouth. Only a mother got away with asking about a person's undergarments. "Yes, Mama."

"Where'd you stow the tonic?" She felt my forehead. I had been sick, maybe sicker than I'd ever been, but the fever had disappeared after the first three days of my cold. Regardless, for the last six weeks she had continued to prod my brow as if convinced I was teetering toward a relapse.

"Under the seat." I'd tucked it there between our dinner and a jug of cider. I didn't want to have to search in the crammed back for the supplies I would be needing soon. Gid had his new vehicle organized just so. He'd purchased it along with the oxen. Though essentially nothing more than a canvas-tented farm wagon, it sported storage chests that fitted snugly inside the box, and its runners, secured to the chain-locked wheels, could be easily removed after winter passed. The vehicle would serve him well year-round.

Grace pitched herself half into the sled to pet the silky head of the dog. "Good girl," she murmured. "Sweet doggie." My sister gazed hopefully at me. "Will you keep her name, Harry?"

"Fancy Gloves? Certainly. It's an excellent name." One that Gideon happened to despise. I smiled slightly, remembering his grumbled "I can live with Gloves, but I'm dropping the Fancy."

I called the pet Fancy for short, just to tease him.

Mama was pulling my coat sleeves over my red mittens. "I can see your wrists," she muttered. "Do you want the frostbite? There." She patted my arm. "You ate the onion I toasted for your breakfast?"

I grimaced. "Most of it." Some of it, anyway, and washed down with plenty of coffee.

"And you have the almanac handy?"

I nodded. The almanac was her parting gift to me. It would provide the exact information on the sun, moon, and tides to let us set our clock. It'd give us the brightest nights to plan our most difficult stretches of travel. It'd tell us when to plant the above- and belowground crops.

In Mama's mind, the almanac was a talisman. With every turn of the moon and shift of the stars articulated in the pages, it would aid and protect us.

"I added peppermint tea to the caddy to help with Gideon's indigestion."

Gid's bellyache was all nerves, but I merely said, "I'll fix it for him nightly."

She rattled off a few more directions, fretted about the packed supplies, then finally sighed, "So you have everything you need?"

"Everything." Even a few items no one knew about, not even Gideon. I hadn't spent my convalescence simply sitting around doing nothing. I'd been wily, concocting a plan and executing it furtively enough that not even watchful Betsy knew about it.

My mother nodded, her whole face creased in a severe frown, like she was concentrating on not crying. After a moment she said in a near whisper, "You can always come home."

My gaze drifted in the direction of our closest neighbor's land, still steeped in darkness except for the start of morning rimming the east. Along the black backs of the mountains, dawn was just a scant redness, as thin as a fresh wound the second before the blood flows.

Not once had I talked to Daniel Long since that catastrophic day in January, mostly because I'd been bedridden and so sick (and, yes, humbled, humiliated, and intent on hiding) that I'd missed meeting and social gatherings. I hadn't helped make up the party that saw off the three Weldses. Except for Gideon, none of the Winters had. Though I won the award for being the sickest, we'd all shared some degree of the cold and thought it best not to give our ailment to the pending pioneers. By the time I'd recovered, Daniel had departed to visit his relatives up north. He still hadn't returned. I wasn't sure if he even knew I was leaving.

Now I felt his absence, in the last minutes of hugs and kisses, tears and reminders. I would have liked to have said good-bye to him. To apologize. Things remained terribly undone between us, like an unfinished seam, with loose threads dangling everywhere.

Gid and I set out across the packed snow, our bells jingling through the gray air. How incongruous the cheerful music sounded. So at odds with our sadness, our shuddering breaths, our wept good-byes.

———

"I'm bored."

Gideon touched the air with his whip. The sled lurched forward. He flashed me a warning glance. "Don't say that. You'll invite bad luck."

Balancing on my lap, the dog licked my neck.

I liked our new pet. Her eyes, the prettiest girl eyes I'd ever seen, gazed at me worshipfully. I rewarded her adoration with a stroke down her back. She whined in pleasure. "Everyone should appreciate me as much as you do, Fancy."

My brother snorted.

"So, Gid, tell me: Where are the gorges we need to circle? The avalanches we have to outpace? The peculiar species of bear that doesn't sleep through the winter but preys year-round on unsuspecting travelers?"

"If we slide into a ditch, I'm blaming you."

"That's extremely unlikely." On this first day, civilization still favored us, and though the roads we followed might have troubled our trip if this had been springtime, the year's ample snowfall had filled the ruts. Plus, the snow wardens of New England clearly revered their jobs. They'd made recent use of their giant rollers to pack and grade the snow, not only along the main stretches but even under the newfangled covers we encountered over two of the bridges. In short, we moved at a spanking pace. "At this rate, we'll make it to the Genesee Valley by nightfall."

Gideon laughed. "Not quite."

For a while, we slid along in companionable silence. The sky, the shade of pristine blue only a winter day can deliver, permitted a bold sun to cull diamonds out of the snow-carpeted fields. Icicles fringed hemlock boughs, and every so often a wind triggered a silent explosion of snow in a tree, spewing loose a weighty cloud of white from a top branch. The accumulation's plunge caused the lower limbs' snow to follow suit.

"How are you feeling?"

I half smiled at Gid's formal tone. My entire family had performed a tiptoe dance around me for the last month and a half, exercising the kind of wariness one employed with the mad and dangerously unpredictable. But my favorite brother had been especially cautious. Perhaps he knew, better than the others, what that January day had cost me.

I didn't want his sympathy. Straightening, I answered briskly, "Absolutely fine. Like a dandelion seed."

"In this weather?"

"Yes. I've slipped away, and I'm soaring toward no-man's-land."

"Few-men's-land."

I nodded. "Bob and Ed probably have their cabin up by now. And of course there's Rachel"—I gave him a sidelong glance— "the love of your life."

His smile slipped. "Too bad it's such a lonely love." He shrugged. "She likes you better than me."

"We're singing chums." I scratched Fancy behind the ears. Her tail swept my lap. "None of them even know I'm coming." The family hadn't advertised my leaving. Most likely, our parents had hoped I might change my mind.

The last encounter with Daniel Long, like an oft-told, terrible tale, replayed in my head. I cringed. There was no changing my mind. I couldn't.

"A dandelion seed," I sighed, running my thumbs over Fancy's silky head. "Unfettered." I wished. Oh, how I wished it were so.

"Beautifully free."

I smiled slightly. He didn't know it yet, but I was about to get even freer.

We happened upon a rude camp close to a trickle of a stream and decided to stop there for the night. A hovel slumped against a hill, the way a mouth without teeth caves into the head. The breeze combed snow from the roof into an airy curl, and a gray oilcloth flapped in the doorway.

The cabin was eerie.

But I refused to become Faint-Hearted Harriet. I grabbed the foot stove and followed Fancy inside. It took a moment for my snow-dazzled eyes to adjust to the dimness. A crumbling fireplace occupied a wall, and the lingering scent of burned wood suggested others had sojourned here recently.

Gideon arranged a handful of kindling on the hearth. "Peddlers probably use the place." He peered around. "It'll do."

Making camp was like playing: Our supper of bread and molasses became a picnic, and the hut, without chinking or a decent door, might as well have been a snow fort. But my brother and I barely exchanged a word. As soon as we finished feeding and watering the oxen, we stretched out by the fire. Gid fell asleep immediately. I shivered under my blankets for a long time.

Middleton seemed many worlds away. Daniel, even farther.

When I awoke, I was alone, with not even the dog around to keep me company. The room, soft with dawn and silent, made me want to go back to sleep.

However, I had work to do. After counting out a minute of

blissful heat, I threw off the blankets and opened the satchel I'd carried in the previous night to use as a pillow. I emptied its contents and listened carefully.

Nothing. Gideon must have gone to the stream.

I smiled, thinking about the shocker that would greet him upon his return.

First, the scissors.

Gideon was talking before he even pulled aside the oilcloth. "Come take a peek at these tracks on the bank with me, Harry." Light, wind, snow, and brother entered the hut all at once. "Could be a wolf's, though we never see them anymore back ho—" He screamed.

Oh, the look on his face.

I doubled over with laughter, and Fancy shot around me, panting, tail wagging, ready to join in on the fun. When I straightened to execute the jaunty bow I'd practiced, just one glimpse of my brother's expression, how his eyes bulged as if ready to pop out of his head and how his mouth remained open in a silent howl of horror, toppled me into another spell of the whoops. "Gid, Gid, *Gid*," I gasped through my laughter. Swiping at the tears on my cheeks, I managed, "You scream just like Grace does when she spots a—a—mouse!" I imitated his reaction and slapped my hands against my thighs and shook with more laughter.

He finally snapped his mouth shut. As soon as I'd quieted to a soft tee-heeing, he said curtly, "I scream just like a girl, and you look just like a boy. Good. God. You are *seriously* dicked in the nob."

"Well, if folks saw me now, most would assume I was dicked somewhere."

"*Harry.* That's disgusting. And you're . . ." He primly pursed his lips.

"A boy."

"Insane."

"Free!"

"Unhinged." He waved a hand to indicate my person. "Fix this."

"I don't want to. Besides, my hair's gone."

"Your hair. Your pretty yellow hair," he moaned. "I'd better take you back home." He ran his hands over his face and gripped his darker (and now longer-than-mine) locks. "Mama's going to kill me."

A little uneasiness unfurled. I'd known he'd be stunned. I hadn't expected him to be tragic. "I'm not going home."

"How—where—when . . ." He thrust his hands toward my apparel and fluttered another wave.

I proudly patted my front. "I made them when I was sick. The girls had to cover my chores. The house was empty. Not even Betsy suspected." I spun around with my arms outstretched. "What do you think?"

"No boy would twirl like that," he answered darkly.

I gazed down at myself in satisfaction. The coat of butternut-colored wool, short and snug, fit precisely over my perfectly tailored linen shirt. I'd bound my breasts, and a heavy tow-cloth vest hid any remaining hint of femininity.

But the pantaloons: They were the best part of my revolutionary regalia. They absolutely liberated my legs. I could climb a stone wall, leap across a stream, hang upside down from a tree, even, if given the chance, ride astride a horse, without experiencing the tiniest bit of encumbrance, the least threat to my modesty. Until now, I'd never realized how symbolic a woman's clothing was: the skirt that twisted around the legs and slowed her down, the hampering, cramping style of her boots, the way fashion dictated just enough exposure of the arms and neck to leave the skin perpetually chilled. Women's clothing was a punishment, a trap.

My new clothes emancipated me. Indeed, for the first time since that disastrous last afternoon with Daniel Long, I experienced a swell of hope. Maybe my future wouldn't be entirely dismal after all.

Gideon pointed at my feet accusingly. "Those are mine."

"They were. What do you care? They don't fit you anymore." I'd uncovered the boots in the woodshed and polished them clean. Shoes were hard to come by, but since Gid was the youngest boy, no one had inherited his outgrown boots.

But he did care. I could tell. He looked positively mulish, standing there with his arms akimbo. "How am I supposed to explain what happened to Harriet?"

"That's the beauty of this situation, Gid. You don't have to explain a thing. Not a single Welds is expecting your sister to arrive with you." I shrugged and conceded, "Of course, they might recognize me." Especially Rachel. But I could depend on my pal to keep quiet.

"Wouldn't count on it," he said flatly.

I grinned. "It's a convincing disguise, isn't it?"

"Frighteningly. Still, it won't work at the Hubers'."

I stared at him blankly. "The who?"

"The Hubers. Promised Mama we'd stop in Londonbury to

pay her old pal a visit. Sally Huber's a great one for letter writing. You can bet she'll mention Gid and the Mystery Boy in her next one."

I shrugged. "So I'll change back to a girl for the visit."

"Ah. And grow out your hair?"

I tackled my scalp with some furious scratching. "Lice. Had to chop it."

He grimaced. "Lovely." After a moment, he said, "I don't know how I'll explain this to the Weldses—my accompanying a perfect stranger into the wilderness."

"I'll be an orphan you discovered, stranded by the road after my poor family was beset by bandits."

He smiled humorlessly. "Oh, sure: because with that beaming face of yours and that chipper prance, you definitely strike a person as a deeply grieving orphan. Please. Not even Ed would fall for that one."

I snickered. He had a point. I didn't want to have to act depressed, especially when, after weeks and weeks of being out of sorts, at times quite desperately sad, I was finally feeling happy. "Then I'm a foundling, currently on the run, having escaped my indentured apprenticeship to an evil silversmith with a brutally heavy hand. You rescued me from homelessness and certain starvation. Now I'm your loyal servant."

He didn't comment on my story, just shook his head. Finally, but very slowly, as if residual shock were hindering his speech, he said, "I hardly recognize you. You look like a stranger. This isn't right, Harry."

I bit my lip. Gid was usually easy to bully. I crouched to pet Fancy and, after a moment of quick thinking, suggested mildly, "You know, this situation might actually work better for us. First off, I can help in ways I couldn't as a girl: clearing, building, and planting right alongside you."

"I need someone cooking, washing, and cleaning."

"I can do that, too. And you won't have to worry about me so much on this trip. A woman you'd need to protect. But who's going to bother a gawky boy? If a storm threatens and we're forced to seek tavern accommodations, no one will question if we're really brother and sister. Let's be honest here, Gid: I can't imagine a more brotherly brother than you, but we don't share blood, and we certainly don't look a thing alike. Instead of stirring doubt and difficult questions, we'll just be two boys set on adventure. In fact, if you decide to linger in the barroom to gather news on roads and conditions, I won't even have to wait in the room for you, worried some seedy blackguard is going to break in and get bold with me. I can just join you." And perhaps try my hand at faro. And perhaps even sample a bit of the gin my parents had always forbidden me to try.

He gave me a dry look. "You don't have whiskers, Harry. I doubt the tavern keeper will permit you to get drunk." He rubbed the fuzz on his chin.

"Then I'll just sit there quietly and listen, like a good boy."

"A scrawny bean of a boy. You look about thirteen."

"See! You can finally be older than me." It had always perturbed Gid that I surpassed him in age by a month. Granted, I'd used my elder's status our entire lives to lay first claim to all sorts of privileges.

His face brightened. "So you'll listen and obey? You'll act as befits a young subordinate? You'll mind my rules and orders?"

"Don't get carried away."

He smiled. "Maybe it could work. What should I call you?"

I frowned. My nickname would suffice, since Harry already tagged plenty of males, but its connection to my true self would surely stir even the dull Welds brothers' suspicions. I shrugged. "You decide."

"Freddy."

"Freddy?" I hated that name. "Can we make it Frederick?"

"Too much of a mouthful. Freddy works. But for how long?"

"However long we like."

"I won't agree to that. What if Mama and Papa travel to visit us or we want to return to Middleton to see them? I'll give this six months."

"Eight. Then I can help with the first harvest, if we have one."

"Fine. Eight months before you're Harry again."

"You might miss Frederick."

"Freddy," he corrected with a frown. "Doubtful. The little gudgeon's irritating me already."

CHAPTER THIRTEEN

When I'd quipped I was bored at the beginning of our journey, Gid had warned me I was tempting trouble. Perhaps he was right, because after leaving the scanty protection of the roadside hovel, we shared a whole day with a contrary wind that seemed intent on shoving us back to Middleton, then endured a subsequent day of heavy snow. We hadn't broached the wilderness yet, but even with the benefit of packed roads, the weather slowed our progress.

Near Londonbury I forced a further delay, requiring some time to scramble out of the new attire and struggle into the old. I felt the loss of the boys' clothes immediately. A girl's dress invited in the chill. Trousers simply didn't.

Mama had assured my brother that the Hubers' address would be easy to find, not only by its proximity to town, the biggest homestead on the first south-side road off the main thoroughfare, but also by its features.

"What are we supposed to be looking for?" I asked, pulling the hood of my cape more securely over my head.

"A spacious breezeway"—Gid squinted through the snow—"and an enormous stone icehouse."

When we finally reached the place that matched our mother's description and, sleigh bells ringing, swept into the yard, twilight was blurring the falling snow. The house, outbuildings, and scattering of trees cast murky shadows across the seamless white.

The door cracked, then opened wider. A stout woman, holding her shawl together at her throat, appeared.

Gid jumped out of the sleigh. He introduced us, reached into his coat, and presented the letter Mama had asked him to pass along.

Smiling, Mrs. Huber pressed it to her bosom. "Please, come in."

When my eyes adjusted to the dim interior, I glanced around with interest. The Hubers' house was generously sized, but its openness spread the fire's warmth thin. Indeed, frost trimmed the door and furred the glass of the single-paned window.

"Will this winter never end?" Mrs. Huber dusted flakes off her dark shawl and gazed at us warmly. "Dear Margaret's beloved Harriet and Gideon. I've heard so much about you—knew about the pioneering, too, just not the precise schedule—and now you're here and such a coincidence. Only this afternoon I was determined to write your mother a letter, then scolded myself for leaving the stone well in the borning room. Ink froze solid. Well, the loft's toasty, anyway, and you can spend the night up there." When we mumbled about not wanting to put anyone out, she exclaimed, "Heavens, of course it's no bother. Wouldn't think of sending you off without a good night's rest and a full stomach. You'll have plenty of rough sleeping and eating in the coming weeks. We can offer you respite for at least one evening." She turned. "Come, girls." She introduced her red-haired daughters, Fran and Kate, younger than me but older than Betsy, and clucked over an absent Sarah, "lately married and now living in your neck of the woods, close to Middleton." Then, like one saving the best for last, she presented her eldest—"Here's my Lance"—and, with a meaningful look: "Seventeen years old. Just your age, Harriet."

The son, shortish like his sisters but with hair more auburn than orange, greeted us cheerfully and gave me a furtive scan.

I automatically returned the look.

Nice but no Daniel Long.

I blinked. The unbidden thought disturbed me. I was supposed to be putting Mr. Long out of mind, not clinging to him like a hoarded treasure.

Lance grinned approvingly at me. After reaching for his coat, he gave my brother a nod. "I can help you put up the cattle."

"I'd appreciate that."

The opening door allowed in a billow of snow that settled as soon as Lance pulled it shut behind him and Gid.

Mrs. Huber fluttered her hands. "Let me take your coat, Harriet. We'll get you closer to the fire. Mr. Huber ought to be back soon. He walked to the stand of maples at the bottom of the hill—has some notion of widening the field that way." While I unwound my scarf and started on the mittens, she said over her shoulder, "Heat some water, Fran." Beaming at me: "You *must* tell me about your plans. The Genesee Valley! All the rage in these parts, too—and so exciting. I want Middleton news, as well. Last I heard from your mother, she was nursing a houseful of invalids. You, especially, suffered, I recall her—" She gasped.

In the process of removing my cape, I had pushed back the hood.

She stared at my cropped hair in horror and even jerked sideways to glance at my back, probably hoping to discover my tresses bound in a tight bun. "Oh, dear!"

I nervously plucked at my fringe.

Wide-eyed, she gave her head a little shake and pressed her lips together as if regretting the outburst, then started over with "Let me take your cape, Harriet. Come to the fire. Right here, it's the best chair. You must be hungry."

"Thank you." I gratefully fell into the rocker and leaned forward to seek the warmth.

Mrs. Huber situated Gid's and my boots on the hearthstone.

Her daughters, one with the teakettle dangling from a hand, stood frozen, their mouths hanging open.

I slouched under the inspection and scrunched the fabric of my skirt. *It's only hair. Not like I'm missing a limb.*

Their mother shooed them. "Warm the biscuits and broth, Kate. Fran, bring up a jar of my strawberry jam." The girls jerked into action, and Mrs. Huber pressed a hand to her cheek, her gaze sweeping my head again. She made a sound of distress. When my brother and her son returned, she hurried their way, as if relieved to escape the sight of me, and set about getting them situated, taking Gid's winter gear, urging him to the other rocker, and chattering the entire time.

Lance followed my brother but paused by the fire to add a piece of wood. Rising, he turned and parted his smiling mouth, poised to speak.

Immediately, the smile reversed itself. After a moment of

stunned silence, he coughed, sidled to Gid's other side, and began to question my brother on his planned purchase of land, wanting the particulars on the parcel's size and his intentions for it, practically performing an interrogation.

In short, avoiding an interaction with me.

I wrinkled my nose at the fire and fought the urge to reassure him on my equal lack of interest. *No need to panic, young man.*

Mr. Huber entered the house, shrugged off his coat, and carried his ax to the hearth. Upon spotting me, the big man did a double take, then struggled to erase his astonishment as Mrs. Huber presented my brother and me. "How do you do?" He pasted on a smile, bowed, and swiftly sidestepped toward the men. After sitting heavily beside his son, he reached for a jar under the bench, scooped out some fat, and began rubbing it over his ax's blade. Soon, he was adding his own questions about the Holland Land Company to his son's inquiries.

I was fine with being ignored and avoided, fine with not talking. Chilled to the bone, I only wanted to get warm, eat, and sleep. I held my hands to the fire, anxious to accomplish the first two goals so I could seek the reprieve of the last. Meanwhile, Mrs. Huber shared recollections of my mother, their youth, and wintertime capers, her tone wistful but her eyes militantly averted from my cropped hair.

The daughters weren't nearly as discreet. They wasted no time in warming up our supper, clearly impatient to resume their ogling. Mrs. Huber ordered the girls to serve Gid and me where we sat by the fire.

As hungry as I was, I had difficulty enjoying the food, all too aware of the girls' stares.

Kate's stitchery was an untouched puddle of threads in her

lap. Interrupting her mother's ice-skating account, she blurted, "Was it the sickness that made you go bald?"

"*Kate.*" Mrs. Huber stopped knitting to elbow her daughter.

"She's not bald," Fran said. She was sitting at my feet, toying with her long red braid while eyeing my short hair. "Bet it was awfully pretty. So golden . . . like the blond locks of a fairy-tale princess."

"Was it the sickness, dear? Did it"—Mrs. Huber cleared her throat—"fall out?"

Everyone, even the men, gazed at me expectantly.

I shook my head and met my brother's wry glance. "It was just a bad case of lice."

A squeak escaped Kate, and Fran, horror filling her face, fell backward and held her hair protectively behind her.

"They're long gone now," I said quickly.

"Of course they are," Mrs. Huber said, frowning at her daughters. "The pests can't survive without hair for nesting." She sighed over her knitting. "But what a shame, what a terrible shame, for Fran's right—your hair must have been a glorious sight, as pale as it is. Still, it will grow, never fear, and in just three or four years you'll have your crowning glory back again." This last assurance she spoke mostly to Lance, her gaze earnest.

He flared his eyes at his mother in warning before shifting a frown in my direction. With a shake of his head, he dismissed me. Then he turned to Gid and asked him about the girth of his cattle.

After being subjected to so much undesirable attention at the Hubers', I imagined the rest of our journey would prove uncomplicated by comparison. I was wrong. It was pure work: sometimes tedious, sometimes hair-raising, and almost always freezing. Alternating with relatively uneventful days sprang stretches of terror, the sled slipping backward when the oxen lost their footing on an icy incline, our road narrowing to little more than a snowy trail snugly winding around a mountain with the yawning gulf below, a stream's ice cracking ominously under the weight of our crossing sleigh, and the world disappearing completely one afternoon when snow began to fall in earnest, and the wind blew hard, and whiteness, spewed from the clouds and whipped up from below, thoroughly blinded us.

I steadied oxen, dragged aside downed tree limbs blocking our way, shoveled, trudged, and leaped. And, happily, no petticoats tripped me. No skirts slowed me down. My pantaloons especially pleased me, but I appreciated the sturdy warmth of all my gear.

The only thing I missed was my hair—though not in the way Sally Huber would assume. I didn't long for it as a lost symbol of my femininity (how *stupid*; men could grow their hair out, too, if they wanted!); I merely wished for its warmth. When I'd worn it in a braid or a loose, low bun, it had partly covered my neck. Now, unless I remembered to wear a scarf, I felt the bite of the wind on my skin. I spent many hours hunching my shoulders, shivering, and sticking my gloved hands in the pockets of the woolen coat I'd appropriated from Gid's boyhood wardrobe.

"Put on your scarf," my brother would sigh, his exasperated tone telling me he was getting sick of reminding me.

I would. Then the next day I'd forget again.

Even more than my gloves, the coat pockets protected my hands. Before we left home, I'd improved them with extra lining, and they were deliciously warm, twin havens against the benumbing cold. In the right pocket I carried around a small treasure and rubbed its smoothness. This was a habit I probably should have broken, since it frequently turned my thoughts toward home and everything and everyone I was missing. Yet, conflictingly, the small charm comforted me in stressful circumstances, like when the axle broke or Fancy went temporarily missing or the mountains, my sleeping giants, slipped from view.

It was the spile Daniel Long had given me a year ago. Every so often, in the rare moments my brother and I weren't side by side, I'd take out the sugaring spout and trail my finger along the carefully carved vine and *D.U.L.*, the three initials I used to mock with the self-assurance of a vain girl certain of her superior appeal.

Finally, I'd trace the initials Mr. Long had included to tease me. *H.S.L.*: Harriet Submit Long. She was someone I'd almost met. We'd passed each other in another life.

CHAPTER FOURTEEN

We stared at the dilapidated tenement for a long time. The porch steps didn't just head up but also keeled sideways and, in two places, sagged before finishing at a porch that was smeared with tobacco-spit slime. The front door was cracked open. Slurred voices and laughter, drunken like the stairs, spilled out of the taproom. To the right of the door, an unseasonably warm breeze swung a painted sign that read TICKLENAKED TAVERN. Behind us, two rickety shacks of slapped-together, ill-fitted logs slumped on the yard between several tree stumps.

Around these remains of trees, chickens wandered in their peculiar fashion, like stout women skirting puddles while wearing too-small shoes with too-high heels. They pecked at the yard, which was unctuous with mud, and circled a solitary young man, my age or a bit older.

This person was neatly dressed in delicate yellow pantaloons, a long-tailed blue coat, and boots that, although caked in mud on their lower halves, brilliantly gleamed around the top tassels. His cleanliness, in contrast to Gid's and my filth, would have sufficed to surprise me. His present occupation guaranteed my astonishment: perched on a stump, with a beautiful chestnut horse tethered to the post behind him and a case open on his lap, he was inspecting a fiddle's strings.

A ruckus brought my attention back to the alehouse. Rear first, a body tumbled through the door. It fell toward the porch, emitted a giggle, and crashed back until it sprawled, arms and legs splayed, like an ugly mat. After disgorging it, the door swung shut.

From our sleigh, Fancy barked once, then, perhaps observing this individual's unthreatening position, returned her silky head to her paws and closed her eyes.

"The devil!" I bent to get a good look at the supine body. "Is he dead?"

Frowning, Gideon grabbed my arm and yanked me away.

"Dead drunk," the man on the stump answered without taking his eyes off his instrument. He pinged each string and murmured, "No harm done. The E's a little flat, but that's more the fault of the thaw than the villains." He reached up and soothed the neck of his horse. The animal answered the caress by dipping her head and snuffling the man's palm. "They're gone now. Don't you fret." The thick woods resounded with a sudden crackling, like ground-borne thunder. At my startled look, the young man smiled sardonically. "Breaking river ice." He splayed a hand. "Welcome to the Genesee Valley in the springtime."

"Spring," Gideon groaned, and cast a mournful glance at our sleigh. From the seat, Fancy raised her sleepy head again and peered inquisitively back at him. I knew what Gid was thinking.

We would have to take the runners off the chain-locked wheels and turn our sled back into a wagon. No point in trying to drive a sleigh when winter gave up its white. Already we'd spent the better part of the journey between Albany and Canandaigua dragging over snow that was half mud. Indeed, just a short while ago when we'd stopped to dispatch a letter to our family, the sleigh had almost gotten stuck in the postmaster's yard. The wheels wouldn't fare much better than the runners if the snow and ice disappeared—not on the wet, pitted, uneven, tree-strewn cart tracks that apparently counted as serviceable lanes in these parts. Too mucky. We'd sink.

The tavern blared another scream of laughter. Just as Gideon reached for the latch and lifted his foot to step over the unconscious person blocking our way, the young man on the stump suggested mildly, "I wouldn't go in there if I were you."

Gid hesitated and turned to face the stranger. "Er . . . why?"

The man rested the fiddle in the case with the kind of tenderness one might perceive in a new mother situating her firstborn in a cradle. He shut and latched the case, then stood. "Because you'll encounter a nest of vipers, that's why. First they'll jostle you to a table. Then they'll chuckle and pat you on the back and ask you all sorts of chummy questions. Then they'll send a couple of rascals into the yard to inspect your enticingly loaded sleigh. Then they'll steal whatever they want from it." He raised his shoulders in an elegant shrug. "I know. Minutes ago, I fell prey to a variation on that theme. They removed the sacks of potash I'd hoped to sell. They nearly stole my horse. I managed to secure the latter at the cost of the former—and saved my violin, too, thank goodness." He patted the case, doffed his beaver hat, and bowed. "Allow me to introduce myself. Phineas Lionel Standen: violinist, horse-man, and impoverished farmer. And you are?"

"Gideon Winter." My brother took a cautious step back from the door and, jerking his head to indicate I ought to follow, made his way down the crooked stairs to the sludgy yard.

I trailed slowly, my backward gaze more wistful than nervous. After all of these horrid days and nights, how I wished—nay, *yearned*—for hot water and a cleansing bath. I itched. I stank. My apparel (my precious, meticulously sewn, and precisely fitted apparel!) was no longer the least bit smart but shockingly filthy. And, oh, to sleep in a bed again! I'd enjoyed a real bed only once during this vicious journey, when we'd stayed with the Hubers. But that had been weeks ago. I was *sick* of sleeping in that wagon.

Phineas Lionel Standen was staring at me expectantly.

"Oh. Sorry. Frederick."

"Just Frederick?"

I gave my brother a sour look. "Mostly just Freddy."

Gid cleared his throat. "Freddy's a foundling."

"Ah." Phineas eyed me dispassionately. "You've more height than years, I think"—his sigh, profound and weary, prefaced a shake of his head—"and your whole long life ahead of you." His tone made it clear I was not in an enviable position.

A laugh escaped me. "I guess a disease could always put the period to my existence sooner rather than later."

One corner of his mouth slid up. "You'll have plenty of oppor-tunities in this wilderness to make a fragment of your life sentence. Wait until mosquito season. Wait for the fever and ague. Wait until your store of wheat runs out. Wait until the feed's gone and you have to hope your oxen can survive by browsing on parched foliage throughout the winter. Wait until you start browsing right alongside them. Starvation. Bears. Wolves. Rattlesnakes." He glanced at the tavern. "Drunkenness. So many simple ways to cut short the complicated syntax of our worldly composition."

I closed my mouth, glanced at Gid, then managed weakly, "Thank the Lord for heaven."

"Well, it's the least he can promise after punishing us with so much hell."

The blasphemous remark, blandly made, left my brother and me speechless.

Our new acquaintance didn't seem to notice. He was brushing his horse's pretty coat with his hand. After shifting the fiddle case, he turned to face the animal's tail and leaned into her side to urge her to raise one of her hind legs. He held the hoof, inspected its underside, and asked, "Where are you heading?"

"The town of Gaines," Gideon said. "Eventually."

Phineas immediately released the horse and straightened. "Really? That's remarkable."

The boyish pleasure lighting his face warmed me to him.

"Though I suppose it shouldn't shock me," he conceded. "It's our area that's currently getting settled, after all. But still. First the brothers and now two more neighbors. Gaines will be a metropolis before we know it."

"You've met Robert and Edward Welds, then?"

"You know them?"

"Yes, indeed. We're all from Middleton, New Hampshire."

"So you must be the friend Robert mentioned. . . ." Phineas's gaze swung in my direction before returning to Gid. "I was expecting a solitary traveler."

"I picked up Freddy along the way." Phineas didn't respond,

merely waited with his eyebrows raised, so my brother added, "He was stranded."

"Desperate and on the run," I corrected, intent on savoring my exciting, albeit fictitious, past.

"After getting out of a bad situation with an unkind employer," Gid said.

"A vicious blackguard of a silversmith," I clarified, "who beat me and threatened to kill me if I didn't slave night and day and answer his every unreasonable demand."

My brother briefly closed his eyes.

Phineas nodded slowly, his expression bemused. "Got to watch out for those wicked silversmiths."

"An unsavory bunch," I agreed.

"Will you search for your family?"

"Can't."

"Oh, that's right. I forgot. You're Mr. Freddy of Unknown Parentage. I wonder what happened to your folks."

"Highwaymen, I suspect."

He smiled. "You would."

I waved a hand at his case. "Do you always travel with your fiddle?"

"If I want to protect it from several grubby, sticky hands intent on ruining it, I do." He pulled gloves of York tan from his coat pocket and, with his odd elegance, slipped them on. Then he brushed the tiniest speck of flint off his coat sleeve. "Marian can't seem to keep the buggers in check and, more often than not, accuses *me* of too poorly understanding and appreciating the inquisitive minds of youth. Inquisitive!" He gave a disdainful sniff. "*Obnoxious*, more like it." He tapped the case. "It's safer with me. Two things matter in my life: my music and my sweetheart."

"Marian?"

"Ha. That's a good one. No." His arm went up and hugged his horse's neck. "This creature. Sweetheart."

Gid and I nodded. What was there to say? The man loved his horse.

"Now. What did you mean by 'eventually'?"

My brother frowned. "Eventually?"

"Yes. You said you were traveling to Gaines eventually."

"Oh. Well, we *will*, but first we need to head to the Holland Land Company in Batavia to make the purchase and deposit."

"Which article did you choose?"

"I didn't. The Welds brothers recommended the two hundred acres west of them."

Phineas blew a silent whistle and wagged his head.

"What?" Gid demanded.

"Not a smart idea, purchasing a lot, sight unseen."

My brother folded his arms. "I can trust my friends' recommendation."

"Because they're clearly bright, those boys."

Gid bristled, but I couldn't help it: I burst out laughing.

Again, that elegant shrug. "Well, the lot might suit you as well as any other. I'm on the other side of the Welds boys, and in truth, the entire territory is a vicious trial. Nothing but wooded swampland."

Gid and I stared.

"All of it?" I asked, vividly recalling the description of snake dens Robert Welds had read to us from one of Mrs. Linton's letters.

"Inevitable, really. Low-lying land under an endless canopy

of trees stays moist. You'll see for yourself." He sighed. "I'll escort you to Batavia." He shot a glare at the tavern. "I have to explain why I don't have the money to make my loan payment and might as well do it now than later."

"Aren't you worried about leaving Marian and the children unattended?" I asked.

He snorted. "She's more capable than I am of defending the family. You should have seen what she did to the bear that tried to attack our cow."

"Shot it?"

He released the tether from the post. "Axed it."

"Heavens." That was impressive. "But won't she fret if you don't return right away?"

He fitted his boot into a stirrup and gracefully mounted Sweetheart, giving her a moment to prance under his weight, then rewarding her with a rub. "She'll be glad I'm not underfoot, 'sawing up a racket on the fiddle,' as she says. That woman has zero appreciation for fine music." He sniffed again. "Truthfully, this will be a pleasant vacation for me—a chance to get away from her tart tongue and that pack of dirty ankle-biters."

These unromantic disclosures left me nonplussed. Perhaps he and Marian had married prematurely, without sufficiently considering their differences before plunging into a lifelong union. I'd never met a man so obviously disenchanted with his mate and offspring.

Gid, however, seemed more focused on the agreeable news that we'd secured a guide for the remainder of our journey, and he and Phineas spent a moment discussing directions and probable difficulties, given the mucky conditions. Finally Gid said, "We appreciate your escort." He tapped a stump with his boot. "But after we take care of our business with the land company, I'd like to make one additional stop in a place called Barre."

"That won't be difficult. It's not far from Batavia. Friends settled there?"

My brother nodded, his quick peek in my direction sheepish.

I grinned. Gid wasn't wasting any time in resuming his courtship.

Before leaving the tavern yard, we turned the sleigh back into a wagon and then followed the river for three days until we came to a section shallow enough to cross. During this time, our guide sparkled with humor, even when he complained about farm life, the iniquities of the three children "infesting" his cabin home—and his wife.

I felt sorry for the poor woman and probably too blatantly wore my sympathy because Phineas said, "Don't be taking her side, Freddy. She's *terrible*. The temper in that woman! Most don't even guess it. Why, if I ate a cherry tartlet every time I heard someone gush, 'Oh, Marian, what a lovely girl,' I'd be a fat fiddler, let me tell you. She fools them all because she hides the meanness so well. Make the mistake of irritating her once in a while, and she'll let it go for weeks, whole months, with hardly a scowl, but what she's *really* doing is saving the anger, storing it up like an army hoarding weapons and ammunition. Then, one day, I'll say the littlest thing, like 'Golly, Marian, that gingham getup could stand to meet a hot iron,' and boom! She'll blast me so hard, it's like there's a cannon hiding in that wrinkled skirt. Ah, well, it's my lot in life to suffer so, I expect."

I was skeptical. Seemed like the person suffering the most was Marian.

After a couple days of this, Phineas took a break from bemoaning family life in order to enthusiastically recount stories of raging torrents, drowning cattle, and pioneers floundering in deep waters and sinking to their deaths.

The conditions inspired the shift in his morbid wit. The melting snow had dangerously swelled the river, and I could easily imagine never making it to the other side. I was constantly clasping the lucky spile in my pocket as we followed along the river's rushing length.

We traveled as much as we could during the frigid hours before and after nighttime, when the ground was stiff with cold, permitting us to rumble over the pitching lanes without sinking into the mud. I got a good amount of exercise popping in and out of the wagon to drag aside broken tree limbs and hack at the dead remnants of trail-webbing vines. So many encroaching branches: It was as if the forest wanted to reclaim itself and swallow the paltry path humans had carved out of its wildness.

I'd never seen such a forest, with its ancient trees, enormous and innumerable. It teemed with animals awakened by the milder conditions. When I needed to venture from our riverside sojourn into the woods for privacy's sake, I stayed as close as possible to the dense edge, certain that trespassing even a foot too far would make me one more intrusion the vegetation would engulf, perhaps holding me in its gnarled clutches to await a wolf's or panther's or bear's dinnertime.

Eventually, I couldn't avoid the fearsome interior, for our journey veered straight into the woods. This, however, only happened after we executed a different terrifying feat: the fording of the river.

With the wagon cracks caulked and the oxen hitched by rope to our horseman guide, we dared the river at its shallowest point, which still seemed dangerously deep. It was a strangely silent crossing. Anxiety had stolen our voices. The entire way, the poor animals' alarmed eyes bulged above the surface of the water. Fancy, with a frantic whimper, scrambled almost to my shoulders.

The great benefit of the crossing (besides, obviously, survival and being able to continue on our journey) was that I achieved the first thorough soaking I'd had in weeks. I wasn't precisely clean, but I no longer reeked. Phineas, of course, stayed miraculously dapper and mostly dry. Afterward, he merely stretched out a long leg and exclaimed, "The Genesee works better than champagne for boot shining."

We had reasons to be thankful for our smart-tongued companion. Not only had he helped in the crossing, but he also (much better than Gid and I ever would) understood the blazes on the trees that had been left as direction indicators by Indians and earlier pioneers. We would have been lost—literally—without Phineas's guidance.

One night by our campfire, fortified with too many drams of Mama's hard cider, Gid tried to deliver a heartfelt speech of gratitude. Phineas brushed this aside and held up his tin plate with its remnant of johnnycake and fried salt pork. "This is reward enough: Freddy's shockingly good cooking and the exquisiteness of the ingredients." He took a bite, chewed slowly, swallowed, and moaned, "*Wheat*. Glorious wheat."

I considered his impassioned sighs and lip smacking. What had he grown used to subsisting on if a quick bread and a few pieces of crackling pork could inspire this level of appreciation?

Catching my perturbed study, he grinned. "Sure beats wild-leek soup."

As helpful as Phineas was, his constant teasing and joking rankled. The only—*only*—times he turned somber were when he mulled aloud about the theft of his potash at the tavern and what was going to happen when he couldn't pay on his land. Then he'd frown at the fire.

Such seriousness was short-lived. He'd resume his raillery all too quickly. My occasional, solitary visits to the woods particularly amused him.

Once, when I returned after a quick trip, he burst out laughing. "Merciful heavens, Freddy. You're not suffering from a stomach ailment, are you? No? Then don't be bashful. We won't look."

His hilarity only increased when I stammered an excuse of shameful bruises left by my previous employer.

"Oh, no, not the evil silversmith again," he groaned through his mirth.

And on another occasion: "You shouldn't be ashamed, Freddy. We are all God's creation, big and small. Alas, some will always be bigger than others. But you've still got a little growing left in you, so don't worry yet. And if you remain on the nubby side, as long as the equipment works, you shouldn't worry. A woman's sensitive spot isn't the hole. You want to head northward to find her paradise. Ha-ha-ha!" His arm, swung over my shoulders for this friendly (and excruciatingly mortifying) reassurance, practically choked me as he doubled over and lurched sideways in his subsequent laughter.

Gid listened to these tormenting teachings with an expression that was part alarmed, part amused, and part embarrassed (for both of our sakes, no doubt). However, he made no move to interfere, and when I muttered under my breath a complaint, his face turned sanctimonious, and he retorted, "Freddy was your stupid idea. Not mine."

In contrast to my great modesty and Gid's milder version, Phineas revealed a remarkable casualness about such delicate matters. Without pausing, he would carry on about the superiority of horses to all other animals while unfastening his pantaloons and relieving himself against a tree.

Even more startling were his bathing rituals, the regular scrubbings he gave himself and his clothes in the river, unmindful of my gape and indifferent to the nippy April air and the cold water. "Cleanliness, dear Freddy, is the secret to good health," he once lectured over his lathered shoulder, "cleanliness and abstinence." Then, with a twinkling smile, he added, "Abstinence from excessive drinking, anyway. Filth and drunkenness are death's boon companions."

In response to my whispered comment on Phineas's excessive washing rituals, my brother shrugged. "It's an English thing."

This could be true. We'd learned that Phineas's family had only recently immigrated to America from Tadmorden, Lancashire, England.

Gid scratched over his right ear. "And not such a bad idea. I ought to brave the frigid water and join him."

I sighed. "Wish I could contrive a good bath."

"Soon." He gave me a dark look. "In the meantime, stop paying such close attention to Phineas's."

I stuck out my tongue and shuffled away, my face hot from the implication. Truthfully, my peeks at Phineas were curious but not lascivious. Oddly enough, instead of focusing on his nakedness, I found myself wondering what Daniel Long would look like similarly occupied in the river.

It struck me as a tragedy of my own making that I'd never find out.

CHAPTER FIFTEEN

Batavia, despite owning the distinction as the Genesee Valley's county seat, was little more than a bare-bones village. Its outskirts didn't so much drift toward the wilderness as slam into it, for trees densely enclosed the town. However, I couldn't have experienced a greater surge of relief entering its precincts had I found myself in Boston. For too long, Gid, Phineas, and I had suffered either the gloom of the woods or, when the sun breached the canopy and sifted through the legion of branches, its bewildering glare.

Entering Batavia, I blinked like a blind girl newly introduced to sight and, since I'd taken to traveling mostly on foot to ease the weary oxen's burden, stumbled into the road and straight into the path of a mule-drawn cart.

"Oh!" I tripped backward. "I beg your pardon."

"Mind where you're going, boy," the owner said testily, yanking his animal out of my way.

Phineas eyed me in amusement. "Follow me." He tapped his horse's sides with his heels and trotted ahead of us along the thoroughfare.

The central office of the Holland Land Company, Grecian in architectural style, anchored the town on the main road where people strode or rumbled along in wagons. When we shuffled into the clean building, I regretted my ragged appearance, but the bespectacled, thin-haired clerk at the front desk must have been used to dirty visitors, for he barely blinked at Gid and me. Indeed, he seemed more struck by Phineas's dapper apparel. His wide gaze lingered on him and the instrument case in his hand before he coughed and shuffled some papers. "This way, please," he said, his Dutch heritage discernible in his accent. He indicated the hallway behind him.

After he escorted us through a doorway and departed with a murmured assurance that we wouldn't wait long, we found ourselves sitting in the richly paneled, book-lined contractor's room.

The graying agent who entered a few minutes later greeted us and promptly unrolled a map. Based on Gid's request, he inspected this map for a moment, trailing his finger along the demarcations sectioning off two long, intersecting roads, Oak Orchard and Ridge, then identifying the Welds brothers' location. As if speaking mostly to himself, he murmured, "A little south of the Ridge, I believe—right here, near what we call the Five Corners. Two hundred and sixty acres." He peered inquiringly at Gid.

My brother, his eyes alight with excitement, nodded and repeated reverently, "Two hundred and sixty acres."

Gid took the article, made his first payment, provided contact and beneficiary information, and signed three papers to secure the transaction. This took all of five minutes.

Then my brother and I waited as Phineas explained the theft of his potash. "I'm afraid I only have the interest due." More nervous than I'd ever seen him, he fidgeted with his instrument case. "I don't know when I'll raise the rest."

The agent nodded. "May I see your article, please?"

Phineas unlatched the case. After opening the compartment under the scrolled end of his fiddle, he removed a few neatly wound coils of strings, a block of resin, and at last, his folded article. Phineas hadn't once played his instrument for us. I wondered when he would.

The agent opened the article and read it. "I'll be back shortly."

We waited for his return without talking. Phineas sat hunched over his clenched hands, Gid stood staring at his contract in amazement, and I sidled along the shelves, eyeing the books and missing Mama's collection back home.

When the agent returned, he passed Phineas a new contract and explained matter-of-factly that he'd waived the back interest, as well as a dollar per acre on the balance.

Perhaps our companion had been half prepared to lose his land, for these revisions left the normally loquacious Phineas temporarily speechless. He finally managed, "How kind. I—I don't know how to thank you."

The elderly gentleman folded his hands over his vested front. "Make your land prosper. That is the company's hope for every industrious settler."

Shortly thereafter, we stood outside the building, and I felt precisely as I had upon leaving the forest: disoriented and stunned.

Gid gazed around dazedly. "That was easy."

"Dropping blunt is all too easy," Phineas agreed. "Let's celebrate. There's an inn down the road." He squeezed the back of his neck and shook his head. "We need to toast the Holland Land Company, the very generous Holland Land Company."

He spoke with absolute sincerity and blew a gusty exhalation: a huge sigh of relief.

We visited the local postmaster to dispatch a letter to Mama and Papa and then made our way to the inn. Though dubiously named Skunk's Misery, the place neither stank like a skunk nor promised misery to its travelers. It was rough-hewn but surprisingly clean. And though my brother's resources had dwindled and Phineas's financial plight was even direr than Gid's, I'd barely touched my savings. So I offered to pay for our supper and rooms—two, one for Gid and Phineas and one for me. If our new friend wondered why I took the single room, he didn't say anything. He probably perceived it as further evidence of my excessive modesty.

After booking our rooms, I requested a bath.

The tavern keeper's wife sourly inspected not just me but Gid, too. "You'll all be getting baths. I won't have my straw-tick beds swarming with bugs."

I was happy to endure the implication that we carried infestations on our persons, as long as I could get clean, and I even paid the extra fees for a bit of soap and additional kettles of hot water.

A loud crash in the back of the building interrupted our transaction, and the tavern keeper's wife excused herself to check on the situation.

The aroma of roasted pork reached us where we waited. Through a set of closed interior doors sprang a shout of laughter.

Gid gazed complacently at the neat accommodations. Phineas, arms crossed, rocked back on his heels and wondered aloud if baked apples might form part of our meal. The successful negotiations at the Holland Land Company had ensured the men's good spirits. They were prepared to enjoy themselves.

Unlike them, I possessed nothing of great value—no land, cabin, spouse, or livestock. Nevertheless, my face undoubtedly beamed the brightest. I was about to visit a hitherto forbidden realm: a taproom.

The tavern keeper's wife returned and directed us to our rooms. "Takes time to prepare three baths. You might want to sup while you wait."

We agreed with alacrity. After following my companions to the second floor, securing Fancy and my belongings in the private room, and trailing Phin and Gid down a different staircase, I headed into the taproom with every expectation of pleasure, as eager as a secret society's novice on the evening of her induction.

It was like entering a noisy cloud. Several farm laborers puffed on clay pipes, and smoke mixed with the fetid odors of sweat, grime, and whiskey.

Phineas's nostrils curled. "Can't smell a single baked apple in *here*." He whipped out a handkerchief and held it fastidiously to his nose. Suddenly he seized my arm and yanked me toward him.

One of the patrons, a burly man, in a burst of jocularity had sent his chair back on its hind legs, straight into my path. Thanks to Phin's quick action, the blow only grazed my thigh.

The sprawling man shot forward, the chair hit the floor with a thud, and he whirled around. "Watch it."

Me? I glared back. "You, too."

Gid laughed nervously and nudged me along. "Take care,

Freddy." He flared his eyes. "First the mule cart and now this. Pay attention to where you're going."

"I don't see how his throwing himself in our way is my fault."

I would have happily stomped to the opposite side of the room. Unfortunately, the only free table was the one after the rude reveler's. Still, its position granted me a liberal view of the space. I sat with my back to the wall and my shoulder an inch from that of another man's—or boy's. He couldn't have been much older than I was surely taken to be, fourteen or fifteen.

With a sideways glance, he gave me a polite nod, then settled a resentful glower on Mr. Rude.

The man, once again, was tipping his chair into the meager walkway and guffawing. He raised his tankard and bellowed, "To my cousin, fair John, our precious little milkmaid."

Around the table, the toast was laughingly repeated with slight variations: "pretty John," "sweet John," "our lovely milkin' lass."

"*Gammon,*" the boy sitting next to me muttered. "I was just helping Mother."

I frowned at the jokester, curious about the insult.

A servant appeared at Phin's side. Balancing a tray with one arm, she swiped her hand on the greasy front of her apron, then passed out three brimming tankards and three plates mounded with pork and potatoes.

As soon as she moved on, I took an eager sip, hoping for a mouthful of the hard stuff, and slumped with disappointment. It was the same old thing I'd always drunk.

Gid gave me a dry look. "I told you they won't serve nurslings strong spirits."

"What are you having?"

He brought his cup close to his chest. "Never mind."

"Hand it over."

"Drink your cider."

"Come on. Just a sip."

Phineas gave the smoky air an indolent wave. "Give the lad a taste of gin."

My brother rolled his eyes but slid his tankard across the table.

I shot my patron a grateful smile and took a gulp.

Merciful heavens!

My throat, immediately inflamed, barely managed the swallow. Tears filled my eyes. Heat seared my face. It took every ounce of my willpower to stifle a coughing fit.

Phineas grinned. "Yummy, hmm?"

Hoarsely: "Delicious." With a shudder, I returned the tankard to a smirking Gid and swabbed my eyes with a sleeve. Laughter roared beside me, with Mr. Rude pounding the table to accompany the blare. I stilled, thinking the hilarity was for me and my unconvincing handling of the alcohol.

It wasn't. Of the table's six occupants, only my young neighbor failed to crack a smile. Obviously, he was the brunt of another joke. "Rubbish," the boy muttered, mortification spelled large in the flush of his pimpled cheeks.

I gave him a sympathetic glance but then turned away. Tavern visiting was a treat for me, one not likely to be repeated. I was here to enjoy myself and determined to do so.

Between forkfuls of pork, my tablemates dove into a conversation about the lake abutting the valley—"as sweeping as an ocean," according to Phin—and the species of fish to be found in the area.

Not a particularly interesting topic to me. I'd spent too many hours of my life gutting my brothers' summertime catches. I studied our surroundings. The table on our left was as quiet as the one on our right was loud. Its occupants sat hunched, somberly mulling over the cards in their hands. I swatted Phin in the arm. "Are they playing faro?"

He and my brother stopped shoveling food into their mouths and followed my gaze. Gid shrugged (he was no tavern expert, either), but Phin shook his head. "Brag, I think."

"Brag," I breathed. I'd never heard of brag, but it sounded exciting. Maybe he would teach me how to play. With a flutter of anticipation, I gazed avidly around me, then twisted to take in the advertisements and legal notices plastering the wall. Between an announcement of a town meeting and a note offering the sale of a goat was a warning about runaway apprentices. I smiled, imagining my name there, then turned again, began picking at my meal, and strained to catch the exchanges in the room.

My ears pricked at a complaint about President Madison, "his bacon-brained General Wilkinson, and the shameful cronyism already wrecking our government." Politics! I leaned forward, hoping to hear more. *This* was what I'd longed to be made privy to: stimulating theories and elevated discourse. Unfortunately, the distant conversation took a mundane turn and began to dwell on the sad state of a neighbor's cow.

I slumped. Mostly these men were just puffing on pipes and drinking.

Maybe the reference to the farmer's cow aroused Mr. Rude's attention, for he reintroduced the milking topic at his table with a more seriously muttered "Damme, it don't make sense, John, adding milking to your chores. Is darning socks next?" He grunted. "You have men's tasks to perform, and if last year's haying was any indication, you could use the practice. Too slow with the scythe, by far." He cracked a smile. "Listen, girl. I can promise you this year, if you don't learn to quicken your pace, I'll be nicking your ankles with my blade to hurry you along."

More red mottled poor John's face. "Stop calling me girl. And I can't exactly practice haying this time of year."

"Then you should be building fences and splitting rails."

"I *do*. I still have time to help Mother. Why shouldn't I?"

He pounded the table once, with a fist. "Because *it's not your work*. That's for Patience to do."

"She's five!"

"Then your mother must handle it herself."

The young man opened his mouth, then seemed to think better of retorting. Instead he seized his tankard and, without even tasting its contents, turned his glare to the side. He caught my gaze in the process.

I smiled. "Your willingness to help"—I shrugged—"well, *I* think it says a lot about your character."

He ran a hand over the back of his neck. "My mother's been very sick."

"Sorry about that, but sick or not, if a woman has her hands full, she can use assistance. Anyone's."

My support, spoken quietly, wasn't intended for the obnoxious man across the table, but he must have heard enough of it because he observed, "Yet another girl in the tavern. You aiming to become a milkmaid, too, girl?"

I narrowed my eyes. The stupid oaf. He reminded me of Matthew. "I don't like how you use that word."

"*Milkmaid*?" He barked a laugh. "Too bad, milkmaid."

"*Girl,*" I clarified through my teeth. "You say it like *cur* or *swine*."

154

"Freddy," Gid said warningly.

I glanced at my brother. "I just wonder he'd make a curse out of the label. Doesn't he have a sister to esteem? A mother to respect?"

The boor snorted. "This has nothing to do with my mother."

"I disagree. When you use *girl* in that degrading way, you disrespect all women, including your mother."

Phineas groaned.

The man sneered. "I see you're a mama's boy like John here. Why don't you go home to your mother?"

"If only I could." Sadness pierced me. I missed Mama terribly. "I'd certainly find *any* mother better occupied than I am. Mothers would never waste their time on this." I dismissed the taproom with a flick of my hand.

"Nor should they. A taproom ain't for females. It's the small reward menfolk earn after a day of breaking their bodies in the fields."

"I don't begrudge hardworking men an hour of leisure, but when does a woman ever reap such a reward?" A moment to sit, without stitchery blanketing her lap and children hanging off her arms? To my young neighbor, I said, "What was your mother doing when you left?"

He scratched his crown. "Feeding fiber to the spindle, I think."

I nodded. "Working. Like always." No evening of fellowship, cards, and liquor for her. As for the Sabbath . . . well, how restful could a day be when there were children to mind? Even a holiday didn't belong to women, not when they had to cook, cook, cook to make the occasion extra special. "You distinguish your mother by helping her. That's more than filial devotion. That's piety. The fifth commandment: Honor thy father and thy mother."

Gid dropped his head in his hands and moaned.

Phin squawked. "Now he's preaching!" He stood hastily and said in a conciliatory way, "Freddy's studying to become a minister."

I ignored him and executed from my seat a small bow to the faithful son. "I respect you for the deference you show your mother. I believe God does, too." Then because I couldn't help it, I added, with more ire than sense, "Only those who break the commandments burn in hell."

The young man darted a fretful peek at the outraged face across the table.

"Did you just send me to hell?" The cousin planted his hands on the table and heaved himself to his feet, scraping the chair against the floorboards in the process.

I blinked. He was big.

"Come, tadpole. I dare you. Say that a second time." Without waiting for a response, he turned to Gid and backhanded the air in my direction. "Is this stripling a relative of yours?"

Gid held up his palms and shook his head.

"Oh, he's his own man." Phin sidled around the table, clamped my wrist to urge me to follow, and hissed in my ear, "Lord Almighty, Freddy, you want to see the man break the sixth commandment, too?"

Gid rose quickly and caught up with Phin and me; then the three of us performed a close-knit shuffle, giving the angry man as wide a berth as the crowded—and now silent—room allowed.

The beast cracked his knuckles and took a step, as if to block our escape.

What have I done? My heart, beating madly, lurched and seemed to land in my throat.

The tavern keeper's wife suddenly spoke. "Your baths are ready and waiting in your rooms." She was standing, eyes wide, arms akimbo, in the doorway. She stepped back. As soon as we stumbled over the threshold, she pulled the doors shut and exhaled loudly.

Phineas whipped out his handkerchief, mopped his brow, and skewered me with a disbelieving glare.

Plowing both hands through his hair, Gid gasped, "Of all the foolish—that man was twice your size. Nay, *thrice*. What were you thinking, Freddy?"

I winced (truthfully shocked by my temper as well) and glanced hesitantly at our rescuer, waiting for her censure, expecting an eviction for inciting trouble.

She merely herded us toward the stairway. "Sam Fry is tiresome, tormenting his cousin that way, and here everyone knows the boy's poor mother just suffered another miscarriage and is as limp as a dishrag. Well, John's a good sort. Hold on." She paused by the front counter to collect three thin towels. Before passing them out, she smiled and, to my astonishment, ruffled my hair. "You're a good boy, too—filthy as a stray mutt but carrying a clean heart. There'll be a slice of apple pie coming up with your bathwater." She winked. "My treat."

CHAPTER SIXTEEN

My near row with the taproom bruiser did not disrupt my sleep. Nothing could. I was too weary and barely managed to keep my eyes open long enough to eat my pie, bathe, and give Fancy a half-hearted washing. Blissfully clean, I slept heavily and didn't stir until the morning commotions in the tavern yard incited my dog's barking. In fact, my companions had almost finished breakfast by the time I wandered into the quiet taproom.

"Why, if it isn't our young radical, Mr. Freddy." Phineas raised his coffee cup in salute. "Stay up late reading some Mary Wollstonecraft?"

Gid folded his arms and sat back. "Or writing your sermon blasting the social ills common in taverns?"

Phin smiled. "Or drafting your treatise in support of the cause of women?"

"Oh, I finished all that a long time ago."

My brother grunted. "How was the apple pie?"

"Excellent." I grinned at his peevish expression. Maybe he would have gotten a slice of pie, too, if he'd stood up for women. But he *hadn't*.

"No one around this early to start a riot with, but there's food. Have a seat." Phineas toed out a chair and nodded approvingly at my outfit. "You're looking as bright as a gold coin."

"Thank you." I had changed into my one spare set of clothes—articles, patched and altered, from my brother's out-grown wardrobe.

Gid eyed me. "I used to have a short coat just like that."

"Really?" I smoothed my hands down my front and patted the tops of my thighs. "Probably similar trousers, shirt, and vest, too."

"Almost assuredly," he answered dryly. He stood and peered anxiously out the window. The glass's ripples and bubbles distorted the sunny scene, weirdly warping the young maple by the porch. "Eat fast, Freddy. I want to make it to Barre by noon."

"I bet you do."

After shooting me a discouraging frown, Gid went to check on our animals. Phineas kept me company while I enjoyed my eggs and bacon. He lounged and chatted until I started a second cup of coffee; then he left, as well, to gather his overnight things from his room. I finished the remainder of my meal and wandered outside, where my brother was half sprawled in the wagon. Most of our possessions littered the yard. Gid was probably organizing the provisions. The few travelers bustling around their vehicles looked like they were doing the very same thing.

The sun shone gloriously bright, completely unhindered by clouds. For the first time on this trip, I realized how *big* the sky was in these parts. Before Batavia, endless trees had roofed us, and I could never see very far ahead through the branchy mesh, but in this cleared oasis, I was able to take in my surroundings. I didn't mind the flat terrain. Without mountains standing in the way, the sky plunged straight to the ground. I raised my face to the sun's beams and breathed deeply, then headed across the yard to help my brother.

"Freddy! Over here."

Phineas was stroking the nose of a fine mare that was tethered to a post. A leather bag hung from the saddle. "What a beauty," Phineas said, when I reached his side. "Such a pretty head: the flaring nostrils, the soft eyes, the shallow mouth. That mouth! She answers the bridle quickly enough. Stand here. Now look at her in profile. See how the length of her back"—he pointed from the withers to the croup—"is precisely one-half of the underline?" With his gloved finger, he drew an imaginary line from the point of the elbow to the stifle. "And here, the distance from poll to withers, then here, from throatlatch to the neck-and-shoulder junction? The two-to-one ratio? *This* is the sort of information you need to pick a quality horse." He gushed about various ratios and distances and how all of these measurements tell a prospective buyer a great deal about the horse's pedigree and temperament.

When he got going on the importance of good balance in a horse, I stopped listening. All of a sudden, this particular horse struck me as more than a beautiful specimen. It began to look like a familiar one. Terribly familiar. Unlike Phineas, I was no expert on horseflesh, but I had the uncanny suspicion that I'd seen this animal (heaven help me, could it be . . . was it possible . . . how . . . *why?*) on *frequent occasions.*

"So you see, Freddy, so much depends upon the slope of the shoulder. Ah . . . what are you doing?"

I could only answer with a shake of my head. I'd unlatched the saddlebag. Feeling like a sleeper trapped in a dream, I slowly reached into the satchel, unbuttoned the interior pocket, and, with my heart pounding and breath suspended, rifled around for a moment before my hands found precisely the kind of thing I dreaded I'd find.

It was a small wooden instrument, a kind of flute, meticulously carved, lovingly detailed, very nearly if not completely finished. I stared at it hard, feeling a prickle along the back of my neck and something akin to a fist in the region of my heart.

When my eyes started smarting, I squeezed them shut. "It can't be," I breathed. But when I forced my eyes open and twisted the instrument around, there, on the opposite side of the last note hole, I saw it: *D.U.L.*

"Freddy?"

I jumped at the sound of Phineas's voice. Scanning the yard, I blindly stuffed the instrument back into the bag, shakily latched the cover, and stumbled away from the fence, my eyes reeling like those of an unbalanced, half-wild, Phineas-unapproved horse. Then, half crouched, I raced toward Gideon.

With a bewildered squawk, Phin followed.

I leaped into the wagon. After scurrying to the back, I squatted low and lifted the bottom of the covering so I could peek out.

Gid folded up the canvas to widen the part. He gazed at me in amazement. "What the devil—"

"He's here," I whispered. "Oh, God, he's here. Get down. *Get down.*"

My brother just stood there. "Who's here?"

"Daniel Long."

"*No.*" My brother blinked. "Really?" He gazed around wonderingly.

"Would you please—*please*—hide? You can't let him see you."

"Who's Daniel Long?" Phineas asked.

"Why can't I let him see me?" My brother's expression turned obstinate. "Whatever your feelings are, I like Daniel."

Phineas looked over his shoulder. "Who's this Daniel Long?"

"The . . . the . . . silversmith."

"The evil silversmith?" His mouth began to split into a grin. Then he saw my face, and his smile fled. "You really don't want to see this man, do you?"

I shook my head and covered my eyes with my hands, wishing I could cover my feelings just as easily. Amazement that Daniel Long would follow me here—for why else would he appear in these parts?—conflicted with a terror that he would discover me like this, disguised as a boy, a living example of hoydenish defiance and plain-as-day insanity.

No, no, *no.* He couldn't find me.

I grabbed hold of my satchel, my pillow for all of these traveling days, and buried a sob in its softness.

"Calm down now, Freddy," Gideon pleaded. He'd finally crouched. As he gazed cautiously toward the tavern entrance, he reached into the wagon and patted my head.

I swatted away his hand. I had torn open my stuffed satchel and, with shuddering breaths, began wrenching out its contents.

"I suppose I could just slip inside and gather the things in your room," Phineas said, his face politely turned away from my tears.

Gideon shook his head. "Fancy's still in there. You know how loyal to Freddy she is. She's sure to get anxious and bite you if you try to carry her out—probably bark up a storm, too. We'll have everyone in the whole tavern out here inspecting the situation."

"I haven't paid the bill yet, either." I unfolded my old dress.

Phineas frowned. "What do you have that for?"

"I wore it to escape."

A laugh burst out of him. "I can't believe a soul would mistake a lanky stick of a boy like you for a girl." Chuckling softly, he shook his head. "A girl!"

Gideon stared at him in consternation.

I choked on a sob of a laugh and wiped my face with a sleeve. "Gid, you know he'll recognize both of us as we are right now. And he knows I'm—I tried to escape as a female. Our best bet is for me to hide until he comes out. As soon as he leaves the yard, I'll slip inside to pay the bill and grab my things. You and Phineas can stay out here and finish packing."

Gideon scratched his head. "But he'll know you're here when he sees me."

I shoved the dress at him. "Not if you're wearing this"—I plopped my old bonnet on top of the folded dress—"and this."

Phineas burst out laughing again.

Gideon gaped. The gape turned into a glare. "*No way*. No chance in hell."

"Please, Gid. *Please*. You have to help me. I can't let him find me like this. I can't. I just *can't*!" My voice had risen alarmingly.

And this—combined with a streaming of fresh tears—turned my brother into a reluctant accomplice.

Before five minutes had passed, in the relative privacy of a dim barn stall, Gideon Winter became Mrs. Standen, and Phineas—ever one to welcome an opportunity for foolishness—dove into his role as Gid's husband.

He played the part dotingly. From my hiding spot behind the barn, I watched him hand my brother into the wagon, adjust the bonnet that hid his too-short locks, tuck the lap blanket around his person, and squeeze his hands meaningfully. For his part, Gid sat as stiff as a statue of someone miserable, maybe a martyred saint, but he grimly remained in character, at least until his pretend husband raised one of his hands to his lips to bestow a kiss. Then he slugged Phineas in the head.

Phineas rubbed his crown. "Now, is that how a good wife should greet her husband's expressions of affection? You promised to love, honor, and obey, remember, my precious sugarplum, my little honeyed love bun, my delectable punch of rum. Truly, I've a mind to take a strap to your sweet bottom and teach you a lesson you won't—"

"Shh." Gideon jerked his chin toward the door.

Daniel Long had stridden outside.

Daniel Long. I could not believe it. My eyes feasted on the sight of him.

He stood for a moment by his horse, absently rubbing her neck, as he perused the yard, his gaze stilling for a moment on our wagon.

Phineas had resumed his tender ministrations, patting Gid's tightly folded hands, teasingly touching Gid's chin, which was tucked to his chest, then leaning in closer, as if to whisper a few endearments in my brother's ear. Our friend could have played Macbeth (or more fittingly, Puck) on Drury Lane. He was that convincing.

And apparently convincing enough for Mr. Long. At last my Middleton neighbor broke his stare and mounted his horse. I waited, my heart pounding, until he left; then I crept toward the men. Gid had wrenched the bonnet off his head and sat scowling. Phineas was practically mute with laughter, hardly able to form a word through his breathless mirth.

I couldn't join either extreme reaction. I was remembering how Daniel had looked—his dear, familiar handsomeness, his tall, strong frame—and how, inexplicably, the entire time I'd leaned against the rough back wall of the barn, I'd half hoped he would find me. Only fear that the discovery would arouse his disgust checked that hope. He had enough reasons to disdain me. I couldn't bear to give him more.

CHAPTER SEVENTEEN

Less than an hour later, with our wagon packed and hitched to the oxen, Fancy fed and snoring softly at my feet, Phineas in the lead, and Gid back to looking like a man, we resumed the final leg of our trip, following an old Indian trail straight north toward the lake.

Within minutes of our leaving Batavia, the forest engulfed us. On either side of the rough path, ancient trees curled over the wagon and made a tunnel for our passage. The early April sunlight penetrated the canopy in a shattered brilliance, dancing on the dew of countless leaves.

"I can't believe Daniel came after you," Gid said quietly. "You all right?"

I shook my head and turned away. I didn't want to discuss Daniel Long, couldn't bear it. Should I have let him discover me and faced his shock? Was escaping that reaction worth never talking to him again? Regret plagued me. Adding to my depression was the fact that I'd lost my lucky spile. The absence of the spout felt horribly symbolic, *prophetic*. I wasn't allowed anything, not even a reminder, of Daniel.

This sobering conclusion kept me from joining in on Phineas's banter. Gid wasn't much use to Phineas, either. I could tell my brother was subdued—and anxious to get to Rachel Welds.

On three occasions along this stretch leading to Barre, the wilderness opened. Every time, a rough clearing appeared, ragged with stumps and uneven fields. In each center, a rude cabin squatted, its window protected with oiled paper and its roof covered in peeled bark, and around each cabin, oxen browsed. On the first property, a cow trudged among them. The other two places also sported sheep. On account of the bells tied around their necks, the animals chimed as they moved.

Outside the third log house, a woman holding up the end of her apron scooped feed from her makeshift pouch and scattered it for pecking fowl. Upon our appearance, she turned and waved.

She looked thrilled to see people. Setting aside my personal misery, I urged Gid to stop, so we could exchange some words with her. "It's the polite thing to do."

He shook his head. "I want to reach Barre."

With just a shouted greeting, we journeyed on. Soon the thick forest absorbed us again.

Robert and Ed had sent my brother one letter since they'd settled in these parts. From that missive, Gid knew how to locate the Lintons' place. Yet when we neared the location, we were hard-pressed to trust the brothers' directions.

The Lintons had started pioneering more than a year ago. However, of the few homes we'd passed, this one showed the least amount of improvement. If anything, the crooked cabin seemed ready to collapse, as if sunk under a curse of quickened age. Perhaps it had been poorly constructed or damaged in a storm. Regardless, its dilapidated condition suggested a complete indifference to the notion of upkeep.

Evidence of slovenly living was also spewed around the wretched dwelling. Eight barefoot children loitered in a yard of muck and refuse. A few pigs roamed between broken bits of boards, snuffled into mounds of rotting food, and split the air with squeals whenever one of the urchins, raucously laughing, pulled a tail or attempted a ride on one of their backs. I'd tied Fancy to the wagon seat to keep her from jumping out, but she strained against her tether and growled menacingly. She didn't think much of this place, either.

When the children noticed our presence, their disturbing activities came to an end. They watched our approach, only breaking their motionlessness to scratch a head or groin. Eventually, the tallest one shoved at the pig closest to him with a dirt-blackened foot and ambled forth, his finger plugging his nose.

Phineas, who'd brought his horse to our side, stared aghast at the homestead, and when the nose picker held his finger close to his eyes, inspected his finding, and slurped it with apparent gusto, our fastidious friend visibly shuddered. "*This* is where Rachel lives?"

"Heaven help her," I breathed. I couldn't believe it myself.

Gid mutely shook his head.

While the ill-mannered child threaded his way around the yard's filth, stopped near our wagon, and gaped, the others flew into the house through an entrance covered with a stained blanket. They erupted out of it again, this time with a man, a woman, and a second woman in their wake.

The man barked a greeting as he crossed the yard. He was a shocking sight: his muscular frame so covered in reddish-gray hair that he seemed part bear. The frizzy tresses hung in his eyes and knitted his chin, throat, and chest together in a wild mat. His apparel was as threadbare as the children's. He wore a shirt that fluttered open nearly to the navel and hole-riddled pants. And he must have injured his leg, for he limped and used a short tree limb as a walking stick.

The woman who followed kept her head down, her shoulders hunched, and her hands and arms hidden in the folds of her black shawl. Her light brown hair, dressed in a thick bun, as gleaming as any girl's, strangely contrasted with her wrinkled face. She reminded me of the house: prematurely aged, folding in on herself.

Not until I registered the identity of the second woman did I find my voice and answer the man's greeting. I jumped out of the wagon and began striding across the yard.

It was Rachel.

While I tried to make out my pretty, robust, neat-as-a-pin singing companion in the disheveled girl, Rachel was clearly trying to figure out me. She watched my approach with bewildered amazement. When I was within arm's reach, she whispered, "Harry?"

I gave the briefest shake of my head. I'd have to explain Freddy, but that couldn't happen now.

Gid also began walking toward the house.

Rachel drew a fast breath but didn't speak.

Suddenly, Phineas yelped. He stood a distance behind my brother, peering in anguish at his recently polished boots. Despite enjoying dozens, perhaps even hundreds, of acres, the Lintons obviously didn't take the time to empty their chamber pots at a safe distance from the cabin. The yard was rank with waste.

And something else. When the hairy man—Mr. Linton, I presumed—swung his cane to whack one of his children out of his way, teetered closer, and opened his mouth to slur, "How do you do?" I determined the second essence: pure alcohol. His whole person stank of whiskey.

He ramblingly introduced himself. My brother had barely finished reciprocating when Mr. Linton clumsily twisted and said to the woman behind him, "Don't just stand there with your mouth at half cock, you idiot. Get some refreshments for our guests." As she skittered back to the house, a ghoulish smile parted the fur across his face. "We ain't got more than a handful of potatoes to feed you, but there's whiskey. Always plenty of whiskey." He laughed uproariously at this. Except for his retreating wife and Rachel, the rest of his household joined in on the guffaws.

Taking in their vacant gazes, I couldn't help but wonder if the children were inebriated as well. A wave of horror washed through me. I felt like a girl who'd gone to a trickling stream to fetch water and discovered a glutted river instead, one with a crumbling bank and a dangerous current intent on nabbing and drowning me. The situation was totally unexpected. Horribly foreign. It was hell.

How had Rachel endured this?

"Thought you'd try your hand at pioneering, did you?" Mr. Linton shook the head rug that was still parted for that gash of a smile. "The wondrous Genesee Valley. The oh-so-great Holland Land Company. Bamboozlers, the whole lot of them. Well, you'll find out. You'll find out for yourself. Wheat's a damned bit easier to distill than it is to mill and turn into money. You grow your grain and then what? No mill in these parts, not quite yet anyway. So you lug it for days to the nearest place along the river and find no cash market for your efforts. You'll learn. Oh, you'll learn." He gave vent to another round of cackles.

"I see," I said. Since Gid had apparently lost his ability to speak and Phineas had stopped a safe distance from our weird gathering (no doubt fearing further indignities to his person), I cleared my throat and asked, "How many acres did you purchase?"

"Just shy of two hundred, and lousier land you never saw." He elaborated, delivering a rant against the "swampy hell of a wilderness."

I wasn't listening closely. My mind was fiercely engaged with another matter entirely.

What were we going to do about Rachel?

I couldn't leave her here. I wouldn't. Not only did she appear miserable and half starved, she looked frightened. For good reason. I'd suffered this place for a mere few minutes and was already scared witless. I sidled closer to her. My breath caught. There were bruises along her neck, as if someone had battered, even tried to strangle, her.

Mr. Linton stopped complaining and lazily followed my gaze. When his bloodshot eyes, like twin fires in a thicket of brush, settled on Rachel, he cackled again. "Pretty minx, isn't she? But damme, too sullen by half. Quit your moping, slut!" And, with a snorted hiss, he raised his walking stick and jabbed her side.

I gasped and instinctively reached for her, but Rachel had stumbled back, crossing her arms to shield herself.

My mind spun. I could barely absorb what had just happened, let alone make sense of the disturbing implications. *Oh, Rachel, Rachel, what terrors have you faced in this cesspool of depravity?*

Amazed my brother hadn't rushed to Rachel's side, I whirled on him. My dumbfounded horror grew. He was staring, wide-eyed with shock, at the ground, and when he did glance up at Rachel, another emotion flitted across his face. Not love. Not compassion.

Disgust.

The reaction was gone as quickly as it had appeared. But I recognized it—I knew I had—and so did Rachel. She dropped her gaze.

I shot him a furious look, unimpressed with the belated apology that now suffused his features.

While the children resumed their torture of the pigs, Mr. Linton started another drunken monologue, this one on the vicious creatures that slunk out of the forest and gobbled up his chickens.

I stiffened with cold disdain. No forest dweller could be more vicious than him. Interrupting the diatribe, I said tersely, "Thank you for your offer of refreshments, but we can't stay. The brothers Welds are expecting us. Rachel? Are you ready to go?"

Her gaze flew up.

"Go where?" Mr. Linton barked. His fire-red eyes slid over Rachel. "She can't leave. 'Tain't decent, her living with those boys and no female to chaperone her."

He was lecturing *me* on decency? "She won't be living with her cousins. She'll be staying with the Standens. The missus there will be her companion until . . ." I scrambled to think of a long-term plan for my friend that justified her parting from the Lintons and blurted the first thing that came to mind. "Until my house is up and Rachel and I can get married."

This announcement at last galvanized my worthless traveling companions. Gid squeaked, *"What?"* Phineas, in a manner out of keeping with his usual eloquence, blabbed, "Er . . . huh?"

Rachel said immediately, "Yes, of course, dearest." Her face shone with relief and hope and something else. Panic. She glanced meaningfully at our wagon. *Hurry,* the look said.

Mr. Linton appeared poised to argue, so I asked her quickly, "Shall I wait here for you to collect your things?"

She threw an uneasy peek over her shoulder and vigorously shook her head.

"Want me to go with you?"

She began sidestepping toward the wagon. "That won't be necessary."

I caught the hint: time to bolt. "Thank you again, Mr. Linton," I said, treading backward.

Phineas observed me with amazement. "Engaged, my ass," he muttered under his breath, when I was close enough to hear him. "You take chivalry seriously, I'll grant you that." Then he began retreating, too, leaping a zigzag around broken crockery and waste, until he reached Sweetheart. He pulled himself into the saddle.

My brother, in contrast, stayed put, shock alive in his bearing.

"Gid," I called.

He jerked into action, mechanically repeated my thanks, and sprinted to the wagon, passing Rachel and me in his haste.

After hefting himself onto the seat, he put out his hand for Rachel.

She ignored the offer, urged me up next, then scrambled in on her own. This put the three of us hip to hip, with Fancy barking at our feet.

Mr. Linton had started to stalk us, his progeny trailing him like an army.

"Now wait one minute—one minute!—you damned jacka-napes." His drunken command had taken on a querulous quality. "You can't make off with that girl. Rachel, I order you to come down from there, ya hear?" His red eyes glaring his rage, he paused to reinforce his command by pounding the ground with his walking stick.

Phineas clucked his horse into a canter. Though our oxen couldn't hope to emulate that pace, they hurried up the rutted trail, too. Gid cracked the whip in the air to urge them to go faster.

Mr. Linton's furious shouts ("You thankless girl! Come back here, I say—come back here!") faded, then disappeared altogether as we put some forest between our wagon and the dreadful man. I was wholeheartedly grateful for the thickness of the wilderness. It felt like an armor protecting us from the enemy.

CHAPTER EIGHTEEN

To drive, Gid obviously had to occupy a portion of the seat, but he might as well have been invisible for all the attention Rachel and I gave him. Our heads touching and backs bowed, she and I made a huddle on the bench, like two exchanging secrets.

"Are you all right?"

Her breath left her in a quavering sigh. She briefly closed her eyes. "Grateful. How did you know to save me?"

"I didn't. We were just planning to visit."

She gave Gid on my opposite side a hard look.

He deserved it. *Stupid, callous boy.* "Never thought I'd find you in such a . . ." What to call that awfulness? I swallowed hard and finished gruffly, "Nightmare."

"It was. God help me, it was." Her hands shook. She clasped them in her lap, checking the tremor. "What are you doing, going by the name of Freddy?"

"Oh, Rachel, we have much to discuss." First and foremost, her ordeal. I desperately wanted to help—be a support, a listener, if she wanted to talk. Would she? Would talking about what had happened make things better or worse?

She wearily shook her head and scanned my clothes. "Why are you dressed like that?"

I glanced at Phineas ahead of us. He was too near for detailed divulgences.

"He doesn't know who you are?"

"No one does but you and Gid." I squeezed her hand. "I'd like to keep it that way."

She nodded and slipped her hand from under mine.

The withdrawal disturbed me. She wanted distance, and the implications of that desire saddened me, utterly overrode my concerns regarding Daniel. What had Rachel endured in that horrible household? The imaginings weighed heavily on my mind. Gid looked preoccupied, too. And Rachel sat silently beside me, her expression broken, like a shipwreck an ocean away from home. Even Phineas rode quietly in front of us without tossing his typical teasing comments over his shoulder.

Off and on until suppertime, I made a mess of comforting my friend. Caught up in a dismal reflection, I'd automatically reach for her folded hands. She'd freeze, then draw her fingers into the folds of her ragged skirt. An hour would pass. I'd get lost in depressing thoughts, forget myself again, and offer her back a pat. She'd jerk away. With a wince and an apology, I finally brought Fancy onto my lap, just to keep my hands busy, so I wouldn't indulge my instinct to mother my friend.

Gid's words proved just as ineffectual as my caresses: "Are you chilled, Miss Welds? Shall I dig out a blanket for you?" And later:

"We'll be stopping for supper soon, but we keep some nuts handy for munching. Would you, ah . . . like some?"

He earned mute headshakes for his efforts.

I couldn't blame Rachel for shunning his advances. He'd treated her miserably.

As soon as we stopped to make camp for the evening, while Phineas tended to his horse and Rachel hurried to the stream to wash up, I found a moment to speak to Gid in private and took him to task for his behavior at the Lintons', finishing with "and then, after never saying a word, you give her—*her*—the grimace of disgust. Why, I was never so amazed and so *ashamed* of you. Do you assume she *asked* for the mistreatments of that house? What were you thinking?"

He raked his hair. "I know, I know; I can't say why. It was just a shock seeing her like that, mired in filthy sordidness, when I was so used to thinking of her . . ." He fluttered a hand over his head before resuming his hair gripping.

"Like a princess in a tower?"

He nodded glumly.

I crossed my arms. "Rachel was never a princess, Gid." For a moment, I dwelled on the exuberant duets and the number of ribald ballads she and I had belted out together. The recollection made me wistful. What had happened to those carefree girls? "But she isn't a slattern, either, no matter what came to pass in that awful house. To become that, she would have had to make some bad decisions. I doubt she was given the right to decide a damn thing."

"I know. I feel awful. I didn't mean it. And I'm really sorry."

I was so disgusted, it was impossible to even listen to his apology. I threw up my hands, turned on my heel, and stomped back toward the wagon. My brother had his work cut out for him if he planned to make up for his despicable reaction.

Frankly, I didn't think he could.

Gideon trudged behind me, and we joined the others. By the road, the oxen were browsing, Sweetheart was nosing her owner's bowed head, and Rachel was sitting in the wagon. She absently scratched Fancy behind the ears and watched Phineas in bemusement.

He was worth watching. Seated on a supine log, slumped and swaying, he was moaning piteously and staring gravely at the ground. I'd never seen him look less like his sophisticated self. Water dripped to his shoulders; damp splotches bloomed across his coat and pantaloons. He must have dunked his whole head in the water, for his hair stuck up in wet points, like spines on a hedgehog. He was muttering, "A shame, a shame, such a crying shame."

Gid rushed to his side. "What's wrong?"

Phineas raised anguished eyes. "Where do I begin?" He made a helpless gesture toward the ground. After a lull, one he filled with awful groaning, he blurted out, "I have some grievances and feel compelled to air them. It's about those horrible Lintons."

Oh, heavens, Phineas wasn't going to talk about the Lintons already, was he? It was too soon, the pain too fresh, for Rachel to be forced to discuss those people. I violently shook my head, but if Phineas noticed, he ignored me. Gid and I exchanged a horrified glance, then, in unison, turned to Rachel. She had paled and dropped her eyes.

"First of all: *this*." Phineas thrust his hands toward the ground.

"What?" I impatiently scanned the place where he sat.

"My boots. My beautiful, expensive, nearly-as-fine-as-any-Bond-Street-beau's polished, tasseled Hessian boots." He shook his fist at the sky and, with the passion and fervency of a knight announcing a holy pledge, declared, "I will *never* forgive the Lintons for what they did to my boots. *Never.*"

My mouth dropped open. His boots did look bad; that was true enough. But soiled footwear? Seriously? *That* was what filled him with anguish? My breath left me in a growl. I wanted to whip off one of his silly boots and hit him in the head with it. How dare he reduce this debacle to such a frivolous complaint?

I was about to try to quell Phineas's rant (he obviously, in his vanity, couldn't conceive how anyone might have suffered worse than him) when he stopped me with another anguished groan and added, "Then there's the recollection of those ghastly children: in particular, the nose picker." He shuddered and added a few gagging noises to dramatize his sentiments. "Why, Miss Welds, you'd ever want to sally forth into the wilderness to become a support to a woman who clearly has no better sense than a hen—truly, how could she have even that much sense, marrying a brute, then decorating their entire parcel of land with disgusting children and all their filth? Well, I just don't know. It's got me questioning *your* sense. Can't help but think you must be either a drunk, too, or completely unhinged."

I gasped.

Eyes bulging, Gid slapped his forehead.

Rachel, sitting ramrod straight in the wagon and as white as a ghost, retorted with icy asperity, "*Obviously*, sir, the Lintons hadn't yet succumbed to inebriated despair when I arrived; otherwise, my cousins never would have left me with them."

"That gross deterioration happened in only two months?" He eyed her skeptically. "Sounds dashed smoky to me. Now don't go flying onto your high ropes. Chances are your cousins, in their rush to start pioneering, didn't poke around or linger long to assess the situation before bolting. Besides, we all know those boys aren't precisely the investigative types."

That was the understatement of the evening. I couldn't resist flashing Gid a look, but not even my brother, always so loyal to his pals despite their remarkable idiocy, appeared ready to defend them. It was one thing to be stupid; it was another to be neglectful. Robert and Ed Welds should have taken better care of Rachel.

He sighed. "Ah, well, it's done now, and when the soup's gone, there's no sense in licking the empty bowl. All I'll say is—and I say this mostly to you, Freddy, since you're young and still face plenty of opportunities to ruin your life—the Linton household is a living example of what I've previously warned you against: too much liquor and too many children. Both will kill you, and very often, one leads to the other."

I glared at him. Mr. Linton was more than a drunkard with one too many children. He was an abusive terror, and if I hadn't been trying to shield Rachel from the subject, I would have said as much. Though Linton certainly qualified as the worst male of my acquaintance, I couldn't like many of the others right now, either—Gid, the Welds brothers, Phineas. The latter's latest buffoonery goaded me into snapping, "Married people do tend to bear children. That's hardly aberrant behavior."

"But do they have to have so many?"

"You get as many as God wills, clodpoll."

He burst out laughing. "God doesn't have a thing to do with it. A couple can enjoy their pleasures without turning out a passel of nose pickers."

I stared at him in unblinking incomprehension.

With indulgent contempt, he smiled, sauntered my way, and

threw a friendly arm around my shoulders. "Freddy, Freddy, Freddy, don't you know anything? How are you going to marry Miss Welds here without understanding a few important matters about the matrimonial bed?" Then, with Gid and Rachel looking on in embarrassed fascination, Phineas shortly explained the matter, in a few words detailing how the mathematical equation of one plus one shouldn't equal three.

I yanked away from him and, to hide my mortification, muttered, "What a hypocrite you are, Phineas. You act as pure and wise as a priestly philosopher, but what about *your* household, the one you're always complaining about?"

He acknowledged the dig with a nod. " 'Tis true, I've got my own share of nefarious nestlings underfoot." Then, with a meaningful look: "And another abomination roasting in the oven, if you know what I mean." Shaking his head, he sighed, "But it's not like I asked for them. Marian simply thrust them on me."

This audacious declaration left me speechless. Finally, I blurted, *"Thrust them on you?* So she's the one who bears all the blame? Of all the cold, callous—oh, I feel so sorry for Marian. What an ill-natured misogynist you are." Playing the victim. Blaming the wife. Hogwash! It took two to twirl around a ballroom.

My heated reaction seemed to startle him, and this further infuriated me.

Just as he opened his mouth, no doubt to defend his ridiculous position, Rachel asked, "Who is Marian?"

"His wife," I answered.

At the same time, Phineas said, "My sister."

He and I stared at each other.

Then he laughed. And laughed. And laughed. Fell down to his

log perch and laughed, keeled forward and laughed, pitched sideways and laughed, rolled onto his back and laughed, and off and on between guffaws, breathlessly, gaspingly repeated, "My wife? *My wife?*"

Fancy responded with excited yips and tail-wagging leaps. Sweetheart whinnied. Gid, eyeing me with amusement, chuckled. I scowled and tried to shove and kick Phineas into silence.

But for the first time that day, Rachel smiled.

Rachel spent the night in the wagon; the rest of us slept on the hard ground under it. And the next morning, we fed and watered the animals, ate a hurried breakfast comprised of cold biscuits from the previous night, restored to the wagon the few provisions we'd unpacked, and resumed our trip.

One traveling day left: I couldn't wait to finish it.

A pink sunrise threaded through the trees and sifted a rosy glow over the dew-slick branches. Rachel's face, in this warm light, appeared somber. But she didn't pull away when I unthinkingly patted her hand.

It would take time—months, maybe even years—for her to recover from what had happened at the Lintons' place, but I would be Rachel's gentle, careful, loving friend and help her through what was sure to be an agonizing healing process.

I was mentally avowing this noble intention when Phineas, ahead of us, circled the reins around his wrists, slowed Sweetheart from a trot to a walk, and peered over his shoulder. His mouth quirked when he took in our clasped hands. "Mr. Freddy: Mighty Champion of the Fair Sex. Ha." He turned to face forward. "Well, Miss Welds, I won't bother asking for your betrothed's view—he's a regular activist—but I'm curious about *yours*. What are your thoughts on book learning among females?"

She shrugged. "I don't have a strong opinion."

"And that's exactly as it should be. Women with strong opinions offend me. Wait until you meet my sister." He grunted. "No wonder my poor brother-in-law succumbed to the fever. With all her unfeminine ways and unfeminine notions, she likely sapped his will to live." He shook his head and added disdainfully, "Marian's a great one for book learning. This is what I think: If women deserve to improve their minds at all, their education should be exclusively designed to enhance their matrimonial worth. Let a woman learn about housekeeping, child-rearing, and etiquette. Make her an example of female submissiveness and piety—a tender paragon of domesticity."

He slid me a sly peep over his shoulder, obviously hoping to provoke my temper. I refused to give him the satisfaction and merely dug a couple of apples out of the satchel under my seat, handed one to Rachel, and said curtly, "Housekeeping, child-rearing, and etiquette? That's it? Sounds deadly dull to me."

As if I hadn't spoken, Phineas went on, "But please, Lord, save us from those god-awful female scholars, intent on poking into the sciences and ancient languages and all sundry of masculine matters, the sorts of subjects their fragile, weak minds simply weren't made to comprehend and appreciate. *Female scholars.* Bah!"

I stiffened but still refused to bite the bait. I bit into my apple instead.

Gid wore a small smile and dry expression.

Rachel, however, was nettled. "Certainly, efficient housekeeping benefits a woman and her family, but I would never advocate for limiting a female's learning to empty gentility. After all, how can a mother raise intelligent children capable of competing for advancement in our free nation if she, herself, can't benefit from a rigorous education and therefore grow her mind?" She drew herself up to her full sitting height, squeezed the apple so hard her knuckles whitened, and glared at Phineas's back. "Pretty picture of family life *you'd* paint, Mr. Standen, if you made every mother a silly gudgeon with nothing to her credit besides a quick needle. What chance would the children have to succeed if all the maternal instruction they received was limited to the banal advice dear Mama crammed into her embroidered samplers?" She harrumphed.

Vividly recollecting my first encounter with Rachel over Mr. Long's maple-syrup kettle, when she'd announced her passion for stitchery, I stared at her in faint surprise.

Ahead, Phineas's shoulders trembled. He didn't turn around but managed to say in a quavering voice, "Why, Miss Welds, I didn't think you had a strong opinion on the matter."

She ground out, "I changed my mind."

The apple hit Phineas squarely on the back of his neck and with enough force to kill his laughter.

"Nice shot," I said.

Rachel sniffed. "Thank you."

Phineas's troublemaking continued the entire length of the sloppy, bumpy road. His conversation irked me. I found myself wishing for Daniel Long's quiet teasing and subtle wit.

Phineas, in comparison, was pure obnoxiousness.

Rachel—unused to his ways and also the object of most of his comments—responded even more strongly than I did. She bristled.

She flung back sarcastic retorts. She huffed and growled in angry irritation. Then, just as she teetered close to clobbering him, he'd say something so silly, she'd gasp a laugh. I barely recognized the person he was dragging out of her with his infuriating verbal pokes and prods. My easy-natured chum had pluck. A lot of it.

When we reached Ridge Road and stopped to eat before heading west, I thought I'd better have a talk with Phineas. After encouraging Gid to try to net some fish in the stream and leaving Rachel to cook what she could from our remaining journey-allotted pantry supplies, I cornered Phineas in a stand of hickories, where he was sitting on a rock and cleaning his boots.

His favorite pastime.

He smiled at me tolerantly as I lectured him. When I finished, he said, "A person can make a religion out of misfortune, Freddy. With you and Gid tiptoeing around Rachel, moping and moaning, acting like she's fatally ill, she might well decide she ought to die for whatever happened in that hellish hovel. Is Linton, the idiot, worth killing herself over? I don't think so. Better for her to put her foot on the suffering."

"And your utter lack of sensibility will help her do that?"

"Of course."

"I simply don't see this as an appropriate time for jokes. What happened to her was not a joke."

"I'm not laughing at her," he said sharply. "I'm inviting her to laugh at *me*. And it beats what you and Gid are doing—basically everything you can, short of sewing Rachel a shroud and handing her a shovel—to suggest her life's over. Well, it's not. A couple of horrible months don't need to define a whole life. A person's got to check the suffering. Grind it into the ground."

"The way you do? More like *dance* on it."

He shrugged—then, indeed, stood and did a little jig.

"You're incorrigible."

"Thank you kindly." He jigged his way toward the wagon, singing a bawdy tune to go with his fancy footwork.

I stared after him, fuming. I *wasn't* trying to show Rachel her life was over. I was taking seriously a serious situation. And if I did happen to own a shovel, I wouldn't hand it to Rachel. I'd whack Phineas with it—or better yet, Mr. Linton. That man was a menace. He deserved a prison sentence.

Perturbed, I trudged toward the streamside fire, mentally replaying Phin's shroud-and-shovel remark. When the trees thinned and exposed the ribbon of smoke threading through the boughs, I stopped short.

Gid and Rachel tarried there.

His face almost bilious in its sickly hue, my brother appeared to be apologizing—probably for his unconscionable reaction at the Lintons'—though clearly not to good effect.

Rachel stood very still, arms folded, frown lowered to the flames. At her feet, beside two silver trout, a handful of yellow flowers was strewn—dogtooth violets, I guessed.

With a flap of his hands, Gid asked, "May I at least be your friend?"

So *more* than an apology. For the love of God! I covered my mouth with my hands. To propose now—after everything she'd just been through? *What a fool.*

Rachel nudged the scattered bouquet with the toe of her boot. The gaze she raised to Gid was cold. Before turning away from him, she said tersely, "You can try."

CHAPTER NINETEEN

"Here, Marian, we have Gideon Winter of Middleton, New Hampshire." Phineas introduced my brother with a nod in his direction. After Gid bowed in greeting, Phineas continued, "And this is Miss Rachel Welds, recently a companion to Mrs. Linton of Barre, but on account of her pending nuptials, currently our guest. I invited her"—he slid me a twinkling smile to acknowledge this rapper—"for she'll be better situated living with us, closer to her betrothed, until the happy day she commences her wedded bliss."

Rachel bobbed a curtsy. She kept her gaze on the floor. I could tell by the hands she folded tightly in front of her and by the way she chewed on her bottom lip that she was worried, probably fretting that her arrival would discompose the other woman. My heart went out to Rachel. How awful to live so uncertainly, with no place to call home.

Marian Gale, Phineas's sister, apparently as no-nonsense as Phineas was nonsensical, took this news in stride and nodded. "I'd appreciate the company. It's been a lonely winter." She smiled at her, then included Gid in that smile. "Congratulations on your engagement."

With an embarrassed glance at Rachel, my brother turned a deep shade of red and shook his head.

Phineas laughed. "Not him. She's marrying Freddy here."

I shot him a dark look. He knew perfectly well the engagement was a farce I'd concocted to get Rachel away from the Lintons. But ever since she'd joined our company, he'd insisted on referring to her as my Betrothed, Beloved, Conquest, and Wife-to-Be, once even using the title Future Mother of Freddy's Brats.

Mrs. Gale was staring at me in surprise, and her brother couldn't resist chuckling. "Hasn't even cut his eyetooth yet, has he? Ah, well, love can blossom in the greenest heart. He'll get his whiskers in time, and Miss Welds will be ready and waiting to shave them off for him."

His sister rolled her eyes. "Shut up, Phin."

I liked Marian Gale already. Perhaps she and I would become friends. Despite her having three small children, she didn't appear much older than me. She must have married very young.

Her expression turned curious. "Are you and Mr. Winter related, then?"

"Nope," Phineas answered for me. "This is Mr. Freddy of Nowhere in Particular." I stood, hot-faced and squirming, as he continued with theatrical gravity: "Halfway through his journey, Gid discovered this poor boy on the roadside. Young Freddy had disguised himself as a female in an attempt to escape his apprenticeship to an evil silversmith. He couldn't return home, for he has none. You see, he's a foundling, his parents having been the unfortunate victims of violent bandits. So he joined Gid, resumed his boyish gender, and at some point (don't ask me when or how) became betrothed to Miss Welds—a sensible engagement, despite his youth, once you understand Freddy's commitment to public reform. The lad has a profound respect for women. I once had the pleasure of witnessing him climb a pulpit and deliver a scathing lecture on the mistreatment of the fair sex. Got quite the reaction, let me tell you, almost incited a brawl, but Freddy got away with nary a scratch and with a generous slice of apple pie, to boot—one he, alas, deemed too small to share with his comrades. Then his safety was nearly compromised a *second* time when the evil silversmith followed our trail to Skunk's Misery in Batavia, but Gid here—a good sport, I have to say—put on the old girly costume and pulled off a decent performance as my wife. We completely confounded the silversmith and hopefully have seen the last of him, for if there's one thing I can't like, it's an evil silversmith, no matter how talented he may be in selecting beautiful horseflesh. Thus: All's well that ends well."

He flourished a hand to present the interior of the cabin, softly aglow with firelight at one end and, at the other, brightened by the vestiges of daylight warmly filling the single window. "Welcome to my humble abode." He tapped the bottom of a ladder with his boot. "The children sleep in the loft. I'll introduce you to the squeakers in the morning. No point in waking them. Enjoy the quiet while you can. They banish all peace the second they stir."

Following this (admittedly ridiculous) summary of my history, I must have looked as mortified as I felt, for Phineas's sister, when she recovered from her blatant astonishment, whisked the air with her hand and said, "Don't mind my brother, Mr., er, Freddy. I assure you: I don't. He prattles on so, I listen to his silly noisemaking with as much attention as I'd pay to a buzzing bee."

This tugged a smile out of me.

Instead of questioning me on the particulars of my Banbury tale, she moved toward the hearth. "You could use a cup of tea, I expect. If you boys want to go out and take care of the cattle, I'll pull together a repast to tide everyone over until morning."

Rachel took a tentative step forward. "May I help?"

"Yes, please." Mrs. Gale smiled over her shoulder. "I can always use a helping hand."

Phineas and Gid strode to the door, the latter gazing around with appreciation and asking a question about the cabin's size.

I dawdled in the doorway.

Rachel and Mrs. Gale made an inviting picture in the gently lit interior: the younger woman tucking a dusky curl behind her ear before rolling up her sleeves and washing her hands in the basin beside the door, and Mrs. Gale, blond and elegant-featured like her brother, though currently quite round with child, carefully stirring the contents of a pot over the fire.

The scene made me long for Mama, who was probably occupied in a similar fashion back home at this hour. And it made me miss gathering with other girls. Maybe I was simply weary of living outside, working against an evening wind that still carried a good bit of winter. But in that moment, I wanted nothing more than to stay put, feel the warmth of the fire, and join in on the women's conversation, which, by the very lilt of the female voice, held the power to soothe.

With a sigh, I trudged outside. In the searing sunset, the

homestead was a small pool of warm, colorful light encircled by the thick wall of black forest. As we'd traveled down the Ridge, Phineas had shared a few details about his property, and I'd learned that he and his sister's family had settled in this location two years ago, each taking a little over two hundred acres on adjacent lots. Since Amos Gale's death seven months ago, Phineas had given up his plan for a separate cabin and focused on improving what his brother-in-law had begun.

Phineas had already cleared a few acres. A rail fence enclosed the land in the front, while a brush fence followed along the sides and the rear. Stumps still dotted the open stretch. In addition, a cleared rectangle of a patch neatly marched along the south side of the house—obviously Mrs. Gale's kitchen garden, though the season was too new for the ground to sport anything. Phineas had added a stick chimney to the house. Smoke wafted out of it and disappeared into the purpling sky.

Though rugged yet, this new home with its sturdy cottage and hard-won fields already reflected the stoic tenacity of its owners. How lovely this place was, compared to the sordid, careless disaster Mr. Linton had contrived.

Early in our acquaintance, I wouldn't have pegged Phineas as much of a farmer, so enthusiastically had he delighted in playing the role of the dandy. But since then, I'd revised my impression. Perhaps Phineas didn't love farming, but I bet he pursued it with grim faithfulness. And for all his tomfoolery, he possessed an honest core. He clearly despised the Lintons and would never permit such slovenly idleness on his land or unconscionable abuses in his household.

I shivered at the thought of Mr. Linton. What a relief to have

Rachel here, safe and close to me, and no longer there, in that pit of terror.

After the late supper, I slept heavily on the floor without waking until my brother nudged my back and sang, "Rise and shine, Freddy." He shrugged on his coat and left to see to the animals.

Along with the adults, one of the children had started his day: a small boy currently having a fit of happiness over his uncle's return. Where he sat at the table, Phineas (not at all like the child hater he professed to be) joked with his nephew and let the boy climb all over him, while Rachel stirred the ash-dusted coals and Mrs. Gale sliced salt pork by a covered barrel. Without turning, the boy's mother ordered, "Shush, Adam. You'll wake the others."

Gid returned to the cabin, lugging a package and glowing with excitement. "What a fair morning. Ready to go, Freddy?"

I groaned. No, I wasn't. I was sore, sick of the outdoors, and exhausted. "Can we eat first?"

Mrs. Gale pointed at the table with her knife. "Have a seat, Mr. Winter. Your land's not going anywhere."

"Marian was never so bossy before she got married," Phineas mused. "Once she started having children, she turned all the rest of us into her progeny, too, forever snapping, 'Do this, do that.'" He made a face at his sister's back.

"Put a plug in it, Phin."

"See?"

Rachel smiled distractedly. "You heard her. Cork it, mister."

"Lovely." Phineas swept a hand in Rachel's direction. "Yet another mother."

Gid approached Mrs. Gale. "I wanted to give you and your brother this, in appreciation for your help and hospitality."

Her eyes widened. "You don't have to give us presents. Your company's thanks enough. We're very happy to have more neighbors."

He shook his head and held out the package. When she set down the knife and slowly accepted it, she smiled questioningly, and he explained, "It's flour. Not an exciting gift, I know, but—"

Phineas jumped to his feet. *"Flour?"*

"Flour," Mrs. Gale repeated breathlessly. For the first time since I'd met her, she showed a bit of her brother's turn for the dramatic. Enraptured reverence enlivened both of their faces. She pressed the package to her bosom, blinked away tears, and said huskily, "You won't come by flour easily or anytime soon in these parts. Are you sure you want to give this away?"

He nodded. Then the two smiled at each other, so warmly a stranger might have mistaken them for long-standing friends.

We didn't linger over our coffee or wait to meet the other children. Gid was practically dancing with impatience. After listening closely to Phineas's directions, thanking Mrs. Gale, and exchanging a stilted good-bye with Rachel, he strode to the doorway and urged me to hurry.

I said my good-byes more slowly. Pausing by Rachel's side, I touched her arm and asked quietly, "Do you feel all right, staying here?"

Her hand came up in a weak flap. Without even smiling, she sighed a laugh. "As well as I can, I suppose," she whispered.

I swallowed. "I'll be back soon." *We will talk. We will make this better.*

She scanned my person and raised her eyebrows.

I nodded. *I'll explain that, too.* We clasped hands for a moment. Then, stifling a moan, I followed Gid outside. I had zero desire to rush back into the wilderness.

There was a track that went as far as the Five Corners, the place we'd first heard of from the agent at the Holland Land Company. This path wasn't sufficiently wide to accept a wagon, so, with Fancy trotting at our heels and straying from time to time to investigate a chipmunk or squirrel, Gid and I set out on foot and followed the track in the direction of our property.

We carried provisions on our backs and drove the oxen for the better part of the day. My brother's first objective was to widen the trail, and we would need the cattle to help us remove the felled trees. Gid's good spirits lasted until we arrived by the Welds brothers' small clearing. "We'll visit them tomorrow," he promised, frowning at the cabin in the distance.

He was probably vexed with the brothers' shoddy behavior, how they'd abandoned Rachel in such a ghastly situation. Maybe he also felt that their negligence had inadvertently led to the current rift. Personally, I didn't think he had anyone but himself to blame for Rachel's coolness. His reaction to her plight at the Lintons' had been cruel. Then to try to make up for it with a marriage proposal? *Idiocy.*

Still, he was my brother, so as I trudged behind him, I asked cautiously, "Do you feel like talking about Rachel?"

He didn't even turn. *"No."* With an edge, he retorted, "Do you want to talk about Daniel?"

I blew a sigh. "No."

Who knew how my brother determined we'd reached our destination? It all looked like the same endless forest to me. But when the sun had slipped low enough in the sky to blaze like a fiery kite trapped in the branches, Gid halted. He dropped his pack to the ground. "This is it."

I shrugged wearily. If he said so.

After felling a few trees for the cattle to browse, Gid took down a dry stub. I made a fire out of it, cooked a hasty supper, then struggled to construct a small lean-to for our night's rest. My brother's mood improved a little as he set about blocking the path to pen in the cattle. He managed a smile when he glanced at my hodgepodge nest. "Looks like the beginnings of a great bonfire."

With a grunt, I heaved a last limb on top of the jumble and, after snatching a blanket out of my pack, crawled into the shelter. A brittle leaf fell on my face. I swatted it away, mentally cursed the roots digging into my back, and squeezed my eyes shut, wishing I could extinguish everything troubling me as easily as I could cut short the day.

Not far from here, Rachel was settling into yet another home. Not far enough from here, Mr. Linton was running his household however he wished, exercising complete authority over his family. His drunken savagery and blatant negligence didn't rob him of this privilege. The law guaranteed his rights, just as surely as it erased his wife's. If I were to marry, who was to say my future might not resemble Mrs. Linton's? Of course, not every man was a Mr. Linton. Daniel Long, for instance.

"What are you doing?" Gid asked outside the lean-to.

"Going to sleep."

"Already?"

Fancy flew in, pounced on my stomach, and washed my cheek with her tongue. I grimaced. "I'm tired."

Lord, I was tired. Tired of unjust laws and the senseless dictates of society, tired of life's challenges, especially for women, who could never be free when they knew so few choices, tired of wading through the wilderness, tired of being cold and sore and uncomfortable, and tired of missing Daniel. Missing him and pretending not to.

CHAPTER TWENTY

The following day, I declined to visit the Welds brothers. Gid thought me unnaturally antisocial, but in my current mood, pretending to be a stranger around two men I'd known forever didn't appeal to me. Even with the threat of bears, wolves, and panthers, I preferred to take my chances alone in the forest, where I could just be myself. Whoever that was.

I spent the morning improving our makeshift lean-to of branches and calling back Fancy when she wandered too far from the camp. While I worked, I worried about Rachel. And I thought about home.

Around this time of year, the family was very likely working with Daniel Long's crew at the sugaring. Surely, by now, with the Middleton nights' sharp freezes and the days' quick thaws, the sap was flowing properly.

I pictured my faraway family and friends hauling the sugar

buckets from the woods, pitching the thin liquid into the great boiling pan, and feeding the fire to keep the sweetness cooking, while the raw air around them sprang alive with smoke and the fragrance of steaming sap, a scent like wood and flower. Would Mama dish out a sample for my little sisters? Were patches of snow still on the ground, so she could cool the ladleful into taffy swirls? Would Daniel pack some of the rewards of the week's efforts into a jar and deliver it to the Goodrich family as a present? This last thought violently aggravated me until I reasoned that the sugaring, if it was under way, must be progressing without Daniel's assistance. He wouldn't make it back home for at least a week.

My hand automatically started for my pocket before I remembered: no lucky spile. No Daniel Long. No home. For the first time, I fully understood the meaning of *homesick*. Missing everyone and everything I used to know—it *felt* like a sickness, a piercing ache in the belly, a terrible squeeze around the heart.

Sighing, I gazed around at the woods. There was plenty of sumac for spouts in these parts, not to mention maple trees for sap. I wondered if Phineas, Mrs. Gale, and Rachel would be spending the week sugaring. It was quite possible, though at Mrs. Gale's breakfast table, Phineas hadn't mentioned it. In fact, the only task he'd discussed was manuring his fields, a chore he clearly dreaded.

My brother and I were a long way from that labor. We had no fields to manure. We just had trees, thousands and thousands of trees. As I thought about the cutting, hauling, stumping, and burning ahead, I winced. Clearing would be a new endeavor for me. I doubted it would be fun.

Gid returned by midday, his expression somber.

I looked up from the soup I'd concocted. "Don't tell me. The Weldses have become just like Linton, despicable drunks."

He didn't smile. "They're sick."

I stopped stirring. "Badly?"

"Not deathbed sick—it's not ague season yet—but the boys are pretty dragged down with colds. I did their morning chores. They're as weak as newborn kittens." He cast a wistful glance at the woods. "Guess I'd better head back. Do you know any of Mama's cold remedies?"

I straightened by the fire. "Sure I do, and I'm better suited to administering them." Gid didn't know a thing about playing nursemaid. "Let me eat a quick bowl of soup, and I'll go in your stead." Might as well introduce my false self to the brothers and get it over with. "You can stay here and chop down trees to your heart's content."

He shook his head. "It's a sickly place, with the boys coughing and sneezing. I've already put myself in harm's way. No point in you breathing the putrid air." He grimaced. "I'll need to warn away Phineas, should he show up searching for the brothers." At my questioning look, he explained, "Bob and Ed were to go to his place this morning to join in on the sugaring. Mrs. Gale made the arrangement in Phin's absence."

"Ah." So I had the timing right. "Let me see to the boys. I'm as healthy as a horse and no use to you here." I didn't know much about cutting down trees. Besides, I preferred taking my chances with the brothers recognizing me than just sitting around and waiting. How boring. "I hardly ever get sick. I'll be fine. Promise."

"Stupid. You *were* sick, a couple of months ago, and exactly like the brothers. No, I'd better go, but I'll be back by suppertime." He drummed up a smile. "Make me something tasty to celebrate my return, and keep an eye on the cattle."

In twenty minutes he was gone, an onion for toasting and some mint for tea in his possession.

After eating, I collected browse for the oxen, played fetch with Fancy, and organized the provisions. When I ran out of things to do, I sat against a tree. Fancy rested her head on my leg and fell asleep.

The woods seemed to curl up closer to me as soon as I stilled. Birds resumed their twittering, and the bare branches cracked against one another. Soft crunching, splashing, rasping, and rustling intermittently joined the birds' bolder racket. It was the low rustling that urged me to my feet. I glanced around nervously, imagining all kinds of wild creatures. Hungry, toothy, venomous creatures.

I spotted Gid's felling ax beside our branchy shelter and went over to grab it, thinking it wouldn't hurt to keep a weapon handy. The sharp blade was square, lipped, and heavy-polled, and it glinted in the dappled sunlight. I gave the ax an experimental swing and liked the powerful feel of it. I swung again, wider this time, and Fancy barked and slunk into our lean-to. "Come back, dog," I laughed. "I won't hurt you."

I perched the ax on my shoulder and swaggered to the stream and back, enjoying the picture I imagined I made: a strapping young man with his favorite tool. I'd like to see a dangerous animal dare to cross me! I strutted some more, and the forest quieted, the only sounds now coming from the quiet munching of the oxen, the trickling stream, and my stomping boots.

The camp, with its proximity to both water and the trail that would become our road, was a good location for a house. Gid probably hadn't settled on a precise spot to build the cabin, but most if not all of these trees would have to go. I gazed up at one pretty specimen: a youngish hickory, its bark shaggily lining the trunk. Then, stepping away from it, I experimentally swung the ax again. Chopping down a tree couldn't be *that* hard.

Shielding my eyes, I stared at the tree's canopy. How far up it went. I smiled, envisioning Gid returning and blinking in amazement at the clearing I'd managed in his absence. Granted, I wasn't sure how I was supposed to hitch the oxen to the trunks to drag them out of the way, but at least some trees could be felled. That would surely be a good start. I eyed the tree once more, shuffled my feet shoulder-length apart, and did a little experimental swinging without making impact, just to gauge my distance from the tree and get a sense of the potential in my stroke. Then I shuffled closer and, swinging with all my might, drove the blade, at an angle, straight into the trunk.

Where it got stuck.

With both hands, I pulled on the end of the handle. The blade didn't even wiggle in its berth. I slid my hands all the way up to the base of the blade and pulled again. Nothing. Finally, I planted my boots on the trunk and yanked. The blade came free so suddenly, I fell to the ground, hard on my back, the ax still in my grasp and, mercifully, not embedded in any part of my body. Arms outstretched over my head, fingers clinging to the handle, I remained on the ground for a moment, alarmed and panting.

This position gave me a good view of the tree's inner branches. With a sinking heart, I watched a robin flutter into the air from a top bough and a squirrel leap from one limb to another. Maybe this was the reason that February was usually the month for felling trees: Fewer animals had started their spring nesting. How many small creatures' homes were Gid and I likely to destroy in the process of clearing for the cabin, road, and field?

Well, the damage was done. I couldn't leave a tree spliced. Feeling like a bird killer, queasy with regret, and still trembling with nerves, I scrambled to my feet and ordered my hands to stop shaking. After taking a deep breath and situating myself by the hickory, I swung again and again, until I finished the notch. I stepped back to examine it. Cleaved a third of the way into the trunk, the cut didn't look half bad.

I lowered the ax and rolled my shoulders, then went to the other side to start hacking from the opposite direction. This back notch went easier, and though the exertion made me ache, a deep satisfaction welled inside me. I, Freddy the Foundling Apprentice, formerly Harriet Submit Winter, could handle any hardship. Blizzard travel? Pff. Raging Genesee River? Not a problem. Capable of taming the wilderness? Just watch me.

I gazed, gloating, at my young hickory, took a final swipe at it with the ax, kept an eye on the canopy, saw when the tree began to waver and keel, and, as nonchalant as you please, strode out of its way, like any expert tree feller would. Simple pimple in the dimple.

This was why I couldn't understand, in my final moment of awareness—immediately after something monstrously large crashed through and splintered boughs overhead and just before this terrible something made contact with my brow and knocked me senseless—how a tree going *that* way could possibly have managed to come *this* way to hammer me straight to the ground.

PART THREE

CHAPTER TWENTY-ONE

Daniel Long explained when I regained consciousness.

Sitting cross-legged beside my supine body, he said, "They call it a widow-maker: a dead bough the felled tree will strike loose, from itself or its neighbor, in the process of toppling to the ground. Bad luck, but you're alive, and you did a decent job on the hickory. Sore?"

I stared, dumbfounded by his presence, and belatedly nodded. The movement made me wince. My aching head was pillowed on something woolly, soft, and familiar. It was his coat. I blinked up at his broad, straight frame and, despite the pain in my crown, experienced a sudden and excessive swell of pleasure, an avalanche sensation, though hot rather than cold. As I visually inhaled the dear, chiseled face with those dear, gray eyes, laughing eyes, even when his mouth stayed stern, I sighed heavily. Was it a surrendering sigh? Perhaps. But I didn't feel defeated. My voice was husky when I asked, "How did you find me?"

"After Skunk's Misery? I backtracked along the trail, then returned to the tavern to ask a couple of questions—learned something there I hadn't bargained for." He gazed at me intently, then abruptly shifted his attention to Fancy, who'd settled on his lap. He patted her absently, as if deliberating something. Finally he plucked a stick off the ground, tossed it, watched the dog leap after it, and continued matter-of-factly, "Once I knew for sure you'd been there, I decided the simplest recourse was to get Gideon's new address. An agent at the Holland Land Company shared his parcel's location. I headed north. The agent's instructions put me in the vicinity of a neat farm—owned by friends of yours, I learned. They helped. Mr. Standen was happy to direct me to the trail for the last stretch, once Rachel Welds verified my identity and he could be certain I wasn't about to force you to resume your apprenticeship. Your name is Freddy, and I'm an evil silversmith?"

"Sorry." I bit my lip.

"At least it's interesting."

I tried to sit up, but as soon as I lifted my aching head off the coat, a wave of dizziness assailed me.

He slipped a hand under my neck and eased me back to the ground. "Not yet. You've got a regular goose egg growing out of that cropped hair."

I dabbed at my tangled fringe. What must he think of me, a girl going around like a boy, making up names and stories? Blushing but without much means to hide my embarrassment, I averted my eyes and gazed instead at the canopy. Was this where I'd chopped down my tree? I couldn't tell; the branches still so thickly knitted the sky. One downed tree hadn't made a difference, not a bit of difference after all.

So Daniel Long had found me, and I knew precisely how. But why? *Why* did he find me? Why did he come looking for me? I blurted it: "Why did you come?"

"Two reasons." He'd folded his hands and rested them on his crossed legs. Head bowed, eyes lowered, he looked like a man praying. "Not long after you and Gideon left, your mother received a letter. Sally Huber of Londonbury wrote to express her pleasure in meeting your mama's fine-looking children"—he gave me a lopsided smile—"and of course to express her condolences over the unfortunate state of your appearance. Your mother was flabbergasted. A case of head lice so severe, nothing would do but to chop off all of that beautiful golden hair? And how had the bugs beset her darling girl—in the winter, no less? What troubling environments had Gideon dragged her precious daughter into? Seedy inns, unsavory taverns? As you can imagine, astonishment became consternation. She was in a tizzy. When your mother shared her concerns with me, I offered to come here and look into the situation."

Oh.

It was as if the terrible widow-maker bough had hit me a second time. I was that flattened. If I hadn't been already on the ground, I would have toppled for certain. When I recovered sufficiently, in a voice that (strive though I did to control it) was filled with too much choke and quaver to be called colorless, I said, "Well. That was generous of you. Remarkably generous. Daniel Long, the best neighbor ever, leaving his prosperous farm right when he ought to be storing up firewood and splitting fence rails and making his sugaring buckets and—"

He frowned. "My cousin can handle the farm easily enough for a few weeks."

As if he hadn't spoken, I went on, gasping, a little wildly: "—and dropping everything to do the neighborly thing and track down the irascible daughter of the Winters. I can't imagine why Mama didn't send Matthew or Luke, especially Matthew, since she could have killed two birds with a single stone, learning what happened to me while keeping Matt from the gaming tables."

"I offered to come here," he repeated, now scowling. "Besides, Matthew's hardly around the farm anymore. He's working for Mr. Goodrich at the mill."

I was brought up short by this. "Paying back Papa?"

"And courting Miss Goodrich."

"*Lydia* Goodrich?"

"That's the one."

I scanned his face, looking for clues, afraid to find them. Tentatively: "And how does that make you feel?"

"Happy for them." He shrugged. "Glad she found a deserving beau. Hopeful for their future." Gently, he took hold of my hand. I'd clenched it against the ground, and he very carefully loosened my fist with his thumb.

I let him. And I stopped breathing again.

"I said there were two reasons, Harriet. The second one . . ." He shook his head. "That last time we saw each other, I—I behaved poorly."

"*You* did?"

He smiled ruefully. "I guess we both did. But I had no right, even jokingly, to lecture you, especially when you were already lashing yourself, and I should have known better than to mind what you were saying, how you . . ."

Rejected me.

I briefly closed my eyes, a pain in my heart joining the pain in my head. "I didn't mean what I said. I never meant it."

He nodded once and went on gruffly: "I shouldn't have taken it so personally. I shouldn't have retaliated. And I definitely should have stopped smarting long before you left. But I couldn't help but believe that perhaps you *did* mean it." He pressed my hand between his wide palms and studied the effect. It looked like he'd found a way to make me part of his praying. "I would have come after you, whether your mother wanted me to or not, even if it was just to see you again."

I inhaled quickly. "You would have?"

"Yes. I hated the way we'd left things. Your departure sickened me. It felt so *final*. I dreaded you'd grown to loathe me. And when I discovered you probably purposely avoided me in Batavia, I almost gave up and went home." He stopped and cleared his throat. "But when I returned to the inn, I found this."

He reached into his shirt pocket, took out the sugaring spout he'd carved for me more than a year ago, and placed it on my palm.

I brought it to my heart. "My spile."

His mouth came up in a corner. "Expected you to toss it when you saw how I'd teased you with the initials."

"Never. This is my good-luck charm."

His eyes flashed, and he said fiercely, *"I'm glad.* When I found it and realized you'd been carrying it with you, I thought maybe . . ." His face turned wistful. "Our situation hasn't been easy for you. You would have liked me better if we'd met later— at a strawberry festival or the Independence Day ball. The fact is I can't remember a time when we didn't know each other. For me, especially in these last few years, that familiarity's been a gift, in the way a fiery sunset or a mighty storm is. The sun always sets, and storms are nothing new, but they seem extraordinary whenever they happen. That's what you've been for me, every time I see you."

Heavens. I closed my mouth. After a moment, I asked, "It is?"

"Couldn't you tell?" He was flushed, his expression, interestingly, suddenly more irritated than embarrassed or enamored. "It was different for you. I think our proximity made me seem dreadful: a tepid, tired sort of fate." I shook my head, but he overrode me with a resigned nod. "Your family, maybe the entire town, knew I wanted you and hoped to make you my wife. I'm not much of an actor, and they could tell, easily enough, which way the wind blew. But I wish they had kept this to themselves. I'm sure their expectations annoyed you to no end. It didn't help that I always came across as kind, capable Mr. Long, the boring, old farmer next door, even though I'm not even as old as Matthew, not even much older than you, Harriet. I'm *not*. Not at all."

His disgruntlement made him look so like a boy, I couldn't help but laugh.

He gave me an abashed smile and turned his eyes to the branches overhead. The sky wore its peculiar drenched look, when the slipping sun, like an overfull cup, spilled light lavishly. He blew a sigh. "I made a muck of things, being perhaps a little too capable and helpful and"—he winced—"prosy and brotherly, confirming what you already thought of me."

"Don't say that." I gripped the hand gently holding mine. "I—I never thought of you as a brother."

"Good," he exhaled. "Because I definitely never thought of you as a sister—just as someone who never fails to amaze me. You're skilled and learned and honest and, well, *very* funny."

I raised an eyebrow. "What about pretty?"

He shrugged, like looks were beside the point, but conceded, "Pretty, too."

"As pretty as Miss Goodrich?"

His mouth quirked. "Did my playing the eligible beau about town improve my prospects?"

"It made me want to kill you."

His smile widened, and for a moment we grinned foolishly at each other.

Then his eyes swept over my person. "What do we do about Freddy?"

I chewed my lip. I wasn't ready to go home, partly because of Rachel. She needed me. I wanted to be here for her. I was also dogged by my promise to Gid to help get him settled.

But mostly, there was Freddy. I had invented him. I wanted to see what he could do. "People here think I'm a boy."

"Do you . . . want to be?"

I laughed at his hesitant expression. "Not forever." Maybe not even for long. I missed Harriet, perhaps not the former Harriet but the one I felt I could be: the Harriet who took risks and had adventures and enjoyed the desire of a man who'd leave everything—*everything*—just to find her. I mentally repeated that last part. I savored it.

But Harriet would have to wait.

"If you can spare the time to linger here, I want to stay on as Freddy for a while. That is, if it suits you . . . Daniel." Uttering his first name, I felt heat sting my face. Yet it was mine to use freely.

He'd given me that right. I smiled. "Then Freddy can quietly slip away." So long, Freddy. Godspeed. Harriet, accompanied by her handsome husband, would most definitely show up in the future to visit her favorite brother, Gid, and friend, Rachel. Before that, however, Freddy would have left the area with Daniel Long and disappeared forever.

No embarrassing unmasking, shocking revelations, or muddled explanations necessary.

Daniel nodded reluctantly. And though his mouth remained unsmiling, his eyes gleamed with mischief. "That will make my objective an interesting challenge."

"What would that be?"

"Courtship. I'm here to court you, Harriet-Freddy."

Not a minute after Daniel made this intention explicit, Gid returned. Between the recent amorous avowals and the effects of getting knocked senseless, I couldn't muster more than a nod as greeting.

Daniel gave him a condensed version of his story, leaving out the romantic parts but eyeing me teasingly from time to time to remind me that, spoken or not, they were still there.

Gid's response veered from relief—glad Daniel had shown up, "because Bob and Ed are sicker than I thought and the good Lord knows I could use some help, for I can't take care of their farm and get my own started at the same time"—to consternation: "What were you thinking, playing with my ax, Freddy? I don't go around experimenting with your spinning wheel. Serves you right, getting your head bashed. No, I don't want to hear how you were trying to help. Keep your hands to yourself!"

Daniel frowned. "That's enough, Gideon. Your sister did a fine job with the hickory. What happened to her could have just as easily happened to you or me." In a kinder tone, he continued, "Listen, I'll take over the Weldses' chores, so you can start clearing." Then he scanned me critically. "I'm worried about your injury, Harriet. Do you think you might recover better under Mrs. Gale's supervision?"

I prodded my head and winced. "Probably," I said reluctantly. I'd rather have stayed with him. But my head *did* hurt like hell. Plus, a day or two at Phin and Marian's place would give me a chance to talk to Rachel.

We decided it was too late to travel. The trip would have to wait until morning. I didn't mind. I liked the idea of spending the night in the woods, warmed by the campfire and with the stars overhead, while Daniel and I savored our reunion.

In the end, I didn't stay awake long enough to eat supper. While Gid started going on about his homesteading plans to Daniel, Fancy pranced my way. I turned on my side to pet her, closed my eyes, and fell asleep. I woke at dawn in a different location—the lean-to—with a sore crown and a breathless curiosity. Had Daniel carried me here?

The trip to the Standen-Gale homestead held none of the tedious discomforts of the previous travel. Even with an aching head, I couldn't help but enjoy the eastward journey. I rode behind Daniel and of course had to wrap my arms around his waist (how else was I to keep from falling?), and of course I rode astride (why not, when I wore britches and didn't have to worry about my skirts scrunching up to my thighs?), and of course I rested my cheek on Daniel's broad back (I had a bruised brain, for heaven's sake).

When we were almost there but not quite, Daniel (whose heart and breathing, so easily discernible under my nuzzling face, had been picking up tempo until both sped at a spanking pace) suddenly reined in his horse.

He twisted and muttered an apology and something about head injuries and taking care but not being able to wait a blasted second longer: all of this crammed fast into a frantic moment. Before he kissed me.

And I kissed him back.

And then, for some time, we kissed each other.

CHAPTER TWENTY-TWO

Perhaps it was for the best that we reached our destination during the noontime meal, when the three children were making a ruckus at the table and Phineas had returned to the cabin to dine and tease Rachel, and Rachel, slapping food onto his plate and stomping back to the hearth for the children's soup, was retorting with vehement sass.

Mrs. Gale was obviously too harassed by a houseful of shenanigans to notice on Daniel and me the evidence of yet more naughtiness: flushed faces, bruised lips, mussed hair.

She had her hands full. I doubted the fairness of adding myself to her worries. But after our exchange of greetings and Daniel's account of my concussion (delivered with averted eyes and a blush, probably because he had recently forgotten all about my injury), she said, "You were right to bring Freddy here," then ordered, "Molly, move over next to Adam. Make room for our guests." A moment later, her fingers were gently parting my hair. "Ouch," she breathed over my head. "That's a good-sized bump. You oughtn't to be sitting up, Freddy. Let's get you into Phin's bed."

This was a berth in the wall opposite the door. Phineas observed my appropriation of his sleeping quarters with a complacent nod, then, peeking at Rachel out of the corners of his eyes, asked, "Are you sure you didn't bump your head on purpose, Freddy? You must be missing your beloved something awful to go whacking your head with a tree limb."

Daniel frowned. I realized I hadn't explained this recent development, sham though it was, in young Freddy's life.

Mrs. Gale sighed. "Could you please, for two blasted seconds, keep your trap shut, Phin?"

I added my own glare in the direction of the troublemaker, then glanced at Rachel, fully expecting her to counter his teasing with a flattening comment.

What happened next, I didn't expect. If his expression was any indication, neither did Phineas. Nor Daniel, nor Mrs. Gale, for that matter.

Rachel, as sweet as honey, gazed at me lovingly, set aside the soup ladle, flowed my way, fluttered open the quilt that had been neatly folded at the bottom of the bed, swooped it above me, and as soon as it settled, leaned down to tuck it entirely around my person. I felt like a swaddled infant, and a panicking one, at that, for throughout these tender ministrations she was murmuring, "I've missed you terribly, Freddy. It was a real trial, watching you leave, and though it pains me—fairly tortures me—to know your poor head's aching, I can't help but be glad you're back, and I promise I'll make your convalescence a pleasant one."

I gaped, Phineas scowled, Mrs. Gale smiled and turned back

to the table, Daniel shook his head in bewilderment—and Rachel, after patting my cheek and pecking my forehead with a kiss, twirled back to the hearth, delivering a triumphant smile to Phineas on her way.

"Use this one." I tapped Ephraim's forefinger. "From the ground now. Good. See? You're getting the hang of it."

Ephraim, Marian Gale's oldest, examined his marble's promising new position. Besides playing with the baked clay balls, there wasn't much to do. Not today. The April wind had picked up during the night, my fifth one with the family, and swept in an early morning thunderstorm. Rain continued to pelt the roof. I was grateful that Phineas, long before my arrival, had finished the walls. Unchinked, the cabin would have filled like a leaky boat.

A wind coursed down the chimney and split the flames with a hiss. Wood crackled, and the earthy scent of roasting potatoes wafted through the room.

"Would you show me how to hoist again?" Six-year-old Ephraim's blond head gleamed in the firelight. Adam, Marian's four-year-old second child, and Molly, for a while longer the youngest at two, nodded into the little hands propping up their chins. They were splayed on their bellies across the floor.

Marian stood at the table, stirring the big bowl's contents with one hand while rubbing her lower back with the other. "Don't let him pester you, Freddy."

Phineas's sister liked me. I could tell. It wasn't hard to fathom why. Minding my sisters for most of my life had taught me well. Here, as in Middleton, I'd taken over some of the childcare, playing marbles with the three little ones, trimming their hair just the previous day, telling stories, and making a kite and showing them how to fly it.

"You're better at occupying them than Phin is," Marian had told me during the washing, my third day here. We had all moved outside to work under the cloudy sky, with Phineas building a fence, Marian finishing the wash, Rachel scouring the edge of the woods for wild asparagus fronds, and Ephraim and me hanging damp clothes on the line. After adjusting the laundry basket to the side of her burgeoning stomach, Marian had glanced in the direction of the field where her brother was dragging a pile of rocks on a stoneboat toward the beginnings of the new fence. "Come suppertime, he starts teasing and gets them so wild they can't fall asleep. Then he complains they're keeping him up."

Matthew and Luke had done much the same with my sisters. "Typical of a man to roughhouse, then whine when the children won't settle the second he's tired of the games." I'd cleared my throat. "Most men, anyway."

She'd eyed me for a moment, then headed for the stream, saying without turning, "But not you, Freddy. You're not at all like most men."

A crack of thunder brought me back to the present and our game of marbles. "I don't mind," I answered. "Watch, Ephraim. It goes like this." Kneeling, I flipped a marble from knee level. The children and I followed the not-quite-round object as it traveled an erratic route across the floor.

A damp gust blasted the room. Rachel hurriedly shut the door behind her and shrugged off her cape. She hung it on a peg, shivered, and patted her damp hair. As she unlaced her boots, she said, "I took him his dinner, but he complained it'd take more than a few hot potatoes to warm him up." She straightened and beamed a satisfied smile. "He's soaked to the skin and looks just like a drowned rat." On her way to the fire, she added airily, "Ah, well, we all warned him this wasn't the day to go traipsing outside. Now he'll probably catch cold and die."

Marian raised her eyebrows. "You don't have to sound so happy about it."

She shrugged. "He didn't have to be so stupid."

I drew up my legs. Rachel sat on the floor beside me and held her hands to the fire. I eyed her curiously. She and Phineas were always fighting, fighting, fighting. Seemed like Phin went out of his way to instigate the squabbles. I wondered why. Was he trying to divert her thoughts from what she'd been through? Or was there a less noble motivation behind his troublemaking? Skittishness, for instance. After all, if he kept the mood light, he could avoid confronting a heavy topic.

Phineas's sister added mildly, "He wants to get ahead in his chores so we're ready for Friday."

"What's happening Friday?" I gave a marble an underhand troll.

Marian twinkled a smile over her shoulder. "We're having a welcoming party for our newcomers."

Rachel looked up. "A party for us?"

I considered what I knew about this place: trees, trees, and more trees. "Who will come?"

"You'll be surprised," Marian said. "We're not the only pioneers around here. We'll whip together a decent showing and have fiddling and dancing, to boot."

I raised an eyebrow. "You mean Phineas actually plays that instrument he cradles?"

"Wait and see."

I turned to share my smile with Rachel.

Her entire demeanor had changed. She was staring, aghast, at the floor. "You won't invite everyone in these parts, though, will you?"

"No, *definitely* not everyone," Marian said. "Don't fret, dear. Certain folks will never step foot in my house." She went back to stirring and muttered something under her breath about louses and jail being too good for some people.

Rachel and I shared a somber glance. Phineas had obviously told Marian about Linton. We didn't want *him* at the gathering.

"What about the Welds brothers?" I asked, finding my friend's hand and giving it a squeeze. *And what about Daniel?* My spirits lifted at the thought of seeing him soon.

"They're better, so I'm sure they'll be here. Phin said Mr. Long hasn't even stayed with them the better part of the week." At my curious look, Marian explained, "He's been working day and night with Mr. Winter, finishing widening the trail."

I grunted. I should have known Mr. Helpful wouldn't linger at the Weldses' any longer than he had to. The man had a bad case of the good neighbor.

Marian rinsed her hands in the basin. "Phin rode out to help them yesterday and couldn't believe what they've done already. The Monday after the party, weather permitting, we'll have a logging bee there and help clear some semblance of a field. Then it's the cabin." She gave me a pensive smile.

Rachel pinched my cheek. (Around Phineas she was my passionate lover. She'd apparently decided that rather than permit him to tease her about the engagement farce, she would goad *him* with it. The strategy seemed to be working. In Phin's absence, however, she turned into my big sister.) "Marian's missing you already."

"Of course." Marian dried her hands on her apron. "Freddy's the only boy I know who's as comfortable throwing together a chicken stew as he is chopping up firewood."

She ought to see what I can do with a needle and thread. "An apprentice picks up a lot of this and that," I explained vaguely before asking a question about the food preparations for Friday.

I barely attended to her answer, too busy thinking about what would happen *after* Friday's gathering. It was time for me to leave. The swelling on my head had gone down, and it was generally agreed I would be able to rejoin Gid at the beginning of next week. And I wanted to. Rejoining Gid meant seeing Daniel. I missed him.

But I still hadn't accomplished what I wanted to do here. Rachel and I needed time to talk, and we needed to talk alone.

Phineas didn't sicken from his rainy-day labors. Instead, the following morning, it was Adam who woke ill, not with a cold but with a stomach ailment that brought the usual assortment of ugly symptoms. The small cabin didn't leave many places to steer clear of the contagion, but Rachel and I insisted Marian let us handle the patient. It wouldn't do for her to risk infection, not in her condition.

We squirreled Adam in the bed I'd lately used. (Phineas, the good sport, had been sharing the loft with the children every night.) The poor boy couldn't find comfort in the feather mattress or our ministrations. All morning and afternoon, he moaned and shivered and vomited on the hour, so regularly we could have set a clock by his heaving. He didn't keep down a drop of broth until nightfall. Fortunately, the sickness proved as fast as it was frightful. The next day, he was weak but otherwise recovered. I escaped the house to help Rachel prepare Marian's kitchen garden for the spring planting.

The brook was high. A warm breeze carried the sound of gurgling water to our moist plot of soil, and the sun shone across the fields and glinted off the rain that had collected in the lowest dips and furrows. Everywhere, puddles winked like silver coins.

I wrenched out a clump of weeds and tossed it onto the grass. Rachel followed suit with a large rock and, smiling suddenly, pointed. "Bluebird."

"Pretty." I frowned distractedly at the creature. Worries swirled in my head, but broaching the gravest one was proving harder than I expected.

"Well? What's first?"

I shoved back my bangs with a sweaty arm. "Peas?"

"Not for sowing. *Talking.* There's Daniel the evil silversmith, Freddy the foundling, the strange fate of Harriet of Middleton. Speak."

"The most pressing subject is you."

She glanced up warily.

When she didn't say anything, I tugged on my ear and blurted, "I don't want to make you uncomfortable, bringing up anything hurtful. But I also don't want you to think I haven't asked you about what happened for my sake, like I'd be too disturbed to handle the details." Leaning on the shovel, I gazed at her steadily. "If you want to talk, I'm here for you." In the distance, Phineas was manuring the field. I indicated him with a jerk of my chin. "He suggested I should avoid mentioning the Lintons, said whatever happened there is over and done with and fit for nothing but forgetting."

"He did, did he?" She flicked him a dark look. "Easy for him to say."

"Yes," I murmured, but then conceded, "At least he was being serious for once."

"Phineas and his foolery." She sniffed. "He means well, I suppose—wants to distract me, make me laugh so I don't cry." She cocked an eyebrow. "Phineas Standen will do whatever it takes to stop a person from weeping." Her gaze turned in his direction. "I should be more grateful. You, Marian, even Phineas . . . good friends with good intentions. But what you're all kindly setting out to do for me doesn't change the fact that there's a man in this area who is a dangerous threat. I don't need to be patted and coddled. I don't want to laugh along with Phin like everything is fine now. What I crave is *justice*. Linton should pay for his wrongs."

"Absolutely he should." But what was the chance of that? Civilization in these parts was too new to sport sheriffs. Even if it weren't, who was to say a court would intervene? The law gave a man the right to inflict corporal punishment on those in his household, to treat the very people he should have wanted to protect as his property, playthings, slaves. "Mr. Linton—"

"Is a monster." She kicked at a clump of dirt. "His family would be better off without him."

"The whole world would be better off without him."

She nodded shortly and tackled a pocket of mangy green with grim determination. "I'm not ready to talk about that nightmare. Not sure if I'll ever be." The roots came loose with a ripping sound. She tossed the weed aside. Like one anxious to change the subject, she asked briskly, "What about you? Tell me. I want to hear the story."

While we worked, I shared it, starting with that long-ago January afternoon of spinning when Matthew's habit of whistling the family's meager funds down the wind came to full light, plodding hot-faced through my reactions, the ugly outbursts and consequences that urged my flight and transformation, and, more easily, touching on the journey's escapades that culminated in Daniel discovering me hammered to the ground.

At the end of the recital, she shook her head, bemused.

I poked at the ground with the shovel's blade. "You must think I'm a loose screw, dressing up like a boy and diving into so much ridiculousness."

"After such an adventure?" A disbelieving sound escaped her. "Only imagine if you'd stayed in Middleton and gone along with the usual routine: baking, ironing, knitting, washing, sewing. You *never* would have known what it was like to get away from so many spools and reels and knots of flax. You never would have tasted freedom. Heavens, Harriet, I don't wonder at all you came up with this masquerade. The real miracle is that we don't all chop off our hair and call ourselves Freddy."

I chewed on my lower lip. Then, abruptly: "You know, I'll be returning to that world eventually."

"With Daniel?"

"Do you think I'm making a mistake?" I didn't. Not anymore. Daniel was proving to be unusually flexible in his thinking. I expected our marriage to be unusual as well. But I wondered what she thought.

"Only you can decide that"—she shrugged—"but I have to admit, back in Middleton I was jealous of what you had with Mr. Long." When I stared in surprise, she added hurriedly, "Not that I wanted him for myself. I simply wished for that kind of affection—the way he cared for you."

"Despite my nature?" Headstrong, outspoken, rash . . . the list could go on and on.

"Oh, no. That's just it. He loves you *because* of your nature." She sighed. "A rare thing, that."

This sank in, and I recognized its truth with a nod. Perhaps our brand of love *was* special. Yet how bittersweet to acknowledge its uniqueness. We should all be loved for who we are.

Rachel stirred the contents of the boiling kettle, then stepped coolly to the side as Phineas and I neared with buckets of sap.

Phineas made a face. "I don't carry any diseases, Miss Welds."

The look she gave him suggested that, in her opinion, his entire person was an unsavory contagion.

I sighed. They were fighting. Again. "Watch out now." With my foot I nudged Ephraim away before adding my sap to the kettle. I cast aside the bucket, slid another log onto the fire, then swiped my dusty hands on my trousers. "Last night's unrequested Bible lesson was your mistake, Phin. You shouldn't have started in on how all evil in the world stems from Eve's transgression in the Garden."

A smile trembled on his lips. "It's not exactly a new theory, and truly, it doesn't say much for Adam, succumbing so—"

Rachel gave him her back. "The children are going to miss you."

The snub made me smile. "I'll miss them, too." And Marian's

hospitality and Rachel's friendship and even (most of) Phineas's jokes. But the missing wouldn't keep me from Daniel.

It was Thursday. Though the party was the next day and we probably should have been inside preparing for the event, Phin reckoned the afternoon might be our last chance for sugaring. "Wind's turning southerly," he'd said this morning.

One thing I wouldn't miss was the perpetual squabbling. To escape another round, I wandered across the yard to the woodpile, where the children were stacking kindling and playing at cabin building.

Behind me, Rachel called, "How many children should we have, Freddy?"

I tripped as I turned.

Phineas shot me an evil grin and repeated my former proclamation about this matter: "As many as God wills."

Rachel sniffed. "Then I hope God gives us many, many children."

Phineas shuddered with exaggerated revulsion.

I couldn't repress my own shiver. This was something Daniel and I had yet to discuss. I didn't want to give birth to a tribe. Thanks to the intriguing information Phineas had imparted on our journey, I knew how to prevent such a fate. Two children would suffice for me.

Marian appeared in the doorway and gave the combatants an exasperated look.

I regained my smile. No matter how irate Marian appeared, it was hard to be intimidated by a woman absolutely round with child.

"Try to be cheerful, friends," she ordered. "We have a gathering to look forward to." Then, hopefully: "I have an idea! Let's practice some music. Phin, you want to warm up your fiddle tonight after supper, give us a taste of tomorrow's tunes?"

"No." He settled the neck yoke across his shoulders. The empty buckets swung on the ends like silent bells. "I don't perform for bedlamites."

"Bedlamites?" Rachel glared at him.

"Anyone wishing for a whole litter of irritating babies is insane."

Thinking I might halt Rachel's answering cut, I asked quickly, "How about some music, Miss Welds? Why don't you sing for us before bedtime?" Singing I knew she loved to do.

"Sorry but no." She turned up her nose at Phineas's departing back and resumed stirring the boiling sap. Loudly: "I don't sing for misanthropes."

CHAPTER TWENTY-THREE

There was certainly no questioning the effectiveness of Phineas and his sister's ability to spread word of their gathering. After cramming the morning hours with food preparations, we had just enough time to scrub and dress the children, then scrub and dress ourselves, before neighbors (if neighbors they could be called, living as far away as some of them did) began to arrive. They came on foot, on mule, by wagon, and one, two, even three to a horse. Undoubtedly, they crossed streams, circled swamps, and threaded through the woods according to the markings on the trees.

I couldn't have provided a background fact for a single one— which guest sprang from prosperous New England stock and which one had entered this wilderness with nothing but an ax to his name. It didn't matter. The guests were consistently young (for who else but the robust and unfettered would be brash and able enough to take on this frontier?) and thrilled for the occasion to gather. They greeted us, veritable strangers, like long-lost friends. Too much solitude in the disparate nooks of the forest had made them ready for companionship.

Marian's oldest two climbed into the oak Phineas had left standing close to the house for shade, and they heralded new arrivals with shouts. The men brought whiskey, the women food, probably more than they could spare. And as soon as Daniel, Gid, and the Welds brothers arrived, Phineas rosined his bow, tuned his instrument, and started the music.

Daniel treated me to an unhurried handshake and a rueful smile before leading lucky Mary Root in a reel. My brother looked glad to see me. After complaining about his and Daniel's recent spell of poor suppers and telling me how much he missed my stews and biscuits, he ambled Marian's way to see if he could be made useful. Bob and Ed Welds introduced themselves, giving no indication of suspecting my true identity, though I'd known them all my life. They just looked happy that I was willing to listen as they explained their recent sickness. Given the account's gruesome details, the other guests could be forgiven for keeping their distance from the haggard brothers.

The cabin had been emptied of its rustic furnishings for the occasion. Most of the guests danced, but a few simply leaned against the wall and enjoyed the music. Phineas played exceptionally well. Perhaps Rachel thought so, too, for she deigned to bring him a refreshment between songs and appeared almost ready to deliver a compliment.

Phineas, predictably, ruined the moment. "Why are you ignoring your betrothed, Miss Welds? I hope you're not so fickle you'd set poor Freddy aside the second more strapping young men with actual whiskers show up."

She snatched the half-empty glass out of his hand.

"I wasn't finished."

"You are now." She looked tempted to pour the contents over his head but reconciled her ire with a tart "Just so you know, your cravat's wrinkled."

He tucked the violin under his chin. "Save your complaints for my valet."

She turned sharply but promptly whirled back around, hands to her hair. He'd shot out his bow, lightning fast, and tapped her crown, like a fairy swatting an unsuspecting mortal with its wand. Smirking, he returned the bow to the strings and merely said, "Whoops," before tackling a tavern ditty.

The cabin seemed to swell with merriment and noise. It was as if each pioneer, for so long living in isolation, had saved up his or her spirits and conversation and now unplugged the cache so that it spilled forth, in words and laughter, with abandonment.

I caught snatches of the men's conversations: the importance of a sawmill and gristmill, plans for crops, and dealings with the Holland Land Company. And I learned even more from the women, for I danced with them. This posed no difficulty. One couldn't be an older sister to two girls and not know how to lead. I met Dorothy, who described the black bear that took off with her hog a fortnight ago, and Ann, who predicted a bad season for fever and ague and gave me her thoughts on the benefits of bleeding and botanic dosing. Caroline, a fine dancer, agreed to take a turn around the floor twice. She wanted to teach and had an ambitious plan to open a district school in the near future.

A couple of hours into the dancing, I stole a few minutes to catch my breath, sip a cup of ale, and mull over what I was learning from my new acquaintances. Phineas, taking a break from playing, lounged with me in the corner.

Gid squeezed through the crowd. When Rachel also appeared, he intercepted her with a bow. "May I have the next dance?"

She gazed at him steadily. "I—I don't think so."

Color suffused his cheeks. Unfortunately, the press of guests made escape impossible, and they stood in tense proximity, turned from each other, until a part in the gathering permitted my brother to slink away.

Was it disinterest or lingering anger that prompted this refusal? I studied Rachel but only detected resignation in her fair face. She looked done with Gid. Maybe turning down his invitation had been her means to clarify that.

Phineas had also witnessed the exchange. With a shake of his head, he replaced his frown with a smile and called, "Oh, Rachel Welds!"

Eyebrows raised, she approached.

"Better nab a dance with Freddy while you can and remind the young ladies he's not available." He looked at me bemusedly. "Upon my soul, for such a young'un, you're drawing some pretty pairs of eyes tonight. Didn't expect the maids of the valley to find you quite so interesting."

"Not just interesting." Rachel seized my hand. *"Interested."* Ostensibly to me, she continued, with considerable feeling, "The fact is, you listen, Freddy. You actually ask questions. Most men simply talk and talk and talk."

"Ah," I murmured. "A hit."

He cringed. "More like a mortal wound." With a plunging motion, he slid the bow in his armpit, groaned piteously, and staggered.

Rachel didn't find this amusing.

"Music!"

Phin peered around the packed room, searching for the source of the demand. "What shall it be?" Then a pointed look at Rachel: *See? I ask questions.*

" 'The Blacksmith's Daughter'!"

"Oh, I love that girl." His bow hit the strings with a pounce.

I led Rachel into the reel and smiled at her sour expression. "I'm waiting for you and Phin to come to blows."

"He's *incredibly* irritating. I don't think I've ever known anyone quite so irritating. I'd like to plant him a facer."

"Don't let his teasing put you in a pucker and ruin your night."

"Ha." She turned her withering scorn in the violinist's direction. "As if he could."

"Good. Because you're supposed to be finding me the most compelling conversationalist."

"Doesn't take much to claim victory in that sport. Consider the lack of competition."

By the end of the evening, I gave up dancing and drinking. My feet hurt. So did my head.

Daniel found me in the corner by the loft ladder. "What's this? The party's prime favorite playing wallflower?"

My pulse beat faster at his appearance. "I'm recovering." I patted the spot next to me.

With a heavy sigh, he situated himself on the floor.

Phineas had struck up a patriotic tune, and the guests were raising their bottles in tribute to our nation. More than one face wore the soppy, weepy-eyed look that so often accompanied drunkenness. "I expect they'll be tarrying until morning."

"Passed out until then, certainly." He folded his arms, his expression turning thoughtful. "Strange how so many came out this way because they longed for wilderness, *wildness*, but now all they can talk about is how quickly they hope to tame it."

"And make everything civilized. I've been thinking the same thing. It'll look like Middleton around here before we know it."

"Sadly deforested."

"You and your trees. What've you been whittling lately?"

"Between helping Gideon clear for a house and widen a road?" He snorted. "Not much."

"Ah. 'Not much,' meaning at least a little something."

"Actually, I've been helping your brother make a gift for Mrs. Gale." At my expectant look, he said, "You'll see it soon." Then, darkly: "And stop making fun of my whittling."

Smiling, I patted his leg. He stilled, then shot me a wide-eyed glance, which only amused me further. "I'm glad you're a whittler. I can't wait to see what beautiful things await me in my future, all inscribed with my initials."

"Spiles, Frederick. Many, many spiles."

Marian and Phineas's gathering ushered in a warm spell, and on Monday at the logging bee, when Gid's lot was graced with some of the same men who had helped fill Friday's music-teeming cabin, I got the sense, in the way they studied the blue sky, that the farmers of the Genesee Valley were anxious for spring. It was time to improve their properties, carve out of the forests another fifteen acres, and plow and plant wherever they could between the stumps and roots. Springtime meant hope, and they turned their trusting young faces to the morning sun, as flowers do.

Despite their obligations to their land and families, they seemed happy to help Gid, and Gid was obviously thrilled with how quickly they began clearing the thick timber. Mutual assistance was a time-honored practice in Middleton, too, but here it was so desperately needed, for to eke out of the forest a meager field required an incredible amount of effort. When the time came, for each of these helpers, my brother would return the favor.

I had borrowed one of Phin's axes for the occasion and chose some youngish maples on which to practice. The stand's distance from the others reassured me. Any mistake on my part wouldn't result in a tree careening onto someone's head. I was especially concerned about the children, though Rachel was doing a fine job of keeping them occupied across the stream, out of harm's way, while Mrs. Gale served food and cider.

Felling trees was difficult work, especially at first, and when I spotted Daniel, I called him over to check my stance and method.

"You've got the right idea." He turned and gazed gloomily into the woods.

That's it? I had been hoping for a personal tutorial, a little flirtation, perhaps some subtle adjustments to my hold. "What's wrong?"

He shrugged. "Just disheartening, spending day after day tearing down a beautiful forest."

I suppressed an impulse to smile at his sweetness. "You're sad about the trees."

"And the songbirds." Sighing, he hefted his ax. "Keep an eye out for flying branches. Some of the men here are reckless."

I looked past Daniel's departing back. My eyes widened. *And fast on their way to drunkenness.* Near the stream, a handful of farmers were tapping bottles and guzzling.

Toward the end of the logging bee, more people than not were imbibing. The whiskey inspired foolish acts. Several men turned the felling into a competition, rushing to chop down the most trees, boasting in shouts, and drinking toasts to every round's victor.

Eventually, I drew closer to my friends, nervous that one of the children or my dog would wander into the path of a crashing limb. *Our* menfolk, I was happy to see, were more sensible than the rest. Daniel stood apart from the displays of sloppy wrangling and merely shook his head, Phineas observed the antics with a disdainful expression, and Gid chewed on his lower lip and mumbled a prayer that no one die on his new farm.

After our cold supper, we sober ones formed a dumbfounded audience. The light was failing, and we kept our distance from the revelries, but we were close enough to witness Ed Welds demonstrate a headstand from a branch of a maple, as his brother stumbled his way with a bottle in one hand and an ax in the other.

Phineas blew a low whistle. "Surviving the fever only to die from stupidity."

Rachel dispassionately considered her cousins. "Women also gather to help one another, but you won't find their sewing or spinning turned into silly, boozy affairs."

"Or contests," I muttered. What was it with men and competition? Did *everything* have to turn into a race?

Marian grinned. "Actually, it'd be fun to see what a quilting would look like if we refreshed ourselves with rum instead of tea."

Rachel's lips trembled. "Do you think we might start wrestling and broad-jumping the sides of the frame?"

The idea tickled the two women into laughter.

Phineas elbowed Gid in the side. "I'd pay to see that event." He smiled at Rachel.

"Me, too." My brother nodded slowly. His eyes, however, were not fastened on his former love interest.

He was watching Marian Gale. And his expression was stunned.

CHAPTER TWENTY-FOUR

If I'd secretly believed returning to Gid's land would afford Daniel and me time to gaze into each other's eyes and recite poetry, the morning after the logging bee corrected any such assumption.

Gid was not a strict chaperone as much as he was an ambitious young farmer. He wanted to work hard and finish things fast. Spring plowing ought to happen in a couple of weeks! The Indian corn had to get planted! And most pressing: We didn't even have a house yet!

Daniel being Daniel meant Gid found a willing accomplice. I was a more grudging one. I didn't mind the labor; I just didn't understand why a little time for relaxation (otherwise known as courtship) couldn't be spared.

At first light, Tuesday began with Gid promptly setting out to work all three of us to exhaustion. Since he and Daniel had widened the trail, my brother had been able to collect his wagon. He was thrilled to be fully reunited with all his tools and anxious to put them to use. He put me to use, too. I spent hours hacking at downed trees and dragging limbs to a burn pile.

And there were still meals to prepare. While Daniel finished maneuvering a massive rock onto the stoneboat in the field, Gid stood by the campfire, ate a piece of bread (too busy to sit and eat his supper like a decent Christian), and said amid rapid chewing, "I can't imagine what this enterprise would have been like if you hadn't joined me, Freddy. Or if Daniel hadn't shown up. What a worker! He's worth a dozen men." He flashed me a smile, swiped the crumbs from his shirt, and added, already turning back to the field, "I'm glad he's still sweet on you, because he never would have come all this way if he weren't."

I grunted. A lot of good Daniel's being sweet on me did. The only intimate knowledge of my beau I'd gathered since joining the men was an interesting detail from this morning: how Daniel's hair kinked up after it dried from its cleansing dunk in the stream, a curliness he clearly regretted, given his grimace and the ruthless way he combed it out. After that, through the smoke of my burn pile, I only caught glimpses of him. He might have been a rare species of animal, a secretive, beautiful, uncommon creature I was only allowed to admire from afar. It wasn't that he avoided me, exactly, only that he didn't take advantage of our proximity. Not even Gid's tyrannical chore delegating prevented *every* encounter.

That night in the covered wagon, as I stared wearily at the darkness, I mulled over this strange self-restraint. Was it born of respect for my brother? Deference to me? He had to *know* how much I'd enjoyed that blissful, if brief, tryst on the way to Phin's.

The truth hit me like a thunderbolt. *Daniel Long isn't just reserved. He's shy.*

Then: *What are we going to do about that?*

On Wednesday morning, when I stumbled, half-asleep and sore, out of the wagon, I discovered the taciturn suitor sipping a cup of coffee by the fire.

"Morning." He rose quickly. "Ready to build a house?"

I rubbed my eyes and took in the camp. In the fog hanging between the trees, Gid was by the stream, tending to the cattle. I brought my sleepy gaze back to Daniel. "House building. Is that your idea of courtship?"

He frowned.

"Forget it." I yawned and stretched, too tired to address our relationship difficulties. "Let's build the damn house."

Which is precisely what we didn't do.

After the previous day's frenzied branch burning, log rolling, rock heaving, and stump digging, Daniel and Gid commenced house building at the pouring pace of old honey crusted on the bottom of the honeypot. They trod around the clearing, measuring off paces, squinting at the sky, pointing in one direction, murmuring about another.

I finally yanked off my gloves and got to work skinning and cutting up the rabbit Gid had snared. The boys would probably want their nooning early to give them sufficient strength to point and putter.

Gid smiled at my exasperation. "You can't just stick a house anywhere."

Daniel was actually on his stomach now, apparently considering the ground's grade. From this undignified position, he said, "We'll have to think about the disposition of the land, the prevailing winds, the arc of the sun—plan the steepest pitch of the roof toward the winter wind, and face the living area to the south."

"Then there's the water supply," Gid said. "Be nice to eventually connect a gravity spring to trickle water into the house."

Daniel got to his feet and dusted his hands. "And the outbuildings, particularly the privy and barn, ought to go where the summer winds can carry the stink away." At my grimace, he shrugged. "No one wants to smell the privy in August. Better to situate the honeysuckle and herb garden close to the house, straight in the wind's path. Makes for a sweeter living space."

"Well." I tossed the rabbit legs in the pot. "Just tell me when you're ready." I headed to the stream to wash the wild leek I'd dug up. This place was riddled with onions. Mama would be in cold-cure heaven.

Once Daniel and Gid finished plotting, the three of us worked together efficiently and quickly. The cabin's logs had already been set aside, chosen for their uniform length and width. It would be a small, primitive structure, though Daniel assured my brother it'd be easy to expand should life reward him with a wife and children.

Gid responded with a sigh.

The logs retained their bark as they went up horizontally, one upon another, expertly notched (this was Daniel, after all) to ensure tight corners and a close adjacency. Daniel, longer than Gid by half a foot, thought it'd be best to make the structure tall enough to allow a big man to walk around the interior without having to stoop.

Over and over again, I hefted up a log's end, held it in place, and put up with Gid's repeated "for heaven's sake, Freddy, don't move, or I'll drop this thing on my foot." The activity, though taxing to my muscles, left my mind free to wander. I thought about how strong I'd grown in the last two months. Trekking across states, clearing poor roads, chopping, yanking, and hauling had trimmed my body down to something wiry. No wonder folks didn't suspect me of being a girl. I was looking more and more like a whip of a boy.

After a while of contemplatively flexing my muscles, I became conscious of a strange gurgling—coming from me. I frowned at my stomach.

"Be still," Gid groaned, as he stood on tiptoe and pushed his log end into place. To Daniel standing inside the structure, he called, "Good on this side."

My belly rumbled again, followed this time by an uneasy flutter.

Darkness collected in the woods, and by the time we called it a night, the moon had long since risen. The rest of the house would have to wait for the morrow. Besides the final thud of two great lengths of wood meeting each other and the last thwack of the ax, the only sounds came from crickets, wood frogs—and my stomach. Its rumbles joined the hums and croaks.

Gid and Daniel said they were too tired to bother with supper, and I was too queasy to touch the rest of the rabbit stew, so I hauled the lidded pot to the wagon to save it for the next day, then joined the leftovers under the canvas cover, liking how the pot's round cast iron sides warmed me and happy to let my arms and legs relax on the feather mat we kept in the wagon.

Through the sliver of an opening between the canvas and the wagon side, I gazed at the stars. They sparkled and winked, caught like fireflies in a great web of branches. I thought about calling out a good-night and sweet dreams to Daniel but supposed Gid would laugh at me.

And Daniel would blush.

So I went to sleep.

When I awoke, for just a second I was beset by the strange notion that I had kicked over the soup kettle. Not that I was drenched. Merely that I felt slow, a body floating in liquid.

The stirrings outside the wagon sounded painfully loud. Wind played the canvas covering like a drum, birds belted songs to one another, and Gid blared, "*Why* isn't she up yet? We've got a cabin to build, and I'm *starving*." Then even louder, "Lazybones! Wake up."

"Leave her be," Daniel said. "She worked hard yesterday."

"So did I."

"We've got johnnycakes in the basket. I'll grab the kettle. We can heat up the stew ourselves."

The wagon lurched with a sudden weight. I whimpered, excruciatingly sensitive to the jostling, and winced when the kettle disappeared from the crook of my legs. In its place, coldness sprang and clawed its way to my bones. I shivered violently.

Sick, I thought, and opened my mouth to say it. The utterance couldn't form. Instead I slipped into unconsciousness.

I came to in time to hear Gid announce, "*Delicious.* Think we'll finish by tonight, then? Even the roof?"

"Don't see why not."

"By Jove, I could eat the rest of this."

"Ought to save some for Harriet."

"Hmm."

Sunshine streamed where the canvas suddenly parted. Even with my eyes closed, I sensed the light and winced again.

"Hey, sleepyhead. Want some bread and stew?"

The mere thought of food made my stomach roil. "No," I moaned, and sighed in relief when the flap dropped and shut out the morning.

"Should have let her sleep," Daniel said.

"Oh, she doesn't mind."

Gid and Daniel started going on about the cabin. In a murky place between waking and swooning, I heard snatches—"mortice the brace . . . hipping joints . . . no difference in the framework, all made to last"—without really absorbing their meanings. It hurt to move my head, let alone think with it. I drew the fuzzy conclusion that I must have caught Adam's infection and experienced a pang that such a small person had suffered so. I was twice his size and could barely stand the torment.

Time passed. Who knew how much? Then light poured into my makeshift chamber, along with Daniel's cautious "Harriet?"

He entered, an action that jarred the wagon and therefore my stomach. Nausea rolled through me. I groaned.

"What in the—?"

His hand touched my forehead. "My God, you're burning up."

How odd. I felt so cold.

He didn't say anything for a moment. Then, abruptly: "Hold tight, my dear."

He disappeared. Couldn't say I was sorry. I wanted to be alone.

Outside the wagon, Gid greeted the news of my condition with a frustrated growl and suggested they transfer me to Mrs. Gale's care.

"But she might spread the illness to everyone there."

"You're right. Damn."

The canvas swished. My brother's voice, impatience lacquered with a thin coat of concern, entered. "Too bad you're sick, Freddy. Hell of a day to pick for it, though." He sighed. "Where do you hurt?"

"Everywhere."

"Head?"

"And stomach."

"Oh, no." The canvas fluttered shut. "Bad news. She's never been one to handle stomach ailments well. Can't toss up her contents. Simply can't. She might improve faster if she could. Once, the whole family dined at the pastor's. Mrs. Cartwright fed us breaded fish. *I* was suspicious of the meal right away. Smelled like the trout had washed up on a bank and soured under a hot sun. Fishy fish, if you know what I mean. Sure enough, within half a day, we were sticking our heads over the chamber pots and vomiting like mad—everyone but my sister. That nasty concoction just stewed in her poor belly, all that god-awful trout that no amount of cornmeal and parsley could doctor, the stinkiest fish you ever did—"

Lord help me. "Stop!"

"You're not helping, Gid," Daniel snapped.

"Oh. Sorry."

A few minutes passed. Daniel slipped in. I felt a sudden weight of blankets, probably the ones he and Gid had been using in the lean-to. I huddled under their warmth. "Thank you."

"Can I get you anything?"

My mother. I whimpered. "Water."

This was shortly provided. I returned to a fitful sleep.

When I awoke again, the light sifting through the wagon cracks had faded to a honey hue. I cautiously stretched. My stomach felt tender and off but no longer wildly disturbed. Mostly, I felt weak.

The canvas parted. Daniel, his hair ruffled and face grave, appeared. "Better?"

"Better."

He sighed deeply, closed his eyes, and shook his head. Then he looked me over and prodded my forehead again. "Still warmish." He clucked. "What can I get you, dearest?"

I smiled weakly at the endearment and dragged a hand out from under the covers to offer him a feeble pat. "A little broth." I wistfully recalled Mama's sick-food tradition of a healthful broth and biscuit. "Maybe a johnnycake, too, if we have it." A bit of something to settle my stomach. I closed my eyes.

He didn't speak right away. When he did, it was a forced "Certainly, sweetheart."

Gid must have been waiting right outside the wagon, for Daniel immediately asked, "We have any griddle breads left?"

"Uh . . . no. Ate the last one for a nooning." Defensively: "I was hungry."

"Harriet wants bread and broth." When my brother didn't say anything, Daniel muttered, "Wish we hadn't gobbled up the stew. I might have spooned some of the liquid in a cup for her."

"Well, heavens, we can surely make a soup."

"You know how?"

"Can't be that hard. But forget the johnnycakes. Wouldn't know where to start with those."

"Your mother should have taught you some kitchen basics before you left home."

Gid's tone was equally testy: "Why would she bother? I had my sister for that. And what about *you*? *You're* the bachelor."

"With Granny Barnes for a housekeeper and cook."

"Then how'd you survive the journey?"

"Dried meats, fruits, nuts. And the same thing we ate the whole time Harriet was at Phineas's—meat roasted on a stick."

"Think she could handle a little charred rabbit?" Daniel must have shaken his head, for Gid continued with forced cheer, "No matter. We can decipher this broth business."

I heard the exchange with utter indifference and felt no compulsion to offer suggestions. Frankly, in my weakened state, talking was too great a challenge. I burrowed under the mountain of blankets and drifted in and out of sleep. Usually, it was the men's talk that pulled me back to consciousness, questions and comments that blended together like a peculiar mental soup:

What can we put in it? Onions. I always see her digging up onions. How many? Don't know. Five, six. Did you skin it? Reluctantly. Glad Freddy usually handles that. Damn. They slipped out of my hands. Never mind. I'll go rinse them. Again. Add a log to that fire, why don't you. You're supposed to be helping. Huh. Seems like there ought to be something else in this. I know! Let me grab Freddy's herbs. Good. Now let's see. Smell this. What do you think it is? Dill? Why not? Sprinkle some in. Not sure if that's enough. Dump in a little more. Is it finished? No idea. How long has it been cooking? Maybe an hour? Poke the rabbit. Feel done? How is done supposed to feel?

I didn't cherish high hopes for the broth, nor did I get any for some hours. Night had fallen by the time Daniel parted the canvas and climbed into the wagon. Over his shoulder, the gibbous moon shone in a sea of clouds and stars.

Gid's face took the place of the moon. "Suppertime!"

The two approached in a deep-crouched shuffle, my betrothed carrying a steaming bowl, Gid bearing a big spoon and lantern.

I braced my body on an elbow.

They looked so eager to please, bringing forth their offerings, sporting solemn faces, acting very ceremonial. They reminded me of the wise men in the Christmas story, presenting frankincense and myrrh to the baby Jesus.

"Thank you." I accepted the spoon with a shaky hand and smiled wanly, determined to like the meal or at least pretend to.

But the spoonful of broth, perhaps more suitably called pickled gamy onion juice from hell, sat like a poisonous pool in my mouth. My stomach rebelled, my nose fought the wafting odiferous onslaught, and like a country closing its only port, my throat utterly refused. With some desperate sounds, it signaled that an enemy disguised as broth was attempting to infiltrate my poor body.

Mouth full, eyes watering, I glanced from one man to the other.

Daniel grimaced. "That bad?"

I couldn't help it. I nodded and wrenched at the nearest tie holding the canvas to the wagon. Lunging up, I spat the horridness into the night; then, with a moan, I fell back to the bed.

Gid blinked.

Daniel cringed. "Want me to get you some water?"

"Please."

CHAPTER TWENTY-FIVE

The next day, as soon as he left the unfinished cabin, Daniel glanced toward the wagon and, at the sight of me, visibly brightened. He tossed aside the saw and walked over, swiping his damp brow with a sleeve. "Good morning?"

I lowered the bucket to the wagon floor. "Compared to yesterday? More than good." At his feet, the canvas cover made white ripples on the ground. There was a second pile behind him: blankets. Crates and satchels littered the space between the two mounds. I was airing and scrubbing everything. First thing upon waking, I'd done precisely that to myself. Now the wagon's interior was almost finished, too.

I dropped the wet rag in the bucket, pushed back my hair, and sat heavily. My strength hadn't quite returned.

Daniel joined me on the wagon bench.

I smiled a little, thinking about last night's dinner disaster. "You here to finish me off?"

His expression turned sheepish. "We couldn't eat it, either. Tried. Ended up dumping the whole kettle's worth far enough away that we wouldn't have to smell it. We ate walnuts for dinner."

"I'll make some biscuits in a bit."

"You shouldn't be pushing yourself"—he frowned, taking in my cleaning project—"or worrying about this."

I shrugged and peered toward the stream. "Where in heaven's name is Gid?"

"Left early for the brothers' place, ostensibly to invite them to his housewarming tomorrow, but really to steal their breakfast."

"Think the Welds boys are better cooks than you two?"

"Can't be worse."

"Never mind. It's the thought that counts." I smiled at his dismal expression and gave him a cheering nudge. "The party's tomorrow? Will the cabin be done?"

"Would have been up today if we hadn't wasted yesterday on a witch's brew." He scanned me critically. "You still look wan."

"Think so?"

He put a palm on my forehead.

I held my breath. *Definitely better.*

"Cooler, thankfully."

"I'm not so sure." I tapped my neck. "Check here."

Frowning, he slid his hand along my nape.

I shivered. *Lovely.*

"Huh. Doesn't feel too warm to me."

I rubbed my waist. "What about here?"

In a flash, his eyes met mine. *"Harriet."*

"Daniel. Please."

His color was so hectic, *he* looked feverish, but he sent his hand along my belly to my side. "You must be fully recovered." He tentatively pulled me closer. "In fact, I think you feel fine. Hmm. Very."

"We'd better make sure," I said close to his mouth.

We did, thoroughly, moving from the seat to the wagon floor and banishing bashfulness along the way. Maybe putting feelings into words didn't come easily to Daniel, but once he got started, he communicated exceedingly well with his hands. *Thanks to the whittling, no doubt,* I concluded hazily before reason gave way to sensations and I lost my train of thought.

Eventually, however, I dragged myself into a sitting position. "Daniel," I gasped. "We have to talk."

He looked up, dazed. "Now?"

I nodded. Gid would be back soon. "I've been thinking a lot about marriage. About"—I cleared my throat—"babies."

With a groan, he sat up. His hands swept down my back. "I am interested in all matters related to the making of babies."

"No." I leaned out of his arms, found his hands, and drew them to my heart. "I mean the *not* making of them."

"Oh." Then his brow cleared. "You don't want any?"

"That's just it. I might. In the future. But not right away and"—I met his eyes—"most assuredly, *not many.*"

His mouth came up in a corner. "That day at the sugaring. You knew I was teasing about the dozen children."

"Even half that is too many for me."

Concern creased his brow. "Your birth mother . . ."

I shook my head. "I'm no wisp of a girl like she was. It's not just the childbearing. Child-*rearing* is hard on a woman. Too many children, and raising them is all she has time to do. I want more than motherhood for my life. I want selfhood." It didn't matter that my middle name was Submit. God hadn't given me a good head and sound body just so I could yield to others' expectations. I would make my own decisions.

"Then we won't have children." He brought my hands to his lips. "I'm marrying Harriet for Harriet—no one and nothing else."

Warmth flooded me. "Well, I might not mind one or two little ones." *Maybe even three.* I thought about this, shrugged. *Or maybe not.*

"Only if you'd like. Doesn't make sense, really, to have a large family, not in New England. Portion off a farm to too many children, and no one gets much of anything. I'd rather properly provide for one or two and keep the family close together than force our sons and daughters far away"—he smiled wryly—"to wilderness like this, where resources aren't yet scarce. One or two. Yes, you're absolutely right."

I looked around, disconcerted. "Didn't think this would be so easy."

"We're simply like-minded." He started drawing me close again.

Eyes narrowing, I braced my hands on his chest. "You're awfully agreeable."

"Well, of course." He kissed my neck. "Because I'm awfully in love."

With Fancy wagging her tail and trotting happily at Gid's side, my brother soon returned and threw us a distracted wave, clearly oblivious to our disheveled appearance. By way of hello, he announced, "It's official. Bob and Ed can't cook, either. Hope you're well enough to keep us from starving, Freddy."

"I can do that." I'd worked up an appetite, too.

Flashing me a smile, Daniel jumped out of the wagon and began organizing provisions. Gid restored the canvas covering, and I hung the blankets from branches, then made a late breakfast.

Full and in good spirits—perhaps inordinately good, for Daniel and me—we set out to finish the cabin, running poles across the walls for the loft and adding a ridge beam and rafters to support the roof.

Lighter than the men, I took charge of the topmost job.

Squinting, Gid watched me attach an oak splint to the half-finished roof. "You're like a cat. Aren't you scared up there?"

"Not any different from climbing trees." I arranged another splint. "I thought house building would be trickier."

By the wagon, examining some basswood he was considering for the floor, Daniel murmured absently, "No great secret to building. No special magic." He looked over with a smile. "A person just has to have the desire and make the effort."

"Desire and effort." Gid grunted and crouched to continue working on the ladder for the loft. "Well, we've got plenty of both."

When we took a break, I taught Daniel and Gid how to mix a batter, fry biscuits in pork fat, and put together a decent soup, letting them do the chopping, portioning, and stirring so they'd remember the lesson. Gid grumbled about the time it was costing him, but I shook my head. "You'll thank me when I'm gone and you're cooking for yourself." Then, with a teasing smile: "No secret to cookery, no special magic. Just takes a little desire and effort."

Hours later, we stopped our work on the cabin. It was almost done but, with the clouds covering the moon, destined not to receive its finishing touches until morning. Daniel took my outstretched hand and walked with me to the wagon. To my brother he provided no false explanation of where he was heading, and I didn't wish him to. My decisions were none of Gid's business.

That night again proved the day's lesson. When it came to ensuring an endeavor's success, there was a great deal to be said for desire and effort.

In this case, however, I couldn't dismiss the possibility of enchantment. I felt spellbound. There was, indeed, some special magic.

The next morning, Gid was gone. Since both his cap and coat were missing, I guessed he was off visiting the brothers or exploring his property. I breakfasted with Daniel, then climbed the ladder to the roof. I'd nearly finished attaching the splints when I heard my brother return.

He was whistling. Loudly.

Lightly swinging a hammer, Daniel wandered out of the cabin and glanced up at me with an amused face. "Giving fair warning."

Gid bore no cheer to go with his whistle. He looked sorely put out. After tossing his coat on the ground, he planted his hands on his hips. "Well, this is just splendid. Headed over to the brothers again to see if they could spare some treenails and found the boys tipsy." He kicked his coat. "Before breakfast! If they keep this up, they'll drink themselves to death. Of all the stupid ways to squander their time. I tried to talk some sense into them, even took them to task for abandoning Rachel at the Lintons', but I don't know if any of it sank in. They're plain *saturated* with whiskey."

"Goodness, that's too bad," I murmured.

"It's despicable!"

I bit my lip and briefly met Daniel's eyes. There was something excessive about Gid's anger. I got the impression it wasn't all for Robert and Ed. It was clear Daniel thought so, too.

Throughout the morning, my brother glared at Daniel and me off and on, glowered at the rough field, stomped around the cabin, and complained bitterly about how much work there was to be done "just to get the ridiculous bumper crop of rocks out of this bloody soil."

I steered clear, but before our nooning, Daniel followed him to the stream. The discussion that transpired clearly didn't prove productive. My betrothed's expression was pure impatience when he joined me by the campfire.

I smiled ruefully. Poor Daniel. First Matthew. Then me. Then Gid. "We Winters are a tedious lot, aren't we?"

"Your brother's acting like an *idiot*." His hand plowed his hair. "One more week, Harriet. That's it. One more. We'll finish the house. We'll fix him up the beginnings of a garden. We'll plant some potatoes. Then we'll go. I don't want a long engagement. We can get married in Batavia."

My smile wilted. So soon? What about Rachel? She needed me even more than Gideon did. And what about Freddy? I wasn't finished with him yet. Then there was my family in Middleton to consider. "Mama won't understand. . . . If we rush this, she'll be disappointed. . . . The lack of ceremony, not having the chance to help me make my dress—"

"We can throw a party after the fact. Let's not wait, Harriet. No one knows us in Batavia. *No one*. Think about that: the lack of interruptions, the privacy."

This was true. Privacy. Blissful privacy. My thoughts returned to the previous night. How *wonderful* it had been. The doubts remained, but now desire, like a commanding song, muffled them. "You're right, Daniel," I sighed.

"Is it a plan?"

"It's a deal."

He beamed a relieved smile. "Shall we shake on it?"

"Heavens, no." I took his hand and pulled. "We can do better than that."

"Gid?" I patted my face dry and ran the towel over my wet head.

"What?" He was kneeling by his stoneboat and didn't bother taking his attention away from the broken board he was repairing.

"Better wash up. Friends will be here soon." When he ignored me, I added cautiously, "For the housewarming."

He threw down his hammer. "What's there to celebrate? Nothing is working out the way it was supposed to."

I gave him a stern look. "Try a little gratefulness. You have a sweeping piece of land and a sturdy cabin." *Not to mention many helping hands.*

"And best friends who've turned into lazy drunks and a sister who just can't wait to flit away, who's gallivanting here and there and everywhere." My burst of laughter only deepened his scowl. "I'm *serious*. It's shameful. Meanwhile, I'm stuck with no family, no helpmate, no—no—"

"Wife?"

He slumped. "No wife." His brow fell in his hands. After a moment, he muttered, "I'm sorry."

I patted his crown. "Things did turn out differently than we expected, but different doesn't mean bad. You have possibilities you're not even pursuing."

"Marian Gale?" He grunted and shook his head. "As if she'd even consider me."

"I think she would. Why wouldn't she? You're a good catch, Gid." I crouched to give him a sideways hug. *When you're not a gloomy fool.*

CHAPTER TWENTY-SIX

Accompanied by the cacophony of the children's shouts, Phineas alighted from the wagon with the finesse of a young duke disembarking from an elegant phaeton. He stood for a moment and scrutinized the new cabin, nodded in satisfaction, flicked a speck off his delicate yellow pantaloons, twisted gracefully but quickly enough for the long tail on his blue superfine coat to enact a jaunty wave at the end, then held up his hands to the driver's seat, where Rachel awaited.

He wore such an expression of tender regard, I couldn't help but gasp. Could the two actually be getting along? Had Phineas relinquished his merciless buffoonery? Had Rachel decided to look past his obnoxiousness?

Apparently not.

His considerate reach ended with the violin case. He drew it down, rubbed its side, secured the handle, and turned.

Rachel rolled her eyes and jumped out by herself.

"You've been busy." Phin smiled. "The place is shaping up nicely."

Gid, more cheerful now, folded his arms and rocked back on his heels. "Thank you. We're working hard. But I wouldn't have finished a third of the labor without Freddy and Daniel."

Phineas acknowledged this with a small bow in our direction.

"It's been fun." Daniel lifted the children out of the wagon: oldest, middle, youngest. He crouched to steady Molly on the uneven ground. "All set?"

She nodded, then fell as soon as he released her.

Rachel collected the girl and situated her on a hip. While I knelt to greet the boys, my friend patted my head. "How's Freddy?"

"Glad you're all here."

Gid scanned the wagon. "Not all. Where's Mrs. Gale?"

Phineas heaved a sigh. "She stayed behind." At Gid's crestfallen look, he added, "Trust me: She wouldn't be good company."

I dusted my knees and straightened. "Not sick, I hope?"

"Just sick of her brother," Rachel said.

Phineas made a face. "Of all of us. She started the day in the strangest mood. Grumpy but inexplicably driven."

"Driven to what?" Daniel asked.

"Clean." He frowned at the excited nephew who was presenting a chunk of upended sod, one grimy finger pointing out a score of wiggling worms. "Very nice. But please, Adam. You're raining soil on my boots." He glanced up. "At least an hour too early this morning, I woke to the distressing sound of vigorous sweeping. As soon as my sister noticed I'd stirred, she began complaining about dirt, how terribly sick of filth she was, how if I had a single care for anyone but myself and my 'silly mare' and my 'stupid violin,' I'd put up the corner shelves I'd promised her, add an extra bedroom, dig a closer well, and build her a decent porch, so people could leave their boots at the door and stop tracking in the horrible outside." Hurt crossed his face. "I'd never seen her so angry. On my weary way to pour myself a cup of coffee, I accidentally shuffled through her sweeping pile, and she hit me with the broom. Me! Her own brother! The very man who has committed his life to her and her spawn's welfare. Slapped me right in the head. With a *dirty broom*."

I was used to Phineas's dramatic antics and turned to Rachel for the true story, but she confirmed his tale of outraged woe with a sad nod. "Truly, she was in a peculiar state: heaving great buckets of water inside for washing, attacking not just the floor but the walls, too, with vicious scrubbing, muttering under her breath about the disgusting Genesee Valley with its awful red, sticky mud. I asked her if she wanted me to stay behind and help her, and she looked up from her cleaning, stared at me—quite unseeingly, if you know what I mean—and said, 'If you want to help me, Rachel Welds, you'll take the children with you, take Phineas with you, and get them all out of my hair. For. One. Blasted. Day. I want *everyone* out of my hair!'" Rachel's eyes widened at the recollection.

Phineas shuddered.

Daniel gazed at me, nonplussed.

"Huh." I could hardly reconcile this description with the Marian Gale I'd grown to admire and like very much.

Gid especially looked struck by the account. "I can't like it. Something's wrong." He stared grimly at the visitors for a moment, then announced, "I'll go visit her."

"She made it perfectly clear," Phin said. "She wants to be *alone*."

"I can't explain it. I just feel . . ." Gid rubbed the back of his neck. "I should check on her."

Phin shook his head. "Don't do it."

Rachel smiled a little. "It's a fine idea." At Phin's squawk, she waved an airy hand. "He might cheer her up. Marian likes Gid."

While Phineas shrugged, my brother, who was in the process of digging his coat out of the wagon, stilled. "She does?"

His reaction—blatant surprise and pleasure—was a welcome sight. I smiled gratefully at Rachel.

She wiggled her eyebrows at me, then turned to Gid to add blandly, "Quite a bit, actually."

"Why, that's—that's wonderful." Gid coughed and abruptly yanked on his coat. "Good, then. If she's fine, I'll be back before sundown."

"You'll regret it," Phineas said.

"I don't think so." Gid tugged on his gloves. "And who knows? Maybe her spirits will have improved. Maybe she'll come back with me." He glanced over his shoulder at the cabin and added, with quiet wistfulness, "I really wanted to show her my new place."

Phin imitated, " 'Maybe she'll come back with me.' " He grunted a laugh. "And maybe she'll kill you."

A look settled on my brother's face. I knew that expression. I'd seen it a decade ago when he demanded Luke give him back his toy soldier. I'd seen it when he set out to court Rachel. I'd seen it when he decided to try his hand at pioneering. I'd seen it whenever he faced a challenge. Pure mulishness. Sure enough, he didn't even acknowledge Phineas's warning with a glance, just retorted, "I'll take my chances."

Daniel and Phineas struck up a conversation about horseflesh, then wandered side by side toward the cabin, leaving Rachel and me to the children's mercy. Over his shoulder, Daniel murmured something vague about wanting Phineas's input on a few farming matters, and Phineas grinned at Rachel and said that she and I—or, in his words, "the love-sick puppies"—would enjoy an hour or two of courtship without a couple of stodgy bachelors shadowing their every move.

Only the speaker appeared tickled by this comment. Rachel scowled at Phineas, Daniel frowned at me, and I shrugged helplessly.

Marian's little ones took no offense at the men's transparent agenda to avoid their grimy presence. After trailing Rachel and me along the woods' edge, splashing in the stream, examining the legendary location where "the great bough knocked Freddy senseless," demanding games involving marbles, eating all of the biscuits, poking suspiciously at the trout stew, then playing pioneering in the wagon, the children were very ready for bed.

Ephraim adamantly refuted this. "I'm not the least bit tired," he yawned. Adam thought the sleeping loft a prime spot to play pirates. Molly began to wail for her mother. But once they were calmed down and arranged, biggest to smallest, on the floor mat and then covered with two big quilts, all three lasted fewer than five minutes into my bedtime story before falling fast asleep.

That left the adults downstairs, just the four of us, no Gid to improve our numbers, obviously no Marian, either. On the root-riddled ground, so weirdly like the outside for an inside floor, we sat in a circle, close to the hearth we'd initiated with its first fire.

Gid's absence began to make me anxious. Why wasn't he back yet? Every time the wind whooshed and the branches rattled, my eyes flew to the doorway, as yet doorless, expecting the oilcloth to part and present my brother.

Daniel patted my back. "Don't worry."

"Marian probably just set Gideon to work on the corner shelves her brother was too lazy to build." Rachel smirked at Phineas, drew in her feet so that she was sitting cross-legged, and smoothed her skirt over her boots.

Phineas shrugged. "Or murdered him with her broom." He was plucking the strings of his violin. He adjusted one of the pegs at the scrolled head, fitted the instrument under his chin, hummed himself a note, tested a string according to the hum, and bowed across the other strings, two at a time, to tune all four, first with peg turns, then by twiddling the tiny screws at the chin end. He smiled at me. "Don't fret. How about some music to distract you?"

"We're not much of an audience." Rachel turned to me. "Didn't Gid invite my cousins?"

I attempted a casual shrug. "They couldn't come." *Too drunk.* Determined not to ruin the evening with worrying, I gave my head a shake and stuck a smile on my face. "So what do you have in mind for us, Phin?"

"A little night music." With a pounce of his bow, he shot into Mozart's *Eine kleine Nacht*, followed that with a movement from one of Bach's Brandenburg Concertos, lingered over a piece by Haydn, then drifted into "something newer," a dreamy work by Beethoven. Though his playing engaged me completely (so much so, I forgot all about poor Gid), I wouldn't have known each piece's composer or title if he hadn't murmured the information between songs.

By the end of Phineas's last selection, Rachel was drooping, her head in her hand.

He tapped her on the knee with his bow. "You're insulting my performance, falling asleep like that."

She yawned and stretched. "It's all lovely, but I'm tired, and that last one was as good as a lullaby."

"Play something for her to sing along to," Daniel said. "That'll wake her."

"Pff. She never sings."

Still not singing? I frowned at Rachel.

She turned an unsmiling face to the crackling fire.

My hands trembled. I clasped them in my lap. Poor Rachel. What Mr. Linton had done to her wouldn't fade as quickly as her bruises had. If only he could be made to pay for his crimes. How *unjust* the world was. Rachel's sadness, her sufferings—they demanded I not leave the Genesee Valley yet. How could I disappear when she needed me most? "That's because you're not playing what she likes," I finally said, desperate to bring back my former singing pal. "She's an old-fashioned girl. Give her one of the traditional ditties."

Holding his instrument like a mandolin, Phineas played pizzicato on the strings and grinned at Rachel. "I have a good tune for you, then, one I know you'll appreciate. It's all about a female's fickleness, scorn, and cruelty."

She gave him a look. "I can tell already I won't like it."

"Everyone likes it." Observing her the whole while, he tucked his fiddle under his chin and began to play.

I recognized the song immediately. He was right: Everyone probably did love "Barbara Allan." They certainly would if they heard *him* play it, slowly, poignantly, beautifully. By the end, we all looked affected.

"That one deserves a second playing," Daniel said.

So Phineas started it again, and this time my betrothed lent his handsome, low voice to the arrangement, singing after the introduction, " 'It came upon a Martinmas day when the green leaves were a-falling. Sir James the Graham of the West Country fell in love with Barbara Allan.' "

Leaning forward intently, with eyes suspiciously bright and an expression that could only be called painfully enthralled, Rachel suddenly added her lilting soprano to the music, joining in with " 'He sent his men down through the town to the place where she was dwelling . . .' "

It was the only time I'd ever heard Phineas fumble in his performance. His bow tripped over the strings, but after a missed few beats, he resumed, playing even more passionately than before and now smiling, a smile of pure wonder.

Rachel Welds possessed precisely the kind of voice to warrant that smile.

The two foes married their talents, watching each other with probably just as much aching desire as the legendary Sir James felt when he looked upon Barbara Allan. After a few verses, Daniel joined in again. And I felt my own sensibilities caught, so much so that when Phineas neared the tragic end, I heard myself contributing with " 'Oh, Mother, Mother, make my bed, oh, make it soft and narrow! Since my love died for me today, I'll die for him tomorrow!' "

Carried away thus, I didn't realize until I reached the last word of the pitiful promise that I'd been given the chance for a solo.

Daniel bit back a smile and trained his gaze on the ground.

Phineas had stilled the bow in the air. He gaped. "Pretty voice," he said after a lull, and abruptly lowered the bow. "You could sing in a boys' choir."

Pretty, indeed. From neck to ears, I felt a burning flush.

A sound escaped Rachel. She pressed her lips together and squeezed her eyes shut. But again, the sound repeated: a muffled grunt. She wagged her head furiously, and all of her shook— visibly shook.

She lost it. On a roar of laughter, she choked out, "Harry, *Harry*."

Conspicuously bewildered, Phineas laughed weakly. "You mean Freddy. Hairy? Not hardly. The boy doesn't even have his whiskers. . . ."

Rachel swiped at the tears streaming from her eyes, slapped her hands together, and fell sideways against me. "The evil silversmith," she gasped through her mirth, "the engagement to me, a perfect stranger—oh, how, *how* can you be so *stupid*, Phin?"

Like one suddenly struck in the cheek, he whipped his head in my direction and jerked forward, as if to more closely examine me in the firelight. "Wait a minute. Are you—"

"Not *Freddy*," Rachel laughed, then shocked the breath out of me by toppling me backward with the force of an unexpected embrace. "Harriet!"

CHAPTER TWENTY-SEVEN

The three youngsters in the loft had had years to grow accustomed to their uncle's fiddling and so slept through his entire concert. Rachel squealing my name, however, was not a habitual thing, and plucked them from slumber. It took all of her and my cuddling to settle them again. In the end, with her on one side of the children and me on the other, this endeavor lulled everyone. Sleep overtook us before Phineas could badger me about my disguise.

I didn't start explaining the next morning, either. My brother's continued absence at dawn eclipsed the Freddy's-not-a-boy revelation. Where was Gid? That was the question on my lips as I peered around the foggy camp, then shook awake Daniel and our visitors, thrusting cups of coffee in their hands and urging their haste. Gid wouldn't let his friends wallow in worry over him, not without an excellent reason. Rachel agreed, and even joking

Phineas and practical Daniel couldn't quite disguise their dismay. If something hadn't happened to Gid, something might have happened to Marian. She was close enough to the end of her pregnancy to elicit concern.

Since Gid had taken his vehicle, the seven of us piled into Phineas's wagon to investigate, and besides my divulged secret hanging over our plodding party like a curious cloud, nothing seemed changed from the day before. Along the newly widened road, we made our eastward way through wisps of mist, looking as we had twenty-four hours earlier. Every member of our entourage but the children now knew my true gender, but I still dressed as a boy.

The other great experience—that magical moment when Rachel succumbed to Phineas's masterful playing and Phineas discovered Rachel's equally masterful voice—might also not have happened. Neither said a word about it. If anything, they looked uncomfortable around each other. Maybe they didn't know how to incorporate this development into their usual contentious exchange.

As we traveled, the sun began to shine through the fog like a fire beyond a veil, setting the woods aglow. The soft red light turned brilliant whenever it grazed the dewdrops that pearled bark and young leaves.

Soon, a brisk wind muscled up the fog. It was a good air to breathe, alive with rich soil, pitch, and growing things. I liked watching Daniel peer around him and take in the ancient woods: the impossibly thick trunks of trees and the wonderfully varied species of plants and animals. How many intricate ways so much life surely converged near our path, driven by need, fear, and hunger.

Daniel caught my gaze. "I'll never see the like again."

"No." We wouldn't in Middleton—and not here, either, not for long.

As soon as we rumbled into our friends' yard, Gideon came to the cabin doorway, holding carefully (and definitely a little dazedly) a swaddled bundle against his chest.

We barely waited for Phineas to pull on the reins before we leaped out of the wagon.

Gid grinned at the approaching stampede. "Look what I did."

I ran up the three steps to the door, laughing breathlessly, "Oh, did you make that?"

We crowded around the new arrival, and Gid stooped so the children could see, too.

"It's as red as a crabapple," Ephraim said.

"And not much bigger." Phineas rose. He glanced over Gid's shoulder. "My sister?"

"Just resting."

Phineas exhaled.

We followed my brother inside.

Marian was half-hidden under blankets in the wall berth, but she was sitting up, knitting, and looking pleasantly peaceful, as if she'd merely sat down to rest rather than recently endured an exhausting delivery. At our arrival, she put aside the needles and yarn and smiled at our soft greetings and the children's not-so-soft celebratory yips and kisses.

Behind them, Daniel wondered aloud, "Is that a robin's nest in the bush?" When the children sped to the doorway, he urged them ahead of him, tossed a wink our way, and escorted the wild ones out.

When the door closed, Gid shuffled past Phineas and presented the baby to Marian, his entire person radiating reverence.

She tucked the infant in her arms and kissed the downy head.

"Well, sister"—Phineas bent to bestow on Marian his own crown kiss—"what is it?"

"A baby."

"Of any particular kind?"

"It's a girl."

"Ah." Phineas smiled at me and bent again, this time to say in a stage whisper, "So is Freddy."

Gid turned to look at me questioningly.

I rubbed the back of my hot neck and shrugged.

In a similarly dramatic voice, Marian said, "I know."

Her brother straightened, disgruntled. "It would have been nice to let me in on the secret."

"It wasn't mine to tell."

"Hmm." He crossed his arms. "So, everything go smoothly?"

"As smoothly as possible."

"Your sister . . ." Gid's voice caught. He shook his head, his face alarmingly filled with emotion. "She's amazing."

Marian gave him an indulgent smile. "I couldn't have done it without you."

"That's just it," Gid said, very serious. "You could have. You truly could have. You had everything under control."

I laughed. "Didn't you help at all?"

"Well . . ." He glanced at Marian, obviously seeking permission.

She shrugged. She wasn't missish.

Color seeped into his face, but his tone was quietly proud when he admitted, "I did catch the baby."

"And cleaned the knife," Marian said. "He cut the cord, too." To Rachel and me, she added, "And never once turned squeamish or fainted."

He beamed. "It was a miracle. The whole experience . . . *miraculous*."

Phineas snorted. "Come now, Mr. Winter. Babies get born every minute of every day."

Gid gave him a very un-Gideon-like look: disdainful, dismissive. Then his gaze fell on the infant girl. After a moment, he said in a voice rough with tenderness, "And every time it happens, it's a miracle."

Marian's eyes welled. Maybe she wasn't as calm and collected as I'd thought. She caught my brother's hand and squeezed. "It is. You're right. It really is."

I had feared exposure for so long that, in preparation, I'd mentally rehearsed speeches to explain my foray into boyhood. For a long time at Phin and Marian's, however, no one pried for details. It helped, of course, that so many of us were packed into the cabin and too busy to dwell on my escapade. Daniel constructed some long-awaited corner shelves as a gift to the mother, Rachel took over Marian's housekeeping chores, I cooked dinner, and Gid traveled all the way to his homestead, then came all the way back, just to present Marian with the ingenious cradle he and Daniel had concocted: a hollowed-out half log that, of course, rocked naturally.

Meanwhile, Phineas, when he wasn't playing with the three older children, resumed his irreverent teasing.

At one point, Rachel's gaze met mine. She flared her eyes.

Phin's jokes were getting old.

Rachel was leaning over the washing barrel, scrubbing the cast-iron kettle, her strong arms agitating the dirty water, when, out of the blue, Marian asked from the bed, "Why'd you do it?"

No need to ask what she meant by *it*.

Before I could answer, Rachel did. "She was sick of being a girl."

Phineas sauntered over. "Sick of being female? I don't blame her. What an awful fate. Hey—" He frowned at the dirty water stain Rachel had painted down his shirt with a slap of her washing rag. "This is my best shirt."

"Go away," Rachel ordered without looking at him. She was practically murdering the kettle with her scrubbing. "Or your best trousers are next."

Later, when Phineas and I found ourselves alone outside the door, he said, "So Freddy's really Harry. Not much of a difference there." He selected three pieces of firewood from the stack on the landing.

"Harry's short for Harriet." I grabbed a handful of sticks from the kindling crate.

"Who likes to wear trousers. And Daniel Long, I presume, likes Harriet. When she's wearing trousers or a dress?"

I smiled weakly. "Both, I guess."

"And now Gideon likes Marian, I think because she reminds him of his mother. And Marian, who enjoys bossing everyone around, grown men included, might just like Gideon. And Rachel hates me because she's decided to hate all men."

"Or maybe because you act like an ass around her."

He smiled sheepishly. "We're deranged, every one of us. Doing things we shouldn't." He grabbed a fourth piece of wood. The armload already reached his jaw, but he was eyeing another piece.

"Take my fiddling. Back home in England, my father—a hard man—put up with my playing as long as I was a boy, even encouraged it at times, liking how my musical bent proved useful at all the junkets, a talent to accompany the contra dances and cotillions. But he wanted me to give up playing when I turned sixteen, saw fiddling as a boy's pastime, the sort of thing you only do as long as you fly kites and throw hoops. He ordered me to focus on the farm and set aside the instrument until I had a son to pass it on to."

"So you moved?"

"So I moved. I knew I had to farm. But here I can do it however I see fit and keep my passion, too. I need music. More than I need a father's approval."

His words got me thinking about the Genesee Valley in a different way. Yes, it was the ideal destination for men like Gid—those New England second, third, fourth, fifth sons who wanted more than their meager inheritance back home would ever give them. But I wondered how many people pioneered for other reasons. Reinvention, escape from rules, freedom to make their own decisions. Or just the chance to be themselves. All of these reasons, they were mine, too.

"I think you did the right thing," I said. "You should keep your music. It matters, if only because you decide it does. Plus, you're very good at it." I reached for the door but hesitated before opening it. "You've got that in common with Rachel. Too bad you two can't get along."

"Rachel." He shook his head, then murmured quietly, slowly, and without a shred of humor, "Rachel Welds terrifies me."

———

Marian shifted the infant to her shoulder and patted the tiny bottom until her daughter burped.

I smiled. The eruption sounded loud in the empty cabin.

My friends had maneuvered the other children outside again, to let their new sister sleep undisturbed for an hour. I'd stayed behind to make Mama's bread dough, so it could rise sufficiently for baking. It was a good recipe. Tomorrow was Sunday, so there'd be no cooking. This would give the housemates some bread to go with their cold supper.

When I finished, I swiped the table clean, covered the bowl, and stowed it on one of the new corner shelves. The interior glowed rosily with the late light. Daniel, Gid, and I would need to leave soon if we hoped to reach the cabin before nightfall.

I perched on the edge of the bench. "You haven't picked a name?"

Marian shook her head. "If she had been a he, I would have chosen Amos, after my husband." She drew her daughter down to rest in the crook of her arm. "Maybe I'll go with Eliza. That was my mother-in-law's name."

I fidgeted with the basket on the table, wondering about Gid, wondering about Marian, wondering about Gid and Marian. "I'm sorry about your husband. Do you . . . miss him terribly?"

"I miss him, for he was a good man: steady, honest, driven. But ours wasn't a love match. My father wanted the union. I was very young. Sixteen. *Too* young." She tucked the blanket more securely around the babe. When she glanced up, her expression was quizzical. "Did you run away to avoid a matchmaking parent?"

"No. I ran away . . ." How to explain this? "To be myself." I shrugged. "Actually, I didn't run away at all. I left with our parents' knowledge, then"—I ran a hand through my cropped hair—"changed along the way."

"*Our* parents?"

"Gid's and mine."

"You don't look anything alike."

"He's my stepbrother, but as good as a natural one. We've been siblings for as long as I can remember."

She nodded, her face lightening with a smile. After a minute, she asked, "And Daniel?"

"Daniel," I sighed. "Well, he's kind of everything: our Middleton neighbor, the man everyone goes to for help and advice, my parents' hoped-for son-in-law, my enemy for a bit, a man who can be aggravatingly competent, but now one of my best friends."

Her smile widened. "In other words, he's your beau."

I nodded.

"A love match," she mused after dropping her eyes to her baby. She didn't need to see my expression to verify her conclusion. I supposed I'd sounded precisely how I felt. In love.

CHAPTER TWENTY-EIGHT

The following week was to be my last in the new territory. Though Daniel, Gid, and I respected the Sabbath, at twilight on Sunday we started the garden and worked well into the night by the glow of the stars and moon, squaring off a space, removing stumps, tweaking out the rocks that made up the earth in these parts, and improving the garden's soil with manure.

The weather had turned warm and dry. High winds blew from the west. Under such favorable conditions, in Middleton, folks might have already prepared their fields. Our tardiness fretted my brother, who paced during meals and worried aloud about finishing the plowing. A man could never grow too much hay and corn. What if he didn't end up with any? He needed to raise at least enough for the cattle's bedding and feed.

While Gid and Daniel turned their attention to the field (one plowing like a bedlamite, zigzagging around stumps, the other digging out the worst of the great rocks and dragging them away on the stoneboat), I worked in the garden and planted the crops that could survive the late frosts. Mama had sent us on our journey with an array of supplies. I selected her pea and bean packages and sowed the seeds directly in the unctuous clay soil. Marian had given me some potatoes with rooting eyes, so I planted those, too, then gave everything a good drink of stream water.

As soon as I finished planting what was seasonably permissible, I set aside the watering can and got to work digging the storage pit for Gid's hay and corn. I'd never encountered such a mean soil: rich but so laden with clay and rocks I could barely shovel it. My progress was disappointingly gradual, and at the end of every day, I had very little to show for all my scraping and heaving. I did, however, acquire a great many aches and pains, not to mention blisters.

The completion of the cabin meant we were sleeping indoors now, a circumstance that protected us from the night's chill but also kept Daniel and me from romantic pursuits. How could we do much of anything with Gid practically in arm's reach? It was awkward. Plus, my brother obviously disapproved.

Exhaustion partly reconciled me to the restriction. We were working so hard, come nightfall we fell asleep quickly. The labor hastened the time, and the week's end beckoned me: the impending travel by horseback with Daniel, a quick service in Batavia to clinch our partnership, and on our journey toward Middleton, plenty of spring evenings under the stars.

Yet reservations plagued me. I felt torn, half thrilled with newlywed fantasies, half anxious about who and what I was abandoning here: Rachel, Gid, and *freedom*, the unquestionable liberties that came with being Freddy. Like a cage trapping canaries, my stomach reacted to my confusion by remaining perpetually aquiver.

Daniel was impatient. I could tell. He broke the news of our departure to Gid over Thursday's supper.

"Monday? Leaving? So soon?" At my nod, he stared at us for a long moment, then looked despondently around his cabin, as if he was trying to picture it without our company.

My uneasiness stirred. "We'll return for visits."

"And I don't think this place will stay empty for long," Daniel said, smiling gently.

My brother's cheeks reddened. He shrugged, lowered his eyes, and plugged his spoon disinterestedly into his potatoes.

I gazed at him in frustration. Maybe his opinion of Marian Gale was a bit too reverent. Was he planting her on a pedestal like he had Rachel? If so, this was becoming a bad habit.

I doubted the efficacy of worshipfulness in courtship. It established unreasonable expectations and invited failure. To be the object of adulation? Well, no one was perfect. Better to love the fact of the person rather than an idealized version. And better to be loved for oneself. Rachel had said as much not too long ago.

For all that its fertile soil promised good crops, the inland location of the Genesee Valley not only complicated transporting produce (abundant or otherwise) to market, it made communication with families back in the old states a challenge. A person here had to travel hours just to reach a postmaster.

Gid and I had dispatched only two letters to our folks since leaving Middleton, one in Canandaigua, right before we met Phineas at that horrible tavern, and one in Batavia, after my brother had signed the Holland Land Company papers and secured his property.

Since Daniel and I would be returning to that latter town in four days, we told Gid to prepare whatever messages he wanted mailed. We would post his along with our own. The carriers who served the post offices rode quickly and would get the letters to Middleton days before we'd reach home.

We wanted to offer to post our friends' letters as well. Paying visits and collecting their messages would give us the opportunity to bid farewell. I dreaded the visit to Phin's. How could I possibly say good-bye to Rachel? It was too soon and didn't feel right—didn't feel *kind*.

On Friday, the very day I planned to call on Rachel, she surprised me with an appearance. I was washing clothes when I heard the sound of wheels clomping and creaking over the uneven road. Before investigating, I hung my brother's shirt from a branch by the stream and left it dripping there.

Daniel and Gid already waited in the yard and stood side by side, one tall, one short, but both frowning and their arms similarly folded.

Rachel arrived with her cousins. In the wagon, the three Weldses sat combed, scrubbed, dressed in their Sunday best, and looking about as cheerful as mourners on their way to a funeral.

I didn't care to see the brothers—they annoyed me—but I was glad to welcome Rachel.

Her answering smile was decidedly strained.

Robert tilted up his beaver cap. "Morning, neighbors." His face, pale and with a sickly greenish hue, contrasted vividly with his red eyes. Even his smile had an unhealthy twist to it, more grimace than grin. He turned to examine the cabin and winced violently, as the motion brought his fiery eyes in the path of the early sunbeams. "Place is coming along just fine. And—heavens—devilish fast, too." His smile slipped as he squinted at the readied field. "Ed and I seem a mite behind schedule this spring."

Ed acknowledged this with a nod that he terminated abruptly. His hands flew to his bare head. He groaned.

Gid's frown deepened. "Care to come in for some coffee? Help wake you."

Or sober them up: whichever was necessary. I glanced at Rachel to see if she was thinking the same thing, but she was staring straight ahead, grim-faced and apparently lost in her thoughts.

Robert sucked in his upper lip and turned questioningly to his brother.

Ed didn't notice. He poked his pinky in his right ear and commenced scraping out wax.

"Not sure if we have time," Robert said. "We're heading a ways down Oak Orchard Road."

"For what?" Daniel asked.

"A big gathering," Ed answered, suddenly alert, "to celebrate the mill going up in those parts."

"We thought we'd invite our cousin along—fear we've been neglecting her." Robert rubbed his brow and peeked at Gid, maybe recollecting the dressing-down my brother had given him the last time they saw each other. He continued in a rush, "Ought to be fun. Wanted to see if you boys could come, too."

"No, thank you," my brother said tersely.

I sighed. How much more ridiculous could the Welds brothers get? They clearly hadn't understood the gist of Gid's recent lecture. He wanted his old friends to get sober and recognize their duties to their farm and family. He didn't want them dragging Rachel along to a frolic so she could watch them drink themselves to unconsciousness and act stupid along the way.

"You can surely visit for a few minutes," I said. "Go in and have some coffee. Gid made biscuits."

Perking up a little, my brother nodded. "They're very good."

I snorted. Ever since he'd taken over the morning bread making, Gid had formed the notion that his biscuits were lighter and more delicious than any he'd ever tasted. To Rachel, I said, "Would you like to see the mushrooms I spotted growing by the creek? Couldn't believe my eyes—it's so early in the season."

"Must be the warm spell," she answered absently.

"I thought they might be a kind of morel but don't like chancing adding them to my famous fritters lest they poison us. Come tell me what you think."

"All right."

I led her through a thick stand of swamp maples. We passed Gid's wet shirt. It sagged from the branch like a flag of surrender. Without talking, we walked along the stream's rushing length. The shimmering water gurgled between rocks and splashed over stones. When we reached the conical-capped mushrooms, I stopped and glanced behind us. I could just make out a bit of the cabin's roof in the distance.

Rachel crouched by the patch and steadied herself with a hand on the damp ground. "These are witch's caps."

"Yes. Deadly poisonous but pretty. Back home we sometimes called them yellow unicorns." With my boot I tapped a felled oak, where a fungus was growing like rippled shelves out of the rot. "I'll stick with these instead." I broke off the brown clumps.

"Chicken of the woods."

"Ever try them?"

"Of course. They actually do taste a lot like chicken." She rose and whisked the bottom of her dress to free the hem of a dead leaf. "Why are we here, if not to identify mysterious mushrooms?"

"You looked troubled. I thought you might want to talk."

She folded her arms and studied the stream. "You and Daniel are leaving soon."

Though she made her words a statement, I treated them like a question. "On Monday. We were planning on coming by to see you and the others this morning . . . to say good-bye and gather any letters you might want us to mail." I stuffed my hands in my pockets, feeling uncomfortable, unsettled, insensitive: a person abandoning friends to their fates. "I'll miss you, Rachel. And the others, certainly, but especially you." I swallowed. "We'll be back to visit. Hopefully as early as next year."

Her gaze was sad. "I'd like to leave, too."

I stared. "With us?" This didn't displease me. I'd give up a romantic journey alone with Daniel to secure Rachel's companionship. Middleton would be a happier place with her there.

She shook her head. "No . . . just run away." She sighed. "Of course, running away implies you have a home you're escaping. I don't have that. Middleton's not home. This isn't, either." She waved a hand, as if to clear away the gloom, and said with forced briskness, "I reckoned you were ready to go. Straight to Middleton?"

"After we marry in Batavia," I said distractedly. Her sorrow pierced me. She seemed lost, and why wouldn't she? It was true: She had no close family, no home. While I tripped along in my pretense, casually killing off my parents, playing a foundling, inventing stories of enslavement and abuse, Rachel was facing—or had faced—much of what I had invented. For real. How oblivious I'd been to this fact. The realization smote me.

"Marry," she repeated, her tone hollow, face morose. "Last night, Phineas asked me to marry him. Kind of."

I jerked upright. "He *did*?"

She bristled. "You needn't sound so surprised."

"Friend." I gazed at her steadily. "You know I think one Rachel Welds is worth a thousand Phineas Standens. It's just . . . Phin? He's different. Paints himself into the picture of the Confirmed Bachelor. Teasing or not, all his verbal jabs at 'the weaker sex' made me think he'd rather disdain a woman than, well, you know . . ." I shrugged, not sure where the unlikely couple stood.

"Marry her," she finished dully. "You're absolutely right. In fact, you should have heard his proposal. For a man who prizes himself on his fancy speech and cleverness, he sounded like a perfect idiot." With a clap of her hands, she killed a hovering mosquito, then wiped her palms on her skirt. "I never saw a person so racked with agony and dread, wrenching at his hair, ending each of his croaked avowals of love with a misguided attempt at humor, a not-so-funny joke that—as you can imagine—suggested quite the opposite of love." She sighed, a long exhalation that rattled, like there were tears caught in her throat.

I gave her a sympathetic look. "He made a cake of himself."

She threw up her hands. "He's a fool. Since I met him, a day hasn't gone by that he's failed to make some stupid remark. Then, out of the blue, he springs a proposal on me! Not once has he ever sat down and talked to me like an adult."

I nodded. He was like a boy who couldn't think of a better way to express interest in a girl than pulling her braid and calling her a name.

"And the *proposal*, Harry." She groaned a laugh. "What kind of person wants to hear a proposal that makes her out to sound like a jailer, like—like a walking, talking manacle?"

I bit my lip. Poor Rachel.

She slowly shook her head, as if still dumbfounded by the experience.

"So what did you say?"

"*No*, of course." She straightened, fists balling at her sides, eyes flashing. "I told him that since my evil, tormenting temptress of a person was such a bugbear to his delicate masculine sensibilities, such a horrible blight to his happiness, I wouldn't *think* of trapping him in the misery of marriage. Then I told him that until he learned to talk to me with a modicum of respect, I couldn't even consider him a friend, let alone a lover. Then I told him to go away."

I eyed her with grave respect. Certainly, I was sorry for her hurt feelings, even a tad sorry for Phineas, who, for all his witty intelligence, was obviously an idiot when it came to women. Rachel's response, however . . . well, I was impressed. That must have been quite a scene. "So you told him to go away, just like that?"

She cleared her throat. "Actually, I told him to mount his precious little donkey and get the hell away from me."

I whistled low and long. "Precious. Little. Donkey. That couldn't have gone over well."

She sniffed. "I'd say it again."

CHAPTER TWENTY-NINE

By noon, the Weldses had long since left, Robert and Ed fidgety with loads of coffee but still cringing from the ill effects of their night of drinking, Rachel glum.

As I flipped the mushroom fritters in the hot skillet, I listened to Daniel and Gid mutter about our plans. It didn't seem sensible to go visiting today, not when Bob and Ed wouldn't be around to give us their letters for home, Rachel also would be absent, and the rejected Phineas (yes, I'd told them about the botched proposal) was probably out of sorts and licking his wounds.

This conversation came to a midsentence halt, immediately after Gid's "Phineas, the poor sap," when a disturbance outside inspired Fancy's fierce barking and announced no other than the unsuccessful suitor.

"Is she still here?" Phineas asked in answer to our quiet greetings, his hands gripping the doorframe and his gaze darting all around the cabin, as if Rachel might be crouching under the table or hiding in the loft.

I shook my head. Gid covered his embarrassment with a fake cough. Daniel invited Phineas inside.

Our guest fell onto the only seat, a stool we'd transported all the way from Middleton, and immediately slumped forward, elbows planted on his thighs, head in his hands. Not a pretty sight, and practically an aberration: His neckcloth hung, untied, wrinkled, and damp over his shoulders, and his shirt collar gaped, as though he'd clawed it open.

Knowing Phineas Standen as I did, these details, along with the crumpled coat, wild hair, and smudged pantaloons, would have been sufficient to disturb me. But the well-fitted boots brought me to a shocked standstill. They were absolutely plastered with mud, straight up to the tassels.

"I'm sorry, Phin," Gid mumbled, his eyes also fixed on the soiled footwear.

Daniel sighed. "Wish it had turned out differently for you."

Phineas covered his face. "It's my own stupid fault. I made a muck of it. Must be queer in my attic." He groaned into his palms. "Stayed out all night beating myself up. When I went back this morning, Marian told me Rachel had left before breakfast, gone with her cousins to a gathering on Oak Orchard. She said they were stopping here first to invite you along. I came straightaway— hoped maybe she'd decided to stay with you for the day instead of going with those brainless gudgeons. . . ." He raised his head and absently patted his coat pocket, apparently looking for a handkerchief that was no longer there. After the abortive search, he grabbed one limp end of his neckcloth and mopped his eyes.

"Heavens," I breathed. When the fritters started smoking, I

started and hurriedly removed them from the skillet. "Here." I thrust the plate in front of him. "Have some fritters."

He shook his lowered head. "I couldn't eat a bite."

"You've got to keep up your strength. You have a trip ahead of you. You'd better go after her."

Daniel and Gid readily agreed, my brother recommending some pretty things to say, and my beau responding to Phineas's "Oh, what's the use—she made her refusal loud and clear" with "Follow her. That's what I did—went after Harriet, and it worked for me."

Phin's eyes regained a hopeful gleam. "You think I should propose again?"

"Yes," Daniel and Gid said together. They turned to me expectantly.

"Well . . ." I winced. "No."

Phin slumped.

Daniel frowned. "No?"

Gid scratched his head. "Huh?"

"Phin does need to go after her, but mostly to apologize." I sighed. "Rachel's situation has never been easy. She's been forced to cling to the fringes of distant family and acquaintances and pay for their support with good-natured usefulness and hard work. Then Mr. Linton happened, and her situation got much, much worse." I looked at Phin soberly. "What she needs now is a friend."

Friendship, kinship, love matches. What a mess we made of relationships—all because of our personal insecurities, fears, and prejudices. At one time, I'd been so critical of Daniel for not speaking plainly about his intentions, yet *I* could have been the frank one. Instead, I'd hidden my cowardice behind the excuse that coming forward with the heart on the sleeve was the man's job.

Daniel, of course, had played his own game to incite my jealousy. How many poor Middleton girls had had their expectations raised as a result? And though I criticized Phineas and Gid for behaving nonsensically around Rachel, I hadn't been a friend to her in the beginning, either.

And now I was leaving. I briefly closed my eyes.

"If you truly care for Rachel, be there for her, talk to her— even better, *listen* to her." I turned back to the fritters in the skillet. "And, for the love of God, Phin, quit joking."

We found ourselves at loose ends after Phineas left.

Arms crossed, Daniel stood in the doorway, his shoulder holding back the oilcloth. "It's Friday. We'll have to figure out next week, Harriet."

I started slipping on my boots. "Yes." But I was shaking my head. I didn't have any suggestions to offer. Frankly, a Monday departure wasn't just unlikely. It was *impossible*. If his frustrated expression was any indication, Daniel suspected the same. Too many circumstances were precariously undecided and dangerously unraveling.

My brother, meanwhile, remained keen on our original plan to visit the Standen-Gale place this afternoon.

That made no sense. "If you want to see Marian Gale, go see her." On the way out of the cabin, I flared my eyes at him. "You don't need us to accompany you."

He sighed and shuffled behind Daniel and me.

In the end, we all trudged across the clearing to do what we could to rid the field of rocks, but we worked slowly. Our quandaries demanded so much energy, we had little to spare for chores.

My gravest concern was Rachel. She'd seemed so troubled this morning, so terribly *sad*.

Clouds filled the sky, snuffing out the sun, and the wind picked up. Leaving the men behind, I headed for the cabin to collect my coat and had just reached the doorway when, for the third time that day, our road was enlivened with the clatter of another's approach.

It was Phineas and the Welds brothers. In the lead, the former charged into the scant clearing on Sweetheart; the latter drove their yoke of oxen, hell-for-leather. They arrived in the spit and crunch of pounded rocks. Beside me, Fancy barked like mad.

When the dust settled, my pulse leaped. Where was Rachel?

As if I'd voiced my worry aloud, a ghastly white Ed leaped from the wagon, ran forward with his hands flapping the air, and screeched, "She's missing! Lord help us, we lost her. There one second, gone the next." He sent up a terrible howl before falling to his knees in the small yard and blubbering into his hands.

I stared. "You lost her?"

Phineas and Robert reached us. Daniel and Gid had started hurrying our way, too.

Drying his perspiring face with his coat sleeve, Robert booted Ed in the back. "Get up."

Instead, his brother pitched forward until he was flat on the ground, facedown. "I want to go home," he cried into the dirt. "I miss Mother. I *hate* it here."

Heart pounding, I raised my eyes to Phineas. "What does Ed mean, they lost her?"

He gazed blindly past me.

I slapped my forehead. "Phin! What happened to Rachel?"

Appearing beside me, Daniel gripped Phineas's arm, a contact that had the promising effect of jolting Phineas into speech. "I don't know what happened. Just that she's missing." He plowed his hands through his hair. "I encountered the brothers on Oak Orchard. They were heading here."

Pouring sweat, Gid joined us and asked breathlessly, "What happened?"

"We lost Rachel at the sociable," Robert said crossly, as if he was tired of repeating himself. "Figured we'd better get you. We need to form a search party."

"What? Lost . . . ?" Gid breathed a disbelieving sound. "What were you thinking, Bob? You've wasted valuable time. You had an entire gathering of folks who could be searching as we speak."

I held my head. *Rachel's missing. Rachel's missing.* This information repeated but eluded me. I couldn't grasp the thought. It was inconceivable.

Ed released a sob.

Robert scowled and retorted, "We didn't have *anyone* to help us. They're all foxed. We'd be, too, if we hadn't been so queasy from last night and too sick to lick another drop of spirits. Not a single person there would be of use to us."

"Explain what happened," Daniel said.

Robert's forehead puckered. "Cousin Rachel, sour-faced as ever I saw her, said she needed some air away from the reek of smoke. She stepped out but never stepped back in. By the time I thought to go look for her—"

"How long would you say that was?" I asked.

"Maybe a half hour, maybe an hour . . ." He shrugged. "She was gone."

Phineas, in a voice laden with regret and fear, suddenly said, "What if she ran away, Freddy—or—or worse? What if I drove her to that?"

The Welds brothers turned to him in bewilderment, but I knew what he meant. I furiously shook my head. "Don't even think it." I looked away from his white face, acutely uneasy myself. How despondent Rachel had seemed by the stream this morning. How alone.

"We won't find answers here," Daniel said. "Let's go. If we rush, we might have some daylight left to search for her." He glanced at Gid and me. "We won't be back for a while. One of us should hurry through the chores that won't wait."

"*Chores*. Oh, hellfire!" Phineas gripped his hair. "I'm forgetting all about Marian and the farm. If I don't make it back by sundown, she'll worry herself into a conniption." His head whipped my way. "Freddy? Would you take care of the livestock and see to my sister and the children?"

"Gid should do it." Rachel was *my* friend. I had to find her.

Straightening, my brother nodded. "I'll whip through the tasks here, then leave for your place."

Before Gid finished the sentence, I was running toward the horses. Daniel caught up with me and said over his shoulder, "Get there as soon as you can, boys. Freddy and I will move faster traveling by horseback. We'll follow Phineas and see what we can discover."

Daniel kept the horse at a steady trot over the uneven ground, but when we turned onto Oak Orchard Road, he hastened her into a canter. I only had to hang on, and this gave me time to think.

Unfortunately, all I could muster was a recollection of this morning, my friend and what she'd said, words that now portended nothing less than disaster: *I'd like to leave, too . . . just run away. . . . Of course, running away implies you have a home you're escaping. I don't have that. Middleton's not home. This isn't, either.*

Why had I let her depart with her cousins? Why hadn't I insisted she stay? Or why hadn't I gone with her? And why, oh why, when she was so obviously wretched, hadn't I told her I would put off a return to Middleton for as long as she needed me? *Selfish, stupid Harriet.* Rachel had been through so much, too much, in her life. How many losses could a person bear?

Daniel urged the horse to go faster. The increased jostling brought me to attention.

He was scanning the sky, his profile apprehensive. Clouds had formed, like dark wraiths joining in a sinister celestial coven. Obliterating the sun, they swung over the surrounding woods with menacing intent. A moment later, thunder growled from the south.

Phineas, not far ahead of us, shouted, "We must be close."

Daniel patted my arm, tense across his waist. "Don't worry. We'll find her."

We rode into the storm, as though we were hastening to greet it. Thunder increased in volume and frequency, and with a resounding crack, the sky broke apart. Rain shot down and soaked us in seconds. But our destination was straight ahead, unmistakable even in the violent weather.

Scattered wagons half blocked the road, and nervous oxen and horses, tethered to the posts along the fence, shuffled and dripped. While the men hurried to the barn to look for a dry place to secure their mares, I raced toward the rain-blackened building, my boots slipping on the road, then the mill's lane, both of which had loosened into mucky streams.

The doors and windows were open. People craned their heads outside and hollered merrily at the driving rain.

"Excuse me," I barked at two beefy boys blocking the entrance.

Instead of simply stepping back, they laughed and lurched out of my way.

I desperately scanned the interior. It sported an entire party of rowdy drinkers, mostly men, sliding and stumbling across a floor not much different from the rain-saturated ground. It was slick and rank with tobacco juice and liquor. Some dancing, of a sort, was under way, but even the fiddler's playing sounded drunk.

Phineas appeared beside me, shook the wet hair off his face, and spared a scorching glare at the offensive musician. "Do you see her?" His eyes searched the gloom.

I ground my teeth. *"No."* How could I make out anything in this crowd?

It was pointless to look for Rachel among the revelers. I couldn't picture her stomaching this event, not at all a lively sociable but more of a drunken mob. She'd seek another shelter—an outbuilding, if one existed—to wait out the storm.

I sidestepped between the strapping boys playing doormen and hurried outside, shivering in my wet shirt. Maneuvering around empty bottles and dips in the ground that had widened into good-sized puddles, I rushed along the building's side, passed an overturned bench, and headed for the back.

The clearing didn't go far before the forest started. A muffled roar sounded from the swift brook that ran snugly along the wheel side of the mill.

Woods or water: how easily either could oblige the despairing who wanted to disappear.

I fought the impulse to panic. Rachel had never despaired in the past. She was a survivor. I sluiced rain off my soaked head, wringing my hair's short length like a just-washed handkerchief. *Think. Remain calm. Stay focused, Freddy.* A hysterical cackle popped out of my throat. Now I was calling myself Freddy, too.

I tried to check these disordered thoughts and concentrate. How much time had passed since the brothers had last seen Rachel? What had she said before parting?

There was *something* I was missing, some blatant possibility I was stupidly overlooking. I sensed this detail, yet it evaded me, like a butterfly fluttering just beyond my net. The nuance teased me back to their account: Rachel's bad mood, her disgust with the mill party, her desire to leave, her wandering outside by herself. I blinked the damp from my eyes and stared at the millhouse, veiled with rain but still raucous with bad fiddling, slurred singing, cracks, and thuds. Things breaking. Bodies falling.

Why, *why*, had those foolish boys made Rachel linger here? Once they saw the unchecked behavior inside, they should have left. Anyone could see this wasn't a fit place for a sensible person. And Rachel, more than anyone I knew, had good reason to find boozy behavior offensive, after all she'd endured at the Lintons.

At the Lintons . . . with Mr. Linton . . .

Drunken, abusive, disgusting, dangerous Mr. Linton.

The tickling half thought at last took shape.

Oh, no.

CHAPTER THIRTY

Mr. Linton had kidnapped Rachel.

It struck me as an absolute certainty, even a God-granted epiphany.

And the revelation galvanized me.

I shot straight for the road, questioning, with livid disbelief, *how the bloody hell* this could have happened. Rachel would have put up a fight. Undoubtedly, at least a few of the attendees had loitered outside when she'd been taken. Were the revelers so drunk or selfish or stupid or callous that the sight of a young woman's struggle couldn't rouse them to action? Or perhaps luck had favored Mr. Linton. It was possible he'd found her on the property's edge. He might have knocked her senseless and made away with her quickly . . .

Oh, God. I ran faster.

The rain had eased to a sprinkle, but the road oozed with rivulets of mud, particularly in the grooves left by wheels. I wasn't certain how many miles away the Linton homestead was but didn't doubt that Mr. Linton, after capturing Rachel, would have absconded by wagon rather than foot. He wouldn't have managed to kidnap her without a vehicle, not with his infirmity. When I'd encountered him, he had walked with a limping gait and used a branch for support.

And as a club.

This recollection of Mr. Linton delivering punishing blows with his makeshift cane compelled me to break into a sprint. My mind spun with terrifying images of my friend being subjected to his ruthlessness. That he had beaten her I knew. I'd seen the bruises around her neck. Even as I had stood in arm's reach, he'd jabbed her in the side. That he had raped her, as well, I suspected. He was brutal, unconscionable. And he had my friend.

This dreadful line of thought made me realize I didn't have a weapon. *Stupid!* I should have grabbed a farm tool from the barn to use as a cudgel or spear. I should have taken Daniel's or Phineas's horse to expedite my chase.

With a skid across the muck, I staggered to a halt, my hands flying to my wet head. What would Daniel and Phineas think when they discovered I'd gone missing, too?

I looked back, guessing how far I'd traveled, wondering frantically if I should return and collect my friends. The empty road stretched to the north like the wet slash of a knife wound. The forest fenced in its sides, the trees' thick upper branches black against the gray sky. Already darkened by weather, the day was fast slipping toward night.

No time to spare. I ran.

A stitch in my side, the ache in my right ankle, and welling fear: I could ignore the first two but not stave the third. What had that man done to my friend? What *would* he do? And would I be too late to stop him?

I jerked up my head and forced myself to focus on a plan. I would tear into that ramshackle cabin and demand Rachel's release. I'd threaten Linton if he tried to stop us.

Threaten him with what?

I slowed to a stop again and stuffed my pockets with good-sized stones; then I plucked, from along the road's slick edge, a fallen branch. Thanks to the storm, there were many, and my selection was big enough to inflict damage.

As I flew toward my destination, the rocks clanked against my sides. The heavy limb, raised over my head like a sprinter's flag, whooshed through the air, its young leaves wetly twitching.

I desperately did not want to mentally prepare for the worst, for the darkest possibility, and strove not to contemplate it. When avoidance proved futile, I tried reason and thought Linton probably wouldn't kill my friend because he had uses for her. Oh, but what cold comfort! There were evils other than murder.

I had to hurry.

Rachel, my friend, my dear Rachel. I strung the words into an invocation, as if in mentally repeating her name, I might summon her, conjure her . . .

And then: there.

In the mist-shrouded distance. A silvery form. An approaching figure.

I slowed. I stilled. I stared. Straining my eyes to make out the person, I discerned first a steady stride, then a swish of a skirt, then a lowered head, then a familiar shape. . . .

For the first time since this horror began, I released a sob. Leaping forward, I cried, "Rachel!"

Her head came up. She flew my way.

We collided in an embrace made noisy with clinking rocks, labored breaths, and weeping.

As soon as we parted, I blinked away the tears and ran my eyes over her, looking for hurts, reassuring myself that she was here, really here, alive and in one piece, and all the while I panted, "Oh, thank God, you're—I never thought I'd—are you—"

Her hands were on her face. She pulled them away to stare at the damp fingers, then closed them into fists and dropped them to her sides. "I never thought I would, either," she said faintly.

I reached for her arm and paused when I realized I still held the branch. Instead of tossing it aside, I switched it to my other hand, then grasped her above the elbow. I wasn't ready to release my weapon. Who knew if we were safe?

I urged us in the direction of the mill. We walked pressed together along our sides, so tightly our legs brushed, making clumsy our strides. I felt we could not get close enough. Could never be safe enough. "Oh, Rachel." The enormity of the situation rattled me, and I stumbled. Glancing nervously over my shoulder, I clung to her tighter. "Did he hurt you?"

She began to answer. A sob cut short the words. She gasped when her wrist grazed her brow.

I halted us and scanned her features. A swelling discolored her temple. My eyes burned. "He did that."

She closed her eyes, nodded.

My breath came fast, like I was still running. I gripped the branch. The bark bit into my palm. "I want to do the same to him."

Her eyes opened. "You can't."

"I can. We can. We have friends. We'll hold a meeting. We'll tell them . . ." My shoulders jerked up. Gnawing on my lip, I shook my head and tried again: "We will tell them enough. There are good folks here, plenty to form a posse, and we'll—"

"He's dead."

I stared. "He's—"

"Dead."

"How?"

"A fit. Some kind of fit." She started walking again, slowly. She looked behind her, strode faster, tripped, but righted herself even as she continued forward in scrambling haste.

"Let me . . ." After lunging to catch up with her, I hooked my arm through hers. She leaned in to me but stared straight ahead, intensely, as if in focusing her gaze on the distance she would reel us more quickly in that direction.

"It was his legs that gave out first. He stood like he aimed to charge me but . . . didn't. Couldn't. He went down, hands flailing. The arms fell wide, splayed from his body, and his mouth spread into a grimace that was like"—she sobbed a thin laugh—"a grin. The whole time, he watched me. He followed me with his eyes. He followed me . . ." She slowed and wavered.

I wrapped my arms around her. "Oh, Rachel, *Rachel.*"

We wept into each other's necks.

When the tears abated, we slogged forward again. It felt like I was bearing my weight and most of hers, too. Hoping talk would keep her from fainting, I asked the first question that came to mind: "His family?"

"Not there. Mrs. Linton left days ago. Took the children. The last of the money. Fled." She scrubbed her face and shuddered. Her hand went to her throat. "He blamed me. Said I gave her the notion. Said I had to . . . to . . ." She shook her head violently and, on a single keening exhalation, finished: "Take her place. After that, he . . ." Another sob shook her.

"I'm sorry, I'm sorry, I'm sorry," I said helplessly, holding her up, wishing there was more I could offer than a litany of apologies and an embrace.

"I know." She pulled away. Then, like someone putting herself back together, she straightened, ran trembling hands over her hair, and smoothed her dress at the waist, again and again. "He ordered me to fix his supper, threatened to kill me if I didn't do his bidding, but then shoved me toward a pantry that held more rat droppings than food." She gasped a disbelieving sound and staggered forward. "Nothing but a bit of cornmeal and lard. Nothing in the garden, either."

"What did you do?"

"I told him I'd have to forage." Her face crumpled. "I hoped he'd release me long enough so I could flee. Instead he tied a rope around my waist with a kind of knot I couldn't unravel."

My breath caught. He'd *leashed* her?

"I fixed his meal." She stared blindly ahead. "And—and that was that. I found a knife on the shelf over the kindling bin and sawed off the rope."

A drum of horses' hooves charged the air. Daniel and Phineas appeared in the distance, their galloping pace blurred by the misty dusk. We hurried to the side of the road. I waved my branch to draw their attention.

But I wanted the rest of the story. And I needed it before the others arrived. "What did you make for his last supper?"

"All I could find." She kept her eyes on the men's approach. "Mushrooms."

Phineas leaped from his horse and rushed for Rachel.

I don't know what she did or how she did it—most of my attention was frozen on the last thing she'd told me—but her gesture made him halt. Emotion worked across his face. He took a deep breath and ironed his expression. The only indication of lingering angst was in how he scanned me—jealously, for some reason. His tone was clipped when he observed, "Nice tree, Freddy."

"Oh." I finally let go of the branch.

Daniel grasped me by the arms. "What happened?"

"Linton kidnapped her."

Daniel stared and mouthed, *Kidnapped,* while Phin's head jerked back, as though someone invisible had delivered an uppercut.

Rachel glanced away from them. "He knocked me out and took me to his homestead"—her eyes grazed mine—"and had an attack not long after we got there."

Fury bloomed in Phineas's face, a red ire. "Where is he now?"

I found Rachel's hand and squeezed. "He's dead."

Silence answered this announcement.

She tugged her hand free and walked to the side of the road. Her arms made a shawl over her chest.

Phin's breath left him in a growl. He whirled around, hiding his face from us, and his fisted hands pounded the air once. "Rachel, *Rachel*"—his back shook—"how I wish I could make him dead all over again."

"Lord Almighty," Daniel breathed. He drew me into a hug, and the motion jangled my collection of stones. He glanced down. "What in the world—"

I pulled away to empty my pockets, aware as I let the stones fall from my hands that I would never again palm a rock without remembering this day—the day I'd planned to use rubble for a weapon.

Then I threw myself into Daniel's arms.

He cleared his throat and murmured thickly, "If you ever run away and leave me like that again, I'll lose my mind."

I clung to him. He'd get no argument from me. I had never been so scared in my life.

The road, on our way back, all but disappeared in the gathering darkness. Had the moon not found an open berth between the clouds, we might have been forced to pass the night in the mill with the drunken guests, somewhere on the nasty floor. However, there was sufficient light for us to cautiously head north. We met up with the Welds brothers on our way, their identities revealed not because we could make out their features but because we heard Ed weeping, "I hate it here, Bobby. I want to go home, to our *real* home."

We called out to them, and Robert joined the crying when we verified Rachel's return. When Daniel finished briefly telling them what had happened, they stammered apologies. She didn't appear to hear them. As we started the journey home, they repeated their apologies. She still maintained a silence. But after the third time Robert wetly moaned about "putting her in a bad spot in the first place, leaving her in the horrible hovel with that drunkard," she snapped, "Yes, you did. And you didn't cry about it then."

Which effectively quelled them.

The closer we got to the Standen-Gale cabin, the more the day showed on her. By the time we reached the property, her teeth were chattering. I helped her out of her cousins' wagon and braced her with an arm around her waist. She would have fallen on the spot otherwise.

The Welds brothers looked ashamed and anxious to leave. With a few mumbled words, they drove their wagon out of the yard.

Marian came to the door. She took one look at Rachel and ordered Phin, Daniel, and Gid to the barn to bed down with the animals for the night.

Not even Phineas argued with the command. The cabin, on this night, was not for men.

A fire filled the hearth. It threw a restless glow on the rough-hewn walls and played across Marian's face, which was already alive with emotion, and glinted on Rachel's lowered head, adding a reddish hue to the dusky length of hair. The hectic light matched our thoughts, the tumult of our feelings. Marian heated water in the kettle, then sat by Rachel, put her arm around her shoulders, murmured soft words, crooned in the way mothers do. I fed wood to the flames to hurry the warming, then helped Rachel when she struggled with the latches on her dress.

The cabin grew hot, but neither the fire nor the warm bath nor a flannel nightgown squelched our friend's trembling. Marian fetched quilts off the built-in bed and tucked them around her shivering frame, from neck to toes.

Rachel rested her forehead on the table. "I don't think I'll ever be warm again." Even her words shook.

Marian covered her mouth with a hand, then rose. She hastened across the room and took down a bottle from the top shelf of the pantry. "Maybe this will help." She poured some golden liquid into a short glass and set it before Rachel.

We made a huddle at the table, my arm around Rachel's shoulders, holding the cape of quilts in place, Marian opposite us but leaning forward to clasp one of Rachel's hands in both of hers, chafing the knuckles, shaking her head, once muttering fretfully, "We need to get you warm." Then, to me: "Shock."

Shock. We had seen the marks on our friend. Marian had administered a salve on two of the rawest spots. But what else could she or I do? What could anyone do? I stared dazedly at the fire, tried to absorb what had transpired, held my shivering friend closer—the entire time feeling altogether foreign. A foreigner to this room, a foreigner to this moment, unfamiliar with even myself, thinking over and over, *We are different now. Who were we yesterday? Nothing will ever be the same.*

How silly I used to be . . . so anxious to toss aside childhood and move on with life. But I was learning something today, a lesson murky and bitter. Liberating feats, daring adventures— accruing such experiences wasn't the essence of maturity. In fact, growing older seemed less about getting things and more about losing them, less about realizing dreams and more about feeling wakeful and alone. Maybe adulthood wasn't really a matter of age at all. Maybe it happened whenever a person at last saw human nature for what it was, for the shape it could take, from the depravity of one to the mettle of another.

Well, I supposed I was good and grown now. I still held the image of my girlhood in my mind's eye but could find no way back into the frame. I didn't belong in the picture.

The hours passed, fast and slow at once. It was as if we were gathered for a wake. *Not* for Linton. He deserved no vigil. I was glad—fiercely glad—he was dead.

No . . . rather, we were keeping watch over the living. Over Rachel. By the hiss and crackle of burning wood, in this room of uneasy quiet, a brooding silence that demanded reverence, a careful broaching in whispers, Marian and I made a small shelter around our friend. And I prayed distractedly, without conscious aim, a pleading *oh, God, oh, God*. When I noticed what I was repeating, I forced myself to make better sense, to form an intention to this petition. What did we need right now besides succor and healing? Clarity. We needed direction.

And then, as morning smudged crimson into the web of branches, quite abruptly it came to me. An answer.

Marian had gone to stand at the window. Though her back was turned to us, I could hear the frown in her voice when she said, "Phin can stay with the Welds brothers at their cabin for a night or two." She turned and gazed soberly at Rachel. "What you need now is some privacy."

This prescription seemed to hit Rachel in a strange way. She pulled her cheek from my shoulder and swept the cabin with a mournful glance. "I would like that. I would *cherish* a little privacy. My own place. Will I ever know what that's like?"

"Yes." I nodded for good measure.

They turned to me expectantly.

"I have a plan."

In the morning, Marian left the cabin to carry coffee to the men. I slipped outside as well and pulled the door shut behind me. I wanted to breathe some cold air.

A few minutes later, I moved to head inside again but stopped when Phineas called me. He stood near the barn. I trudged across the yard.

Hollow cheeks, heavy eyes: he obviously hadn't slept well, either. He nodded absently at my greeting. "My sister said I'm to stay with the brothers."

"Just for a night."

He palmed his unshaven jaw. His hand fell to his shoulder. He gripped it and gave the cabin a melancholy glance. "She doesn't want me around."

I knew by *she* he didn't mean Marian. "Oh, Phin . . ." I sighed. "She *needs* you." His music and charm and laughter. "She'll need all of her friends." Now more than ever.

He tried to smile. "Thanks, Freddy."

I squeezed his arm and turned.

An hour later, Daniel and I left for my brother's homestead. Behind us, in Phineas and Marian's cabin, Rachel was finally asleep. Marian hadn't discussed my plan with her brother yet, but she didn't need me there to do that. Gid had already gone south to see to Linton's burial, then head to the Holland Land Company with the hope that the record on the Linton property might have contact information. The family had to be informed of the man's death.

I was glad for my brother's absence. I needed to talk to Daniel alone, and since clouds had gathered in the sky for a repeat performance of yesterday's weather, we did so in Gid's cabin, as soon as we finished the morning chores.

When I reached the end of what I had to say, Daniel nodded. He was sitting beside me on the floor, cross-legged, elbows braced on his thighs, hands folded, head down. "I knew we wouldn't leave. Not with all this upheaval." He looked up, his eyes sad. "But I guess I didn't expect one of us to go and one of us to stay."

"It's not forever. Only until wintertime." I said this cajolingly, reassuring myself as much as him.

"That's more than half a year." He gazed at me glumly for a moment. "Are you sure this is for the best?"

I nodded.

Ed Welds needed to return to Middleton. Robert Welds maybe less so. But neither could remain in the Genesee Valley, not in the way they'd been living, practicing too little farming and dousing their insides with too much liquor. If they went home to straighten themselves out, they'd leave behind a small, serviceable cabin. "Rachel can keep her cousins' place while they're away," I said. "She needs time to herself." Desperately. "There's no way she can get that if she continues on with Phin, Marian, and the children. And I can help Rachel, staying with her if that's what she wants me to do." I wrung my hands, hoping she *would* want that, for safety's sake. I didn't like the idea of her living alone. "Or staying with Gid but visiting her daily, making myself useful. Being a friend." A better one than I'd been in the past.

He smiled a little. "As Harriet or Freddy?"

I shrugged. "As myself." Those two, they didn't seem like different identities now. They were both me, just a person struggling to figure out what to do, what to be. I was only beginning to realize the answers.

Yes, Rachel needed time. But perhaps I needed some more, too.

"And tomorrow I get to escort Robert and Ed back to Middleton."

"Because they'll likely kill themselves, trying that journey on their own." I was only half joking. It was a wonder the brothers had made it here alive in the first place. "Of course, they have to agree to the plan. But I think they will. They owe Rachel. Plus, they're not happy. Back home, they can trade their labor for earnings and restore their squandered savings, all while basking in the doting affection of their mama." I took Daniel's hands, trying to keep my voice light when a telltale quiver kept sneaking in, trying to do this right thing when much of me desired a different course of action. "And you can correct all the errors your cousin made while he tried to run the farm in your absence." Daniel had been gone for such a long time already. It was impossible for him to linger in these parts for another handful of months. He had too many responsibilities back home.

He squeezed my hands and said gruffly, "I'll whittle away the lonely nights, making you a wedding present. A cedar-lined chest would be nice."

"Carved with my initials?"

"If I can fit them all."

My laugh tripped on a sob. I stared through a sheen of tears at our clasped hands. "Then come back for me, please, right after banking-up season, as soon as the snow begins to fall."

"Bringing the Welds brothers with me?" He sounded less than thrilled at the prospect.

"Ed is probably better off staying in the bosom of his family. Maybe just Robert."

"And where will Rachel go then?"

"I don't know. I'd love to convince her to return to Middleton with us, but she might want to stay here. She could easily earn money with her needle and spinning. As people pour into this valley, roads will improve, mills will multiply, farms will start turning a profit, and opportunities will grow, particularly for domestic services. More men than womenfolk will settle here at first. Rachel won't have trouble finding work." Then, wistfully: "She might even save enough to lay a stake."

He sighed but didn't comment. The Holland Land Company wouldn't let a woman purchase a parcel. He knew that as well as I did.

But why not? Why in God's name not? I gave my head a shake.

"I bet Phineas would sell her a portion of his property."

I glanced up, startled. "You're right. He owns hundreds of acres he hasn't even touched."

Daniel nodded. "He's been improving Marian's land."

I pondered this possibility. Rachel could handle her own homestead. She could do whatever she wanted. She wasn't poor Rachel in my mind, not anymore. Not with the way she faced adversity. She'd survived more obstacles than anyone I knew.

"Or the three of us"—he cleared his throat—"we'll all head back to Middleton together."

I smiled. He was a good man. "I'll miss you, Daniel."

He tugged me nearer. "How much?"

"Terribly." I wrapped my arms around him, relishing his strength. I wiggled closer to relish it better.

We stayed in that tight embrace for a long time. I wanted to prolong it for hours, for days.

But with a sigh, I pulled away. On impulse, I ran my finger along his chest, starting with an *L*, then an *O* . . .

"Are you initialing me, Harriet?" he teased.

I finished the word. "Yes." For I was that word, too: not just a Freddy or a Harriet, but what I carried in my heart. What I felt for this man.

"Good. That makes me yours."

"Then don't get lost or stolen." I kissed him. "And I will reclaim you soon."

ACKNOWLEDGMENTS

I am grateful to my agent, Rebecca Stead, for her wisdom, patience, tremendous skill, and humor, and my editor, Liz Szabla, for her expert guidance and generous enthusiasm. And many thanks to Karen Sherman, Melinda Ackell, Liz Dresner, and the rest of the wonderful Macmillan team for their outstanding assistance.

Several friends provided ideas for sources, lent me useful books, and encouraged and advised me at different stages of the writing process, including Alethea Johnson, Jennifer L. Johnson, Jennifer R. Johnson, Gwen Oosterhouse, Amy Gaesser, and Sheila Stewart. I especially want to thank Diane Palmer, who introduced me to the firsthand accounts compiled in Arad Thomas's *Pioneer History of Orleans County, New York*, gave me access to the archives belonging to the Orleans Chapter of the Daughters of the American Revolution, answered my questions about the Genesee Valley pioneers, and read an early draft of this manuscript. Special thanks, as well, to Sharon Root, whose family letters, memorabilia, and stories deepened my appreciation for and understanding of the western New York settlers' experiences. And I am grateful to librarian Adrienne Kirby, who graciously lent me dozens of books from her personal collection and taught me a great deal about our local history. And a warm thank-you to my bright friend Anna Symons, who also read an early draft of this novel and offered sound advice. I am obliged to these dear women. So much of what they lavishly shared engendered the seeds of this narrative and fostered its development.

Thanks to my students, who delight and inspire me and who, over the years, have helped make this Lake Ontario fruit country the place I call home.

Sincere thanks to Douglas Carlson, cherished mentor.

Heartfelt thanks to my best friends and siblings, Noelle Swanson and Robert Ostrom, for their unwavering faith in me. Affectionate gratitude to all my family, far and wide.

And deepest thanks to Michael, Lily, and Quintin, the loves of my life.

GOFISH

MELISSA OSTROM

When did you realize you wanted to be a writer?
Not for a long, long time. In fact, as a young child, I didn't particularly like to read. All I wanted to do was play. I ran wild with my friends until sixth grade. At that point, the kids who'd once enjoyed fort-building, bike-racing, potion-mixing, and neighbor-spying with me lost interest in these activities. They got "too cool" to play. That's when I turned to reading. Characters took me on their adventures. They let me keep playing. So my love for reading definitely bloomed belatedly—as did my interest in writing. I just began crafting stories nine years ago, around the time my daughter was born. I remember feeling frustrated with some of the main characters in the books I was reading: they weren't kindred spirits. That's why I decided to try writing. I wanted to create characters I could love and imagine as friends.

What did you enjoy doing when you were a kid? What are your hobbies now?
I was your typical grubby kid, always playing outside and getting dirty, concocting puddle "soup" with dandelions and daisies, jumping into the puddles, then hauling mud out of the puddles to make "pies." Around the age of ten, I turned to a more productive (though no less filthy) activity when my

mom gave me some packets of seeds. From then on, I had a yearly garden, just a squarish plot of earth packed with snapdragons, larkspurs, zinnias, pansies, and sweet alyssums. My hobbies (come to think of it) haven't changed much. I still enjoy gardening, as well as throwing pots in my pottery studio and experimenting with exotic ingredients and new recipes in the kitchen. Of course, I also love to read. Hiking and doing crafts are fun, too.

What was your first job?
Technically, I've been working since the age of eleven. I used to babysit regularly and also shared a paper route with my brother Robbie. But when I turned fifteen, I got my first *real* job—as a waitress at a nursing home. Every Saturday and Sunday, I worked from 7:30 to 3:00. I served the older residents (all women) their breakfasts and lunches, cleared the tables, loaded and unloaded the dishwasher, and handwashed the pots and pans. But between these mealtime activities, there was plenty of time to *not* work: I'd "test-taste" Martha's fabulous cooking, gossip with Beth the aid, hang out with the older ladies, and read, read, read. The residents were very sweet, regularly sharing their books with me. Every paperback they slipped me was a romance novel. I have a vivid memory of sitting in the Warner Home living room with a plate of Martha's paper-thin sugar cookies and a steamy Johanna Lindsey historical novel. That was a great job.

What book is on your nightstand now?
Paulina & Fran by Rachel Glaser. I just started it.

How did you celebrate publishing your first book?
The pub date was a Tuesday, and I had a book club meeting that evening, so I couldn't go out to dinner with my family.

But my husband worked from home that day, just so he could take me out for lunch. The entire day, in fact, felt festive. The Twitter writing community really shines on such occasions. So many lovely people wished me a happy book birthday and tweeted nice things.

Where and when do you write your books?

I write in my office early in the morning, while my husband and children are still asleep upstairs. I enjoy this solitary time, the quiet coziness of the house, the crackle of the fire in the wood-stove, the moon in the sky, a delicious cup of coffee, and what-ever story I'm endeavoring to tell on the computer screen. Even if I don't manage anything else, writing-wise, for the rest of the day, if I can strum up five hundred words in those wee hours and inch along a narrative, I'm satisfied.

What sparked your imagination for *The Beloved Wild*?

The Genesee Valley's history has interested me ever since I moved to Orleans County in New York twenty years ago to teach English at Kendall High School. In the early 1800s, dur-ing our country's first wave of westward expansion, many young farmers left the comforts of their New England homes and settled here, after purchasing their parcels from the Hol-land Land Company. This Lake Ontario fruit country still fosters prosperous farms. With its sweeping lake, orchards, quaint cobblestone houses, and the Erie Canal, the Genesee Valley is an excellent place to live and aptly named: Genesee comes from the Seneca word for "beautiful valley."

But though the area's history has long intrigued me, I didn't come up with an idea for a novel until one day when I was trudging around an old cemetery. While searching for a patch of trilliums that I'd spied the previous spring, I came upon a family plot that caught my attention. The names and dates on the antique headstones suggested that one man must have had three consecutive wives. The nearby infant burials provided an explanation.

I wondered what it would have been like for a girl to grow up in the early nineteenth century when pregnancy and childbirth posed grave risks to women. Worse yet, since society prescribed marriage as the only suitable future for a girl, how nearly impossible it would have been to avoid these dangers! I imagined how a girl would feel about this, especially if her own mother had died giving birth to her. My character Harriet Submit Winter sprang from this woolgathering. And Harriet *does* find a way to escape her lot in life. She disguises herself as a boy.

What is your favorite word?
Tenderness.

If you could live in any fictional world, what would it be?
Elizabeth Bennet's, for sure. I'm a sucker for British Regency romantic novels, and they don't get better than *Pride and Prejudice.*

Who is your favorite fictional character?
Lucy Maud Montgomery's eccentric, imaginative, brilliant, passionate, and adventurous Anne Shirley. She's easy to love.

What was your favorite book when you were a kid?
Anne of Green Gables. I read the novel when I was eleven years old, and it immediately turned me on to reading. I adored the entire Anne series. (Montgomery's Emily books are wonderful, too.)

What advice do you have for aspiring writers?
Read widely, write regularly, and *commit* to your wordsmithing. Published or not, your works have value: They're profound exercises in creativity and manifestations of your unique imagination. Writing is a magical endeavor—truly transformative and deeply satisfying. Whatever else you do to pay the bills, make writing your *real* job, your passionate vocation.

What would you do if you ever stopped writing?
Die, probably. I've fallen in love with writing. I can't imagine not doing it. I don't even want to try.

AFTER SURVIVING AN ASSAULT AT AN OFF-CAMPUS PARTY,
Maggie escapes her college town and moves in with her aunt in
an isolated cabin. But the trauma Maggie hoped to leave behind
has followed her, and her troubles intensify when she begins to
receive messages from another survivor. Will Maggie muster
the courage to answer her emails and speak out?

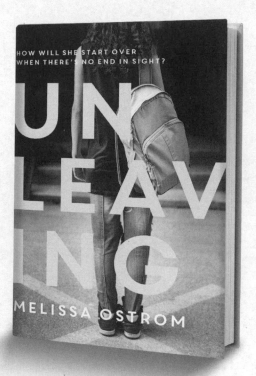

Keep reading for an excerpt.

1

IN THE SEPTEMBER of her nineteenth year, Maggie Arioli did not cover a slender mattress with an extra-long fitted sheet. She did not thrill over the single dorm room her sophomore status at Carlton College would have won her. She did not buy expensive textbooks. She did not lug books or anything else down campus sidewalks shadowed by trees, their leaves green but leaning toward gold. She did not admire the elegant marble pillars or trust the keepers of the columned edifices to edify her, shape and improve her, deepen her like a well and then fill her with wishes. She did not sidle between young men or young women or gaze up at the mountains of two ranges. She did not walk by McCullers Hall, with its white cupola, or the Stanton Center and its bell tower. She did not visit the musty quiet of Swan Library. She did not enter the electric sparseness of a classroom.

She prepared to leave the valley, put the mountains behind her, and stay with her mother's sister, Aunt Wren, in New York, not the city but the state, a western portion and probably, in general, an infrequently imagined place. The aunt, whose artwork entailed communications with larger, livelier worlds, said as much to her niece during the awkward phone conversation when the arrangements were made ("for your sabbatical," as Maggie's mother had lightly coined it).

"It feels like an apology," Aunt Wren had said, "clarifying not the city, the *state*, pointing out the seven-hour distance between my version of New York and other people's. I'm between Rochester and Buffalo, I'll say. Then it's: Oh. Where it snows so much. That's what we've got—weather."

As if to prove it, from nine in the morning until three-thirty in the afternoon, the span of the September trip, rain fell with increasing violence. Through the initial sprinkle, as her mother drove, Maggie mentally said good-bye to Vermont—Carlton, in particular, not just her college town but her hometown. She was half-mournful. The other half of her: *Fuck this place. I never want to see this fucking town again.*

Scotia. Amsterdam. Green interstate signs, alternately Something-Spa and Something-Falls, signaled her and Mom's proximity to Saratoga destinations. Their route took them close to a hillside town over a river. Dark buildings, severe and brick and incongruously ruffled with gingerbread trim, sat blank-windowed on their craggy inclines above the brown water, like hopeless giants reduced to their lace-edged underwear and contemplating death by drowning. New York, Maggie decided, was bleak and ugly.

Then suddenly, the mountains disappeared. Just like that. The earth flattened. She couldn't see what was coming. She couldn't see what she'd left behind. What she saw was sky, and rain filled it.

Bleak and ugly and *flat*.

The weather worsened after Syracuse. Her mother, leaning forward, gripped the steering wheel with both hands. Like a thundercloud, her dusky hair had answered the moisture in the air with threatening billows, a surge in frizz and curls. She usually would have remedied the anarchy with a hairband and ponytail, but this morning, she didn't seem to notice, not even when she glanced in the rearview mirror. She changed lanes, flexed her hands, and rolled her neck.

"Want me to drive for a while?" Maggie dabbed at her hair. Similarly huge.

"In a storm?" Mom shook her head. Woods lined both sides of the thruway, and the trees drooped in the rain. "Too much of this, and we won't have a pretty fall. It will ruin the foliage."

"Yeah." Good. Maggie pictured her old campus sopping, the leaves ripped off the branches and plastered to the ground. Maybe Carlton College would flood. An apocalyptic deluge.

They got off Interstate 90 at Exit 45 and took I-490 into Rochester. The highway became a dizzying loop that wound around skyscrapers, billboards, river, and stadium. Mom attended to the GPS with the concentration of someone expecting to get lost. Which could happen. She had only a hazy idea of where they were going. Aunt Wren was Mom's twin but, for three decades, more of a distant acquaintance. The aunt had gotten out of Carlton at eighteen, almost as soon as she'd tossed aside the tasseled graduation cap. Her trouble had been with their parents, not her sister, but Mom had never shared Wren's contention with their folks. That difference of opinion had landed Maggie's mother in the disowned camp, until last October, when poor Grandma and Gramps died in a car accident. Mom and Aunt Wren had talked more since then.

Maggie eased back and closed her eyes. She ordered her body to relax.

Cut it out. Grab her hands, Matt. Fucking relax, okay?

Her eyes flew open.

"Lake Ontario Parkway's up ahead. Won't be long now." The traffic had trickled off. Though lightning split the sky and the windshield wipers' speedy sluice could barely keep up with the downpour, Mom exhaled and smiled a little. "Go ahead and take a nap. I can figure out the rest."

Maggie frowned. What was her mother talking about? She hadn't played navigator once.

The implication was nice, though. Her mere presence helping, comforting.

She closed her eyes again, willed her brain shut, too. She didn't sleep. Couldn't. Hardly ever anymore. It was like she'd lost the knack.

Aunt Wren lived at the dead end of a dirt road called Ash Drive. A generous person might have called the place rustic. However, holding open a screen door patched with duct tape, Aunt Wren, herself, hollered through the heavy rain, "Welcome to the shack!" and beckoned with a wave.

Maggie stared at the aunt. This could be no other than the

aunt. She looked just like Mom but also (in the severe haircut, threadbare jeans and flannel, and unmade-up face) totally different. Bizarro Mom.

From inside the car, Maggie's mother smiled nervously and raised a hand. She had her car door cracked, but instead of leaping out with her own shout of greeting, she scanned the property and murmured in hollow astonishment, "Holy crap. What a . . ." The smile looked ready to collapse. "I'm just not sure about this, honey."

This: the aunt's unpainted hovel; Lake Ontario, like a molten metal beast gnawing the pebbly shore that crept all the way up to the porch's crooked steps; the woods on the other side, black and grim and wet; and the yard, oozing mud and collecting puddles, the entire surface looking diseased, covered with lesions and sores.

Mom took a deep breath, like a person preparing to dive into the sea, shot out, and slammed her door. Running in a crouched position, head bowed, arms awning her hair, she zigzagged around the reddish pools that bubbled in the torrent.

Maggie clumsily got out of the car and shut the door. Thunder cracked. Startled, she jumped, lost her footing on the slick ground, and almost fell. *"Shit."* Lightning illuminated the lake. It was an arresting sight, like electricity galvanizing a monster. Maggie hurried toward the porch, keeping her eyes on the muck and sand.

Mom and Aunt Wren had disappeared into the house, and when Maggie entered and shoved the wet hair from her eyes, she found the sisters, laughing and crying at the same time, embracing and rocking together and saying in bursts of emotion, "My

God, you look just like Mom," and "*I* do? Then you do, too," and "Can you believe it, Min? Fifty. When did we get so old?"

The kitchen was plain—no fancy appliances, not even doors on the cupboards—but big, clean, and fragrant with yeasted bread and damp wood. A pendant lamp hung over a farm table. The copper pots above the stove echoed this single source of light and gave the room the warm hue of a polished penny.

A noisy penny. Rain pinged overhead, indicating a metal roof, and thunder rumbled. Behind the crying, laughing, roof tapping, and sky rumbling, something else added to the racket, a regular shattering from a distant corner of the cabin.

It was like standing inside a percussion instrument.

Aunt Wren pulled away from Mom and nodded at Maggie. She swiped her face with a red plaid sleeve. Then her face— heart-shaped, big-eyed, long-nosed, eerily like Mom's—softened. The sweetening of the expression prepared Maggie for something like a hug, so when the aunt abruptly turned and shouted over her shoulder, "Jesus Christ, Sam, will you give it a fucking rest? I've got company here," Maggie actually flinched. Her back hit the screen door. It swung open and banged shut.

The aunt flared her eyes and shook her head. "Sorry about Sam. He's mad and taking it out on the rejects." She made a swiping motion, as if explaining would be a waste of time.

Steadying herself with a hand on a chair, Mom untied her sneakers and introduced her daughter and sister. Then Maggie found her right hand captured and squeezed and patted like a ball of dough.

"I'm so glad you're here, Margaret." Over her shoulder, Aunt Wren said, "She's got our hair."

"And frame."

Aunt Wren raised the kneaded hand, as if to lengthen out Maggie and improve the view. She hummed agreement. "More hair and legs than anything."

"But her dad's brown eyes."

The aunt grunted. *"Him."* To Maggie, she said, "You can keep the Bambi eyes, but nothing else from that one, you hear?"

"Poor Jim. God—since high school!—you've had it out for poor Jim." Mom pulled a band from her pocket and drew her hair into a ponytail. "The nicest guy and the best of fathers."

Bor-ing, Aunt Wren silently mouthed, dragging a wry smile out of Maggie. "An accountant." She announced this flatly, as if the profession said it all. With a final squeeze and slap on the knuckles, she released Maggie. "What's first? Want to change into something dry? Are you tired?" She planted her hands on her narrow hips. "You've got bags under your eyes. A nap sound good? You can put on your pajamas. Or take a bath. Want to take a hot bath? Or eat? I made soup and bread. How about a tour? Want the ten-second grand tour? The best part's outside, but you brought a storm with you, so that'll have to wait." While Maggie was deciding which question to answer first, the aunt asked, "What do you think, Minerva?" Her mouth curled at a corner. "Goddess of wisdom. Patron sponsor of the arts." To Maggie, she said, "Minerva. Can you believe that shit? And here *I'm* the one with the artistic talent."

"Jeez," Mom moaned through a laugh. "Let's not start that up again."

The aunt collected the wet jackets and hung them by the door. "She got Minerva, and I got Wren—a common little brown bird."

"With a beautiful song."

As if Mom hadn't spoken, the aunt said to Maggie, "You can see from the start our folks weren't big on fairness."

Mom's smile wilted. She held a shoe in each hand. "That's not true."

"Says the favorite."

"According to you. For heaven's sake, it hasn't even been a year since they passed. Have a little respect."

"Respect would be hard."

"They didn't love me any more than they did you."

"Want some evidence to prove otherwise?"

"Oh, please."

But the evidence. Where's the evidence? Until the police release their statements . . . Maggie shuddered, pressed her hands to her ears, and ordered herself, *Don't.*

Aunt Wren, poised to snap a retort, glanced at Maggie. She covered her mouth.

Mom gave the slightest shake of her head. "Show us around."

"Good idea. This way. Then you can wash up while I throw together a salad. We'll eat and get you to bed early."

The glimmer of the kitchen died in the gloom of the windowless hallway. Dazed, Maggie trailed her mother. The aunt led the way through the cabin, narrating as she went: "Note the wide-plank pine floors, all carefully preserved with the original dents and gouges" and "Even the paint on the walls is antique, totally authentic."

Maggie tried to focus on her surroundings. They trudged into the living room. Rippling gray and blinking whitecaps filled the windows. Back in the hallway, the aunt swung open a door. It was her bedroom. The woods stood close to this side of the cabin and threw its shade, like an extra blanket, over the small space. The bathroom came next. Mom oohed and aahed at the sight of the claw-foot tub and pedestal sink, then Aunt Wren nodded instructively at an opposite door in the hallway ("Linen closet"), a second door ("Studio"), and patted a bannister. Maggie looked up. The staircase was so narrow and steep, it hardly qualified as a staircase. More like a ladder.

"I've only got two bedrooms," Aunt Wren said, "one below and one above. You're up there, Margaret. In the loft."

Mom, determinedly chipper, said, "Wow. The whole second story—all yours."

"Go on," the aunt said. "Take a look. Watch your step. That one's cracked. Keep meaning to have Sam fix it. No, check the right side. Feel the switch?"

"*Ouch.*" Maggie rubbed her head.

"Whoops. Sorry about that. You don't want to straighten there."

Maggie found the switch. And for the first time in a long while, she experienced a stirring of pleasure. The room was . . . something else. She shuffled away from the light switch, half-bent until she got to the peaked portion.

The space spanned the length of the cabin and held the warm redolence peculiar to attics. Its wooden floors, whitewashed walls, and sparse furnishings—just a dresser, a bedside table, and, positioned under three abutted windows, a quilt-covered bed—were made homey by the pitched ceiling. The room was all roof, and it pinged softly. The rain must have let up.

The short wall to Maggie's right held drawers; the wall on the left, embedded shelves, crammed with novels. But the windows perfected the loft. The ones close to the staircase overlooked the trees, blackish green in the gray afternoon, except where early autumn streaked the canopy with ochre. The room was like a nest. No, grander: an aerie. She crossed to the windows over the bed, where the lake roiled. Now it was the lookout on the mast of a ship.

In her breast, she experienced a tightening—a flicker. Maybe she could do better than just hide here.

When she returned to where the women waited at the foot of the stairs, Maggie gripped the bannister and bit the inside of her lip to stop a tremble. "Thanks, Aunt Wren." She cleared her throat. "I like it."

The aunt cracked the studio door and stuck her head in the opening. "Sam? We're coming in, okay?" She sidled forward and held the door to her side, like one blocking a view into a dressing room.

"Fine." A wealth of not-being-fine crammed into the syllable.

The aunt hesitated. "Where's Kate?"

"With Dad."

Her fingers, curled around the edge of the door, fluttered a tap. "Linnie?"

Clank, clatter, thud. "Take a good guess." A stomping crescendo. Then, closer to Aunt Wren: "Don't tell Dad, okay?"

She shrugged, noncommittal and disapproving, then widened the door with her foot. "Meet Sam, my assistant."